Death of a Queen

CHRISTOPHER ST JOHN SPRIGG

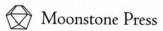 Moonstone Press

This edition published in 2019 by Moonstone Press
www.moonstonepress.co.uk

Originally published in 1935 by Thomas Nelson and Sons Ltd

Introduction copyright © 2019 Moonstone Press

ISBN: 978 1 8990 0005 0

A CIP catalogue record for this book is available from the British Library

Text designed and typeset by Tetragon, London
Cover illustration by Chrissie Winter and Charlie Fischer
Printed and bound by in Great Britain by TJ International, Padstow, Cornwall

Contents

Introduction

Death of a Queen, which appeared in 1935, was the last conventional whodunit to be published by Christopher St. John Sprigg before his untimely death in the Spanish Civil War. Originally subtitled "Charles Venables' Fourth Case", the story is set in a small Balkan country, "Iconia", whose leaders have appealed for help with a sinister development. Shortly after arriving, Venables must deal with the death of the eponymous monarch and solve an "impossible crime".

Many "golden age" books have a plot (or subplot) involving an imaginary European kingdom, often on the brink of revolution. The inspiration for this subgenre was "Ruritania", the setting for Anthony Hope's best-selling 1894 novel *The Prisoner of Zenda*. Ruritania became the basis for hundreds of imitations (Lutha, Graustark, Ixania, Riechtenburg and Evallonia, to name but a few) as well as parodies—the Marx Brothers' film *Duck Soup* features Groucho as the dictator of mythical Freedonia. The Ruritanian setting became so well known that Sprigg refutes it directly in *Death of a Queen*. When Venables complains: "This place sounds dreadfully like Ruritania," his colleague replies: "There's nothing Ruritanian about Queen Hanna."

Sprigg read widely across history, anthropology, politics, sociology and linguistics, and he puts this knowledge to good use in *Death of a Queen*. He devises Iconian history, heritage and architecture with an enthusiasm and realism that add to the book's appeal. Reviewers took note and it was widely praised both for its cleverly constructed mystery and for its skilful prose. "The action of this cheerful murder tale is most un-Ruritanian in that it does not creek at all but leads us smoothly, by means of an ingeniously intricate path, right up an Iconian garden. Mr. Sprigg packs a stout last-minute punch," wrote "Torquemada", the pseudonym for E. Powys Mathers. Dorothy L. Sayers reviewed it for the *Sunday Times*, stating: "Mr. Sprigg strikes exactly the right note for this kind of extravaganza; with enough gentle humour to make the absurdities of his one-horse kingdom entertaining and enough romantic glamour to keep the murders in key."

Sprigg ran an aeronautics publishing business with his brother and wrote numerous short stories, book reviews and aviation textbooks, as well six other detective novels. Around the time *Death of a Queen* was published, he began a passionate conversion to Marxism. He adopted the pen name Christopher Caudwell for his serious literary work, publishing a well-regarded Marxist critique of poetry entitled *Illusion and Reality*. In late 1936 Sprigg joined the International Brigade and drove an ambulance to Spain. Encouraged to return home by friends and family, he instead stayed on and trained as a machine-gunner. In letters home, Sprigg argued: "You know how I feel about the importance of democratic freedom. The Spanish People's Army needs help badly; their struggle if they fail, will certainly be ours to-morrow." He was killed in action on 12 February 1937 at the age of twenty-nine.

For many years, Sprigg's fictional work was forgotten; the last few years have seen a resurgence of interest in his detective writings. It is a delight to see *Death of a Queen* back in print.

The visitor to the Balkans who has sufficient time at his disposal should stay at least one day in Isorb, capital of the historic little kingdom of Iconia. Unfortunately none of the hotels can be unreservedly recommended. The Hotel Victoria is, however, clean by Balkan standards. There is a fine Romanesque chapel attached to the Milö Palace. When there, the visitor should not miss the crypt. The guide will explain the legend appertaining to the silken 'Curse of the Herzvogins' on view there. Do not tip him more than one dracon. The excellent modern buildings in the Vio Victorio, a contrast to the surrounding squalor, are interesting. Experienced travellers speak highly of the view to be obtained on a barge trip up the Iranian River, but the warning previously given about the use of insect powder in the Balkans should be borne in mind. The old Roman aqueduct at Theria is worth a visit...

LOCKHART'S GUIDE TO THE BALKANS,
PAGES 15—16

Chapter I

THE MYSTERIOUS MR. SHILLINGFORD

When Charles Venables returned from lunch at four o'clock he found a telephone message waiting for him. It was from Superintendent Manciple, who asked Mr. Venables to come round and see him, on an urgent matter, at half-past four that day. He was to ask for Room No. 352/AL, New Scotland Yard.

Two years ago a peremptory message from Manciple, then an inspector, had resulted in the arrest of Charles Venables. But Venables and Manciple had long forgiven each other that little error for which, to tell the truth, Venables was quite as much to blame as the Scotland Yard man.

Venables was puzzled. "Have there been any murders while I've been away?" he asked Clavering, the assistant news editor of the *Mercury*.

Clavering scowled at the *Mercury*'s privileged crime investigator. "Not that I know of. There might have been a murder if you had taken much longer over your lunch. Heflin has sent a messenger to find you twice already this afternoon."

"One must eat," said Venables humbly.

"Why don't you?" answered Clavering rudely. "The last time I had lunch with you I don't remember seeing you consume anything solid."

Venables decided not to answer this, and walked moodily back to his room. By this time it was necessary to take a taxi if he was to arrive at Scotland Yard by half-past four.

He seemed to be expected at the Yard, almost anxiously expected, thought Venables, being used to a far more off-hand reception in these official halls. He was pounced on by a policeman and piloted swiftly to the Superintendent, whom he found busy with three visitors.

Venables greeted Manciple with a cheerful salutation. The detective himself was not a cheerful man; nor yet could he be described as gloomy. The fat creases of his broad face were arranged in folds which gave it an appearance of imperturbable, Mongolian inscrutability. Whatever Manciple's views on the functions of the human face may have been, he plainly did not include among them the office of expressing the feelings of the possessor. By repeated prodding, Venables had discovered a keen and somewhat malicious sense of humour behind Manciple's impassive exterior, but the bright jest with which he greeted the Superintendent now fell on unresponsive ground. Manciple's formal reply suggested that the matter for discussion was serious. Venables accordingly looked carefully at the visitors.

The first, on the right, a pale individual in a black hat, Venables decided was a minor poet. Possibly a Communist. In the centre was a blond giant, who looked like a Scandinavian athlete, in a suit almost certainly produced by an English tailor. On the left was a slim, dark, foreign-looking young man. An Italian, guessed Venables.

The Scandinavian athlete stared at Venables blankly out of his very blue eyes, and then turned to the Italianate young man.

Manciple rose and introduced Venables to the minor poet. "This is Mr. Venables, about whom we have been speaking.

"Mr. Lancelot of the Foreign Office," explained Superintendent Manciple to Venables.

Venables felt a trifle disconcerted at his wrong diagnosis of the pale individual. But, as it turned out later, he was not altogether wrong. Mr. Lancelot had in fact published verse, and he was suspected by some of his colleagues of Marxist leanings...

Mr. Lancelot now took over the burden of introduction. He drew Venables towards the Scandinavian athlete, holding the journalist firmly by the left arm, as if in fear that he might run away. "Mr. Charles Venables, sir, of the *Mercury*," he said to the giant. Then

Mr. Lancelot gave Venables a penetrating glance sideways. "Mr. Shillingford," he whispered in Venables' ear.

The dark Italian was not introduced. He appeared to be a kind of appendage, secretary or such-like, of the Scandinavian giant. Venables' guess as to his nationality was, however, partly confirmed when Mr. Shillingford referred to him later as "Luigi."

At the moment, however, Venables' attention was concentrated on something odd about Mr. Shillingford's manner, and indeed about Mr. Shillingford himself. This athlete (surely no one but an athlete could have that huge torso, and that clear skin) spoke perfect English, without a trace of foreign accent. Yet Venables stuck to his first impression that the man was not English. There was something Continental about the cast of the features, the close crop of the hair, the heavily beringed fingers, and salmon-pink silk shirt...

Mr. Shillingford, still seated, extended his hand to Charles Venables graciously and gracefully, rather as if he was giving a pet animal a bun. Luigi had risen from his chair, and Mr. Shillingford, lifting it in one giant hand, moved it in front of him. Then he motioned Venables into it, patting him gently on the arm as he seated himself. "Excellent," the giant murmured encouragingly. Venables felt more than ever like a household pet.

Suddenly something clicked in Venables' brain. Twice before he had met this manner, this queer blend of haughtiness and almost menial affability. The first time it had been the Hereditary Grand-Duchess of Georgina, and the second the ex-King of Kossovia—his only two encounters with royalty. This particular manner was, of course, the inevitable badge of the tribe of royalty, as clearly marked as the professional manner of the lawyer, the doctor, or the priest. The Scandinavian athlete then was a royalty of some kind. Hence, no doubt, the presence of Mr. Lancelot from the Foreign Office. The question was—what illustrious name did the rather ridiculous incognito of "Mr. Shillingford" cloak? Was he a full-blown sovereign, or a princeling? Hardly the former, thought Venables, or surely they would have heard of his arrival in England at the *Mercury*. Venables decided to go for the latter.

"Thank you, your Royal Highness," he murmured as he seated himself in the chair.

Mr. Shillingford and Mr. Lancelot exchanged a glance—Mr. Shillingford's was inquiring, Mr. Lancelot's humble and deprecatory. "Very acute..." murmured Mr. Shillingford. Even Manciple nodded approvingly.

"Mr. Shillingford came to us for help," explained Mr. Lancelot. "He came at the request of his mother."

Mr. Shillingford nodded solemnly in confirmation.

"They—he—want someone possessed of some experience in—er—investigation to look into certain events which have occurred in their—house." Mr. Lancelot cleared his throat. "For a variety of reasons it is undesirable to employ what I may perhaps call local talent." Mr. Shillingford here showed his fine white teeth in a grin. "Unfortunately, anxious as we are to help them, it would not be in order for us to lend Mr. Shillingford any of our agents. I therefore brought him along to the Yard. Superintendent Manciple takes the same view as we do. I feared he would. So it then became a matter of finding some private individual to undertake the task. Superintendent Manciple recommended you very warmly," ended Mr. Lancelot, with an inquiring lift of his eyebrows.

Venables felt genuinely surprised. Although he was now on friendly terms with Manciple, he had never supposed the detective had anything but good-natured toleration for his unofficial activities. At the same time he felt it necessary to make some small protest.

"What about Murphy?" he suggested. "Or Hind? Or Garrick?" All three he named had formerly been C.I.D. men, who had retired and founded private investigation *bureaux* of their own.

Mr. Lancelot pursed his lips and frowned. Manciple explained the frown. "It's more your line than theirs, Venables. Whoever takes on the job has got to keep his end up in—er—Mr. Shillingford's house, and mix naturally with everyone, and so forth. Murphy and that crowd would not do at all."

"Not at all," said Mr. Lancelot decisively.

Venables understood. Murphy and Co. were good souls, but they might not fit unobtrusively into the atmosphere of whatever palace Mr. Shillingford came from. Venables was not sure he would himself, but Manciple evidently had a touching faith in his ability to mix on equal terms with the Royal Household.

"The real question," went on Mr. Lancelot, "is the attitude of your paper. Obviously the last thing His Roy—Mr. Shillingford—wants is publicity. You would have to get leave from your paper and come in a purely private capacity."

"Any sum in reason," murmured Mr. Shillingford.

"My Chief would speak to your editor, Mr. Grovermuller, if it would help," added Mr. Lancelot.

"I don't think there will be any difficulty," answered Venables. Apart from the fact that he had a holiday due to him, recent comments from his news editor, Heflin, had made it clear that he was not, at the moment, by any means considered indispensable at the *Mercury*. There had been an unfortunate scarcity of first-class murders lately...

"Excellent," said Mr. Shillingford, rising. "Consider it settled. The sooner you can come the better. Luigi here will look after everything for you—the visa of the passport, and so forth. I am so glad you can come." The blond giant showed his excellent teeth again in a smile.

Venables felt a slight objection to being thus hurried off into the unknown. "May I ask, sir, for what city I am bound?"

"Isorb," answered Mr. Shillingford, looking at him expectantly.

"Ah, the capital of Iconia," commented Venables promptly.

Mr. Shillingford smiled again, and extended a gracious hand. As he left with Luigi, ushered to the door by Superintendent Manciple and Mr. Lancelot, he turned. "Luigi will ring you up at your offices in an hour," he said. "It will be nice if by that time you have been able to arrange your leave. Then later we can have a chat together. I am delighted you can come, Mr. Venables."

Mr. Venables bowed. The door closed and Mr. Lancelot patted the journalist on the back.

"Stout effort that, seeing through his incognito! I thought you would drop a brick when he mentioned Isorb. Ninety-nine out of a hundred people in this country have never heard of the place. But evidently you know all about it."

"I had it in a crossword puzzle the other day," answered Venables frankly. "*Town in Iconia, word of five letters*. And that is all I know about it. You'll have to tell me."

"Oh, well, what do you want to know?" answered Lancelot, a little disappointed.

"To begin with, who exactly is this Greek god? At first I took him for Sweden's hope in the Olympic Games."

"Yes, he's an impressive-looking Johnny. He's the Crown Prince of Iconia. H.R.H. Augustus Crispin Maximilian, known to his friends as Gustav."

"But how does he come to be such a good imitation of the common or garden English gentleman?" asked Venables.

"Oh, he went to Eton and all that."

"Who is the King of Iconia?" asked Charles. "His father, I suppose?"

"There isn't one—it's a queen. This chap's mother. Queen Hanna—or Queen Anne, to give her name its English equivalent."

"An unfortunate name. We all know what happened to Queen Anne," complained Venables. "This place sounds dreadfully like Ruritania."

"There's nothing Ruritanian about Queen Hanna," Lancelot answered. "She's an elderly, strong-minded, bad-tempered, and at the moment badly scared old woman!"

"Why scared?" asked Venables, interested.

"That's your business, old chap," said Mr. Lancelot evasively. "Gustav will tell you all about it later. It's why she sent her son over here. As far as I can gather, what she really wants is a private detective in the Palace to protect her."

"Hold on," exclaimed Venables, a trifle annoyed. "I can't do that sort of thing. I don't propose to shadow her everywhere in big boots. That's not my line of country at all. Murphy would be the ideal—"

"I don't think they expect you to do that, Venables," interrupted Manciple blandly. "From what the Prince told me, I understand his mother wants someone she can confide in. Someone like yourself who would appear intelligently interested in her troubles, and at any rate make a show of finding the villain. In other words, the Prince does not take his mother's fears very seriously."

Venables became more cheerful. "That sounds better. It ought to be a good holiday. But look here, Lancelot, how on earth am I going to appear intelligently interested in the Queen's troubles without knowing a word of Iconian, if there is such a language?"

"There is," admitted Lancelot. "It is a corruption of Romaic Greek, with Slav inflexions."

"Good God!"

"But the Court and official language is English," went on Lancelot. "To be perfectly candid, we practically own the place. Of course we don't interfere in politics as long as the lads behave themselves and only shoot their own citizens. They discovered oil there a little while back, and the fields have been developed entirely by British capital; that's how we got our foot in. For that matter British influence goes back to a much earlier date, when King Augustus VI, a godson of our George IV, became enamoured of the English political system (God knows why), and got some minor notability of the day—the second Lord Champneys, if I remember rightly—to come over and reorganize Iconian affairs on similar lines. I don't think it was a great success. However, the country appears to keep going without any first-class revolution."

"I see. Well, that's a help. I never was good at languages. I hate to confess it, but I don't even really know where this place is. How big is it?"

Mr. Lancelot looked a trifle pained. Later Venables learned that he was the Foreign Office specialist on Iconian affairs, and the author of several books on this remote kingdom. Charles discovered this when, as he was leaving, Mr. Lancelot suggested his books might prove useful to him, and thoughtfully provided him with a list of them. Charles conscientiously purchased the lot.

"Iconia is about as big as Yorkshire," Lancelot now explained. "It is a pocket of land trapped between the Danube and the Transylvanian Alps. Rumania, Yugoslavia, and Bulgaria are all her neighbours. Iconia escaped the various troubles of the Succession States partly because of its isolation, partly because of the extreme backwardness of its development (the oil was found only recently), but mainly because neither Mr. Lloyd George nor President Wilson—nor even Clemenceau—had ever heard of it. It was originally a part of the Roman province of Thracia, then of the Byzantine Empire, and during the Dark Ages some petty Gothic chieftain seized it. The present ruling dynasty, the Herzvogins, are supposed to be descendants of those original noble brigands. There is a legend—"

"I really must be getting back to the office now," interrupted Venables hastily, seeing that Lancelot was embarked on the full flood of a favourite topic. As it turned out, he was wrong to interrupt, for the legend which, in all probability, Mr. Lancelot was then about to recount had an important bearing on the puzzling events that are the subject of this book. However, Venables could hardly be expected to guess this. "I must catch Grovermuller before he goes. Good-bye, Lancelot! Cheer-oh, Manciple. Thanks for the recommendation!"

Manciple turned to Lancelot after Venables had gone. "You deal with the Iconian mails from our Embassy, I believe," he said. "I shall be rather interested to hear what happens to our Venables in Isorb!"

Chapter II

THE AFFABLE PRINCE AUGUSTUS

G rovermuller made no difficulties about Venables' request for leave, and freed him as from that afternoon. Luigi came round to see him in the evening, and now introduced himself as Luigi Pavellicini, personal private secretary to Prince Augustus. He was a pleasant-mannered young man who spoke English with only a trace of accent. He evidently knew London well, and, Venables gathered, was equally familiar with most other European capitals.

He was also discreet, for he turned aside all Venables' questions with smiling but noncommittal retorts. He himself volunteered only one remark about their destination.

"You must not expect too much of Isorb," he told Venables. "It is not much larger than the average English market town. In fact, I myself have seen a cow lying down in the middle of the Vio Victorio—the equivalent of your Piccadilly—while four soldiers endeavoured to persuade it to move to one side." Luigi shrugged his shoulders. "But the inhabitants do not like to be reminded of the comparative insignificance of their town. The Prince is different, of course. He is a man of the world with a sense of humour. But his mother, you must remember, unlike the male members of the ruling house, was educated in Iconia."

Luigi left Venables packing on the large scale the prospect of palace life suggested.

The next morning there was a message asking him to come round to "Mr. Shillingford's" Park Lane hotel. The Prince's small entourage was accommodated in an expensive suite overlooking the Park, and His Royal Highness himself was being shaved in the hotel's most luxurious bedroom when Venables was shown in to him. Gustav waved him into a chair, while his valet suspended his shaving brush to allow the Prince to greet him.

"Luigi is out at the moment fixing things up for you," he said. "Let me introduce you to my equerry, Count Markonyeff."

A young man with a monocle, a highly polished pink face, and a microscopic black moustache, bowed with military precision to Venables. His English had a trace of foreign accent.

"Leave us for a moment, Mike," Prince Gustav told him. The young man disappeared, and Venables was left with the Prince, his valet, and the overpoweringly modernistic wall design in black and yellow marble which adorned the walls of the room.

"You are probably wondering why you have been sent for?" went on the Prince. "It is not easy to explain in this twentieth-century atmosphere." He indicated the fresco. "When you get to the Palace, above all when you have met and spoken with my mother, you will understand it much better."

"Am I right in supposing the Queen believes herself in grave danger from some unknown source?" asked Venables.

Gustav was silenced for a moment by a second application of lather. When the razor had removed it from the neighbourhood of his mouth, he answered.

"It is nothing so simple as that. I am afraid you will not really understand it until you have seen the Queen. We are a mediæval people at heart, Venables, and although I myself don't believe in all this kind of thing, all the women at the Palace—and half the men—certainly do."

"Is it a supernatural danger then?" asked Venables, puzzled. "A personal one? I don't quite follow."

Gustav fixed on the journalist a bright-blue stare. Venables— who was beginning to be interested in the Prince and had already decided he was intelligent—returned the gaze with his extremely penetrating green eyes. Gustav was silent under his scrutiny for a moment. Then he rubbed his face briskly with a silk handkerchief as his valet released it, motioned the valet out of the room, and went to sit nearer Venables, an imposing figure in his brilliant scarlet dressing-gown.

"I'm going to be frank with you, Venables!" said the Prince. "Although you may not think it, I chose you a good deal more on my own personal judgment of character after meeting you than on your police chief's recommendation. Now listen. My mother is a genuinely great woman—a woman of immense strength of character and real shrewdness. But during the last few months, for some inexplicable reason, she has changed. It is not always easy, even for me, to make out what is at the back of her mind," mused the Prince. "Like many other successful rulers she believed in concealing her motives, perhaps even from herself, and she still keeps up the habit.

"You won't be long in Iconia without hearing some silly talk about what is called the 'Curse of the Herzvogins.' The details of the legend are unimportant. You will hear them soon enough. The point is that she has now begun to take that idle tale seriously. She talks now about some great 'Act of Propitiation'—it sounds ridiculous, doesn't it?—which she proposes to perform to avoid the curse. Here again you will understand better when you hear it from her own lips."

"It will help me a good deal, sir," answered Venables, "if you will be still more frank with me. Is there, in your opinion, the slightest ground for your mother's fear? Or is it a pure delusion? In which case, I take it, my appointment will be merely a gesture?"

Prince Gustav frowned as if he thought this a trifle too candid, and then changed his mind. "You are quite right to ask. The answer is that in my opinion it is a mere delusion; but it is possible—just possible—that there may be something behind it all. And that is what I want you to find out. In your position it would be easy for you to play up to my mother's fears. It would also be profitable." Gustav grinned. "I know, of course, that you will give them neither more nor less weight than they deserve. In fact, that is why I am happy to leave the matter in your hands."

Venables began to like the Prince—not that he had not been favourably disposed towards him from the first meeting. On the face of it the whole business sounded just what Lancelot had hinted at—an old woman suddenly possessed by a persecution complex like many another ageing person. But because she was—in theory, at any rate—an absolute ruler, instead of being laughed at by her friends she was upsetting the Palace, and had sent her eldest son scurrying to England to beg help from the Foreign Office and from Scotland Yard, who had skilfully shifted the responsibility on to the officially insignificant shoulders of Charles Venables.

Venables did not flatter himself that, if the matter had been much more than this, Manciple would ever have suggested his employment. It was his duty, therefore, to listen sympathetically to the Queen, do his best to soothe the old lady, and meanwhile amuse himself in Isorb, which he did not doubt he could do very well.

At the same time, Venables reminded himself, the Prince had suggested in all seriousness that it was just possible there was something behind it all. He hoped so, for the sake of his lingering reputation as a criminal investigator.

Meanwhile, Gustav had got up and had taken off his dressing-gown, revealing himself in shirtsleeves. His trousers, Venables noticed, were in excellent taste, but the shirt was execrable—an even brighter pink than the shirt he had been wearing the previous day. Gustav must have interpreted his look, for he examined the shirt carefully in the mirror.

"It is a bit lurid for England, isn't it?" he said with a grin. "The truth is, Rosa insists on choosing my shirt materials for me, and her tastes are a bit exotic. But, of course, you don't know Rosa. You will be meeting her in a moment at breakfast. You will breakfast with me, won't you?"

"I have already breakfasted," admitted Venables, "at the unearthly hour of ten o'clock." It was then half-past eleven.

"You are an early bird," said the Prince in all seriousness. "But you will be able to have some coffee with us, surely."

Gustav's valet had now appeared, and helped him on with his waistcoat and coat. The Prince then insisted on Venables accompanying him into the other room—an alarming cube in which the floor was white and the ceiling of dark oak, jointly making the room appear upside down. The furniture was chromium plated and sketchy. Coffee and rolls were being set on the table. Venables recognized two of the three occupants of the room, Luigi and the equerry, Count Markonyeff. The third, a woman, had her back half turned from him, but she moved as the Prince entered.

"Rosa," said Gustav, "this is Mr. Charles Venables—Signorina Rosa Pavellicini. Mr. Venables has been chosen as the Queen's adviser. He will be returning with us to-morrow."

Rosa was magnificent. Venables admitted it at once. Her features were classical—an adjective often misapplied but which fitted Rosa perfectly; her creamy white complexion added to them a suggestion of being carved from antique sunlit marble. You could examine them as much as you liked without detecting a line where the carver's invention had been unworthy. Such features needed living up to, and Rosa realized it. Her coal-black hair was worn long, and was braided to make the most of her broad brow and drop gracefully on the nape of her neck. Even her smartly cut dress was evasively reminiscent of Greece.

Venables took all this in, and wondered meanwhile if she were Luigi's sister. The name was the same, but there was nothing at all ideally classical about Luigi's blue-chinned monkey-like little face. He learned afterwards that Luigi was a cousin.

"Need we go back to-morrow, Gustav?" asked Rosa, after smiling at Venables and carefully arranging her bare arms before her in a Grecian vase attitude. It was remarkably effective, and the blatant modernisms of the room were temporarily softened by its impressiveness.

"I love London. I think all we Romans love London more than any other town but our own, Mr. Venables," she confided.

Rosa, as Venables subsequently found, was fond of talking about "we Romans." Another Italian member of the Royal Household later informed him maliciously that the Pavellicinis were and always had been Neapolitans.

"We can't possibly stay any longer," answered Gustav firmly. "You can come another time. You know my mother asked me to get back as soon as possible."

A frown marred for a moment Rosa's perfect brow. "Oh, that!" she said. "But is there really any need to take it so seriously? It is all so absurd—"

Whatever he himself might say about his mother, Prince Augustus evidently did not allow others to permit themselves disparaging comments upon her. He gave Rosa a piercing glance which visibly shattered her. She bowed meekly forward, arranged her beautiful arms afresh above the glittering silver coffee service, and murmured humbly:

"Two lumps of sugar, is it not, Gustav? Do you take milk with your coffee, Mr. Venables?"

Venables' respect for the Prince went up again. On first encountering Rosa, he had been afraid that perhaps after all this picturesque Prince was another of those rulers who ruled by a woman. But quite plainly Rosa was kept in her place. The Prince's look alone had been sufficient...

"Do you mind flying back, Venables?" the Prince asked. "There is an Iconian air force bomber waiting at Hendon, all fixed up to carry passengers. Iconia does not as yet possess an air liner.

"It is a British-built aeroplane," he added, seeing a faint expression of hesitancy cross Venables' face, "and our pilots and engineers are all trained under British officers on loan. Our bulky luggage would go on by train."

Venables accepted enthusiastically. He had been dreading the inevitable rattling across the heart of Europe to the remote Balkans.

They left next afternoon, and stopped the night at Paris. By the late afternoon of the next day they were gliding down on to Iconia's only aerodrome, a plateau on the foothills of the Transylvanian Alps from which, even after they had landed, they could see Isorb lying below in the distance, a misty city of grey stone, nursed in a bend of the Iranyi River, that ancient and little known tributary of the river Danube.

Chapter III

THE ROYAL HOUSEHOLD

I sorb—from the aerodrome a misty city of grey stone and crooked roofs—separated into something more individual if perhaps less picturesque as they splashed and bumped their way in a Rolls–Bentley over its mud and *pavé*. The city straggled disgracefully, and on closer acquaintance there was more wood than stone in the buildings. The streets were generally nothing but narrow chasms between strings of hovels, without pavements to the streets or threshold to the doors, so that the transition from street to domestic interior was abrupt. Indeed, the family generally seemed to flow over into the street, in which one would find from time to time a few articles of furniture, and, of course, invariably the scattered kitchen refuse of the houses and a pervasive unpleasant smell.

There seemed no wealthy quarter to the town, but in some districts more than in others, a great sprawling villa would rear itself from the clustered buildings, separated from its poorer neighbours by a huge walled garden.

Oil apart, Isorb was based on an agricultural country, and so there was no precise demarcation between town and farmsteads. Fields of wheat straggled almost into the centre of the town, and the streets were crowded with herds of cattle, gaily painted wagons loaded high with agricultural produce, and peasants who could be told from citizens only by a certain aimless and surprised stare as they wandered about sightseeing or marketing.

A feature of Isorb was the bridges—bridges which seemed to record every age of architecture—mediæval bridges with pointed arches flanked by shops; eighteenth-century bridges, on whose arches

reclined dolphins and nereids; a revoltingly ugly railway bridge of
Victorian inspiration, and, as if consciously to complete the series, a
modern bridge of unadorned concrete. Although the river obviously
meandered, it seemed to Venables odd that they should have to cross
so many bridges in one journey. Later he guessed that the Prince had
ordered this roundabout route, with rather touching pride, so that
they could see the Vio Victorio, to which the concrete bridge led.

Venables might have been more impressed by the Vio Victorio
had he not remembered Luigi's anecdote of the cow. The surface
was asphalt; there was a wide pavement; and on either side were
modern stone buildings, large shops, restaurants, picture palaces,
offices of oil companies—buildings as self-consciously dignified
and ill at ease as those of Regent Street. Then Venables saw, dominating the other end, some kind of triumphal arch. It appeared of
modern design, yet, for some queer reason, it was already ruinous.
Most of the statues were headless or limbless, and large cracks were
visible in the main structure. Their cars went round it instead of
under it, and as they passed Venables noticed a board marked with
what, judging by its flaring red paint, was the Iconian equivalent
of "Danger—Keep Off".

He turned to comment on this to the Prince. But Gustav merely
frowned, and said coldly, "Yes, it is falling down," and then, turning
away, became pointedly engrossed in conversation with Rosa. Luigi,
who was seated beside Venables, giggled and began to tell him the
history of the arch in a low voice.

"The arch is a monument to Iconia's greatest and best-loved
statesman, Paul Vergotin, who died ten years ago," he explained.
"Enough money was raised by public subscription to build a magnificent memorial arch of marble and bronze, and one was accordingly designed by our leading sculptor, Bröny, of whom you may
have heard. Unfortunately, when the committee of famous Iconian
politicians came to hand over the funds, the regrettable fact was
discovered that for various reasons, into which I had better not

go"—Luigi grinned maliciously—"they had dwindled to about a quarter of their former sum.

"It was therefore necessary to build the great arch of plaster instead of marble. At the opening ceremony, which was performed by Queen Hanna, Bröny became so incensed at the degradation of his great artistic conception that he broke through the cordon, rushed at the arch, and started banging at it with his umbrella. Before the police could stop him, he had destroyed the allegorical figure of Plenty, completely obliterated Virtue Triumphant, and decapitated Justice. Since then the monument has been slowly collapsing." Luigi shrugged his shoulders. "It amuses you? Well, the whole story is typical of Iconia."

The Italian was a good raconteur, and Venables enjoyed the mocking story. However, he wondered, after all, whether Luigi was so discreet as he had at first appeared to be.

After the arch the Vio Victorio relapsed abruptly into hovels and petty shops. They turned off to the left. They had now swung round almost completely and were facing the direction from which they had come. Then, through a break of the houses, dominating the skyline, rose, ridge behind ridge, the bulk of the Transylvanian Alps—white-capped, mist-veiled, remote. The town at once seemed to become more important with that portentous background...

Here, with no preparation in the way of avenues, they came suddenly upon the Milö Palace. Its façade sprung to an impressive height, flanked by a huge wall of massive, vermiculated stone which ran down one entire side of a long but narrow street. Opposite it was merely squalor. The façade itself was magnificent baroque. Enormous pillars rushed up through five storeys to support a gigantic pediment, in which rioted a confused and battered medley of gods and symbolical figures. But everything led up to the enormous gateway with massive bronze leaves, through which the cars now swung, while the black-bearded green-coated sentries presented arms, not very enthusiastically.

The cars drove into a small courtyard, arcaded and dark on two sides, but here, facing their entrance, was another and more magnificent arch, through which they drove into a still larger open space. This was the centre round which the whole building was planned, and all the most important rooms of the Palace overlooked it. Terraces and stairways composed an impressive setting for a luxuriance of ornamental marble pools and statuary. Nymphs lightly extended vases to gaping tritons, Neptune tapped a rock with his trident, dolphins cavorted—evidently some Iconian monarch had attempted to revive on a small but still ambitious scale the glories of Versailles and *le Roi Soleil*.

Playing jets of water were obviously needed to give life to the setting, but when they entered the fountains were dry and the pools muddy. Venables noticed a frown on the Prince's face as he looked round, and wondered whether the non-performance of the fountains had something to do with the frown or whether it was caused by graver matter. A moment later he caught sight, behind a pyramid of struggling gods and giants, of the end of what was manifestly a line of washing, incompletely masked by the pile of statuary...

"Queen Hanna is still in residence here," murmured Luigi, pointing to the Royal standard which floated from a cupola, and on whose yellow background a blood-red eagle reminded Venables that (according to one of Mr. Lancelot's excellent books) the Herzvogins claimed, by some obscure marriage with a Palæologos, to be direct descendants of the Byzantine Emperors. "Generally she leaves about this time for the winter Palace."

Before he vanished into the recesses of the Palace, the Prince turned to Luigi. "Show Mr. Venables to his room. He will, of course, dine with the Chamberlain." He waved a farewell to Venables, and went.

To Venables' surprise Rosa now bade good-bye to the party in the courtyard. Her farewell to the Prince had evidently been spoken in the car. "You must call on me, Mr. Venables," she said, extending a hand languorously, her head bent a little forward, so that the curve of the neck blended with the run of her shoulders in a classic pose. "Any Thursday. Luigi will bring you."

He had expected—wrongly as it turned out—that Rosa would live at the Palace. He watched her, drooping gracefully in the back of the Rolls–Bentley, as it purred out of the courtyard. Then he followed Luigi inside, preceded by a slightly sinister bearded flunkey who had pounced on what little luggage Venables had been able to bring in the aeroplane. To his consternation Venables discovered that he was expected to sleep in a room of which the walls, ceiling, and floor had a background of bright blue, to simulate the effect of a sky. All over this background, without any regard to the law of gravity or the natural division of a room into sides, top, and bottom, sprawled an eighteenth-century version of the Apotheosis of Hercules. (Hercules, Venables remembered, again thanks to one of Lancelot's invaluable little books, was the legendary ancestor of the Herzvogin family.) The effect at first was vertiginous, and was made definitely worse by the presence of queer-shaped mirrors in unexpected places, such as at the foot of the bed, so that one confronted one's own face when one woke in the morning. Later, however, he grew used to walking with bare feet over the cold bodies of nymphs, gods, monsters, and classical vegetation.

"We dine at eight here," said Luigi at the door. "If you ring that bell"—he indicated a golden cord depending from the head of Charles's bed—"the fellow will show you the way. Tell him you are dining with the Chamberlain. If you have any difficulty in finding your way back, ask for the Blue Room."

Venables was late. The curiosities of his remarkable room had delayed his dressing, and on top of that he had not realized that to reach the Chamberlain's apartments from his room involved about ten minutes' hard walking. The four men and two women waiting in the anteroom gave him that look of half-veiled relief which generally greets the late-comer on these occasions.

The Chamberlain, Count Ferdinand Mapponyi, was an unmistakable figure. A thin man of about forty, prematurely stooped, but with a fine head, his huge hooked nose and the small, sharp eyes twinkling behind it made him look like some temporarily domesticated eagle. A sweeping iron-grey beard fell in two forks over an expanse of shirt and white waistcoat, which could not be described either as spotless or immaculate. They were, on the contrary, liberally besprinkled with snuff.

Count Mapponyi greeted him with a formal affability.

"Welcome, Mr. Venables. I am glad to hear you are joining our little household. You will, I understand, give us the pleasure of your company at meals? Your valet will tell you the times," added the Chamberlain, with an apparently casual glance at the great clock on the mantelpiece. "There is no formality here. I have put you between Miss Janet Fotheringay, who is Governess to His Royal Highness's children, and Mr. Brightholme, who is assistant to Dr. Robor, our Physician."

After the glories of the Blue Room, Venables had expected an Arabian Nights' luxury from the Chamberlain's apartments. He was disappointed. Both the anteroom and the dining-room were papered with a fruit-covered wallpaper of the late Victorian period. Venables had time to note the title of three engravings before he was introduced to Miss Fotheringay—"The Stag's Last Stand," "Cattle Drinking in the Highlands," and "Baby's Sunny Hours." The sofa on which the two ladies were seated was of red plush...

Miss Fotheringay, after being introduced, offered Venables a portion of her hand, scrutinized him carefully, and said, in the tone of one asking a question:

"Gloucester?"

"I beg your pardon?" he asked, puzzled.

"Are you one of the Gloucester Venables?" explained Miss Fotheringay patiently.

"I am afraid I am not," admitted Venables.

Miss Fotheringay accepted the apology and seemed momentarily at a loss for conversation. Venables attempted to supply the deficiency.

"We had quite a decent trip over from England," he said cheerfully. "It was Rosa's first flight. She was quite amusing."

"Rosa?" asked Miss Fotheringay, her lips pursed.

"Signorina Pavellicini," explained Venables.

Miss Fotheringay's nostrils quivered as if she were near an unpleasant odour. "I have never met the Ballet Mistress," she said. "Do not trouble to discuss her further."

Fortunately, even as Venables staggered under this blow, dinner was announced.

Venables had hoped for a drink before going in, but the cocktail habit had not reached the Milö Palace.

Miss Fotheringay evidently belonged to a generation which had been taught to walk properly. Although as tall as Venables—a height exaggerated by the thinness of her arms, her gaunt features, and her tightly coiled hair—she floated in on Venables' arm like a ghost, the ghost of Victorian deportment.

Charles at first felt conspicuously nude, for his shirt-front alone seemed undecorated with some insignia. He was relieved, after a second look, to find his other neighbour, Brightholme, equally unadorned.

Brightholme was a cheerful ginger-haired fellow, who seemed disposed to be companionable. "The grub's awful here," he muttered, as he saw Venables look for a moment at the watery soup before putting his spoon into it. "It'll take you a week or two to get used to it."

"It will," agreed Venables, after a mouthful of the soup. "It wouldn't be so bad if it were hot."

"The food's never hot," explained Brightholme. "You see, it starts out hot from the kitchen, but by the time it reaches here, quarter of an hour later, it's quite cold."

"Will you take wine, Mr. Venables?" interrupted the Chamberlain, talking across the plate of Miss Fotheringay, who sat next to Count Mapponyi.

Venables brightened. "Thank you."

"We have a nice hock," murmured the Chamberlain. "Or perhaps you would prefer champagne?"

"I think I should," admitted Venables.

The Chamberlain made a sign to the wine steward, and turned again to Venables. "It is the custom for each member of the household," he said blandly, "to deal with the matter of wine separately."

"In other words," murmured Brightholme, his words audible only to Venables, "the drinks aren't free."

"Quite," said Venables to the Chamberlain. "I think perhaps, after all, I will take some hock." He felt compelled to invite Miss Fotheringay to take wine with him. She accepted, and at once became more gracious.

"I hope you do not find your room draughty, Mr. Venables," she inquired benignly.

"Not yet," he answered.

"The draughts are terrible in the Palace," she complained. "Have you met the Queen?"

"No. You see I have only just arrived."

"The dear Queen. I almost worship that woman! You know—although, of course, I would never presume to mention it to her—we are in a way related. I have the blood of the Stuarts in my veins."

"Really?" said Charles, who was becoming bored by Miss Fotheringay. "Good old Nell Gwynn, eh?"

Miss Fotheringay shuddered. "Most certainly not. There is nothing dubious about the Fotheringay ancestry, I am glad to say. I am only a humble member of the family, but a Stuart was my great-great-grandfather—on my mother's side, and, of course, King Augustus III married a sister of the Cardinal Duke of York. It is quite exciting for a humble little governess like myself to think of this connection, so far back in the mists of history."

Venables felt it was quite time to end this conversation.

"Are you one of the Glasgow Fotheringays?" he asked coldly.

His remark had the desired effect. Miss Fotheringay's nostrils quivered. "I have never heard of them," she said stiffly. "I have never been to Glasgow. My people live at St. Andrews." She turned her head and entered into conversation with the Chamberlain.

"Bravo!" murmured Brightholme approvingly. "Old Fothers takes a bit of choking off. But now she's got that bit about the blood of the Stuarts off her chest she'll be all right. I say, Venables, we're all seething with curiosity about you down here. Is it true that some-one has pinched one of the Crown Jewels, and you've come from Scotland Yard to nose him out?"

"I have not come from Scotland Yard, or anything like it," said Venables. "As for why I came here, I don't quite know myself yet."

"Quite right, of course," answered Brightholme, disappointed. "You must be discreet and so forth. Well, if I can help you, let me know."

"Thanks," replied Venables. "You can help me quite a lot. Here is something to begin with. What exactly is the position of Rosa Pavellicini at Court—apart from the—er—well, the obvious? I should like to know, as I seem to have dropped one brick already."

"Her official position is Ballet Mistress," explained Brightholme. "Not that Rosa knows anything about dancing, but it is a polite fiction always adopted by the Isorb Court. Half of the title is correct, after all. Fothers doesn't approve of her, and often remarks how different life at the Palace is from the home life of dear Queen Victoria. And indeed it is. Did you like Rosa, by the way?"

"Yes, I thought she was quite amusing."

"Um," answered Brightholme noncommittally. "She'll be losing her job soon, you know. The Prince's engagement will be announced shortly. The fiancée-to-be is staying at the Palace—Princess Vera of Kossovia. You'll meet her later. She's an awfully good scout. And as Gustav is a perfect gentleman, Rosa will be packed off before the announcement is made."

"Poor Rosa!"

"Oh, she's all right. She'll get a good pension and a villa up at Theria—that's the Iconian health resort on the hills. She is probably looking forward to it."

"I was told Miss Fotheringay taught Gustav's children. Is he a widower, then?" queried Venables.

"Yes. Their mother died about four years ago. Princess Hilda of Georgina. She was rather sweet, I'm told, but a delicate thing. According to Miss Fotheringay, the draughts of the Palace were too much for her. There's nothing delicate about her children—they're twins, by the way—Petro and Petra. They're absolute devils."

"Oh, I don't mind children," said Venables, in happy ignorance of the character of the Royal twins. "Who are the two old boys opposite me?"

"The little bald-headed man—bit like a monkey, isn't he?—is my chief, Dr. Benedict Robor. Royal Chirurgeon—Court Doctor, you know. He was a pal of Dr. Glastonbury of Bart's, my old chief—that's how I got this job."

Dr. Robor could hardly have heard Brightholme's whisper, but at that moment he directed at Venables a look of piercing scrutiny from a pair of sloe-black eyes. His face, seamed with hundreds of fine wrinkles, looked for a moment malicious and cunning. He drew both hands from his forehead to his mouth, on either side of his nose, with a gesture that seemed habitual with him, and then resumed his conversation with his neighbour, a thin, ascetic-looking man, in the fifties, wearing pince-nez and with a lock of hair sweeping poetically on to his high brow.

"That's Professor Carolos Andreyi he's talking to," explained Brightholme. "Theoretically he's Royal Tutor. In practice it's a sinecure, and he spends his time browsing among the State papers. You see, Miss Fotheringay is educating the children at present, and as soon as Petro is old enough he'll go to an English school."

So far no one could describe the dinner as a cheerful one. None of the men, except Venables and Brightholme, was drinking. The food, magnificently served certainly, and running to several courses, was so outstandingly poor in quality as to discourage conviviality. Venables was therefore relieved to notice that the lady on the Chamberlain's left—a fat elderly woman with a puffy face and quantities of straggling flaxen hair—seemed to be hilarious.

"Good old Naomi," whispered Brightholme—"I should say the Countess Naomi Tacora. She is the Mistress of the Wardrobe, and takes precedence of the ladies of the Household."

A little incident followed which was either missed or politely overlooked by the other members of the party.

The Countess signalled to the wine-waiter, who glanced at the Chamberlain and then prepared to serve her, not for the first time. The Chamberlain frowned, leaned across, and murmured something in the Countess's ear. At the same time he motioned the wine-waiter back.

An expression of fury crossed the Countess's flushed face. Venables could not catch the words that she hissed at the Chamberlain, but they drew forth a small red spot on each cheek of his patrician face. He shrugged his shoulders and turned away, lips compressed, eyes disapproving...

The Countess's wide-mouthed brandy glass, designed to hold a mere spoonful, to be swilled round the glass to release its bouquet, was filled, at her request, to the brim. Venables, fascinated in spite of himself, watched her consume it in a couple of minutes without blenching.

Venables decided it would be indiscreet, until he knew Brightholme better, to question him about the Countess Naomi's apparent weakness. However, there was plenty of other information he might reasonably seek from Brightholme, and now some words of the Prince's flitted through his head, and made him ask the young man:

"Can you tell me what the Curse of the Herzvogins is?"

The effect on his companion was considerable. Brightholme half-turned and looked at him with quite a new interest.

"Crummy!" he ejaculated, "is that why you are here?"

"As I told you before," Venables reminded him, "I do not know why I am here. What is the Curse, and how could it possibly have anything to do with my arrival?"

"It's like this," answered Brightholme, reflectively stirring his coffee—coffee which Charles had found undrinkable. "The second Herzvogin to reign in Iconia was Augustus the Clerk, a weak, well-meaning kind of fellow. His younger brother was a lad who thought he could rule Iconia much better. Unfortunately Augustus was prolific and had five sons, all of whom stood between their uncle and the throne. One day, so the story goes, the father and the five children were found strangled with a silken cord. Of course everyone suspected the brother, but it was never proved. The rope still exists to-day, and is in the Museum in the Chapel crypt. I'll show it to you to-morrow if you're really interested.

"Well, the Curse is supposed to originate out of this piece of mediæval devilry. There is a little Iconian jingle—it means roughly that the throne will never devolve in the direct male line, and that no ruler will reign longer than Augustus the Clerk, who is supposed to have occupied the throne for thirty years."

"And do they really believe in that sort of rot?" asked Venables curiously.

Brightholme shrugged his shoulders. "I don't know. The ignorant peasants do. Everybody at Court laughs at it, but one has a feeling sometimes that half of them do believe in it, in a way, at bottom."

"But surely," pointed out Venables, "either the Curse is true or not. It's categorical enough. Either the Iconian crown has never descended in the direct male line or it has. And either no Herzvogin has reigned more than thirty years or he has."

"No, it's not so simple as that. It is true there has been a constant tendency for the crown to skip about. Uncles and cousins are always inheriting, and there have been six women monarchs of Iconia. But, of course, Iconian Court politics has been fairly lurid in the old days, and the very fact that the Curse exists has probably made uncles and cousins do their little bit to help out the prophecy by bumping off the Heir Apparent."

"Still," Venables pressed him, "have there been authentic cases of direct male descent and of long reigns?"

"Several," agreed Brightholme. "But the superstitious easily explain that. On the principle that it's a wise child who knows its own father. A bit hard on the mother, of course, who was probably a most virtuous and honourable queen, but it's an explanation that can't be disproved, and that saves the face of the prophet. For, of course, if the Heir Apparent is not really of Herzvogin blood, the Curse is fulfilled even if he does come to the throne."

"I see," said Venables. "Thanks a lot. You seem quite an authority on Iconian history."

Brightholme disclaimed this. "I got most of this line through yarning with the Professor. He becomes a bit boring after the first hour. He doesn't himself believe the legend of Augustus the Clerk, by the way. He says Augustus died peacefully in his bed, and that the five children all perished in a local plague. As for the famous silken cord, he swears it is only a nineteenth-century bell-pull. However, I prefer the popular version of the story."

It was at this moment that the Countess Naomi rose, perhaps a little unsteadily, to her feet. The Chamberlain made as if to stop her, and then apparently thought better of it. He leaned back watching her, an inscrutable expression on his aquiline face.

"Dear friends," began the Countess, addressing the table at large in a mournful voice. All traces of cheerfulness had deserted her puffy face, which now looked inexplicably woebegone. "Dear friends, how many of you remember that it is thirty years to-day since poor little Prince Maximilian breathed his last?" The Countess Naomi glanced unsteadily up and down the table. "I remember him so well—such a charming little boy, the hope of us all. And then he died. And my poor little boy Sergio had died before that." Maudlin tears stood in the Countess's eyes.

A chair scraped as Dr. Benedict Robor rose abruptly to his feet. He glared fiendishly at the speaker, bowed to the Chamberlain, and left the room.

Venables heard Brightholme's whistle of amazement. "What on earth possessed Naomi to lead off like this?" he muttered. "She's generally as quiet as a mouse when she gets tight."

"Who on earth was poor little Maximilian?" asked Venables, in a pause during which the half-drunken woman, still on her feet, appeared to be attempting to pull herself together.

"Maximilian was the son of Queen Hanna's brother," explained Brightholme. "He was the heir to the throne. I believe he died of spinal meningitis. The point is that Dr. Robor attended him and also treated Naomi's little son Sergio. Well, you can imagine what Court gossip is. It was whispered that poor old Robor had made a bungle of the treatment of both kids. One scandal-mongering old lady-in-waiting—she got sent back into the country for it—said that Robor had poisoned Maximilian. You can imagine how tactful—"

But the Countess was speaking again. "Some memorial is due…" she muttered thickly, looking at Professor Andreyi through glazed eyes and tottering slightly. She lifted an empty glass slowly. "Let us drink to the memory of poor—"

She broke off as a peremptory hand was laid on her shoulder. The glass slipped from her fingers, and she turned. Luigi Pavellicini had entered the room quietly, and now stood beside her.

"Her Majesty asks you to attend her at once," he said aloud.

With an instinctive gesture the Countess put her hand to her straggling hair as if to straighten it. Then she hurried out of the room.

"Naomi's for it, poor wretch! She's a perfect martyr to delirium tremens!" commented Brightholme. "She'll be sober all right by the time the Queen has finished with her."

Luigi sat down beside the Chamberlain in the place vacated by the Mistress of the Wardrobe. Miss Fotheringay—now the only lady left—rose and left the gentlemen. Her exit was, of course, a model of deportment in leave-taking. Luigi carelessly ordered some cognac and asked the Chamberlain to join him. The Chamberlain agreed, and the five men talked idly together. Then the Prince's secretary turned to the Chamberlain.

"Look here," said Luigi, "H.R.H. was a bit put out by the state of the Grand Courtyard when he passed through. He ordered me to have a word with you about it."

"What did he object to?" asked the Chamberlain coldly.

"Well, for one thing, the fountains were not playing."

The Chamberlain gave a groan. "Does His Royal Highness realize that those fountains cost God alone knows how many dracons an hour when they are working?"

Luigi shrugged his shoulders and ordered a second service of the cognac.

"To be perfectly frank, H.R.H. neither knows nor cares. You know his attitude in these matters."

"I do. I do," muttered the Chamberlain. "But what is to be done?" he went on. "I can only respectfully remind the Prince, Signor Pavellicini, that the fountains will play day and night if only the Chancellor would consent to an increase in the Civil List. If not," the Chamberlain threw up his long white hands, "I cannot work miracles. I wonder sometimes how I manage as it is."

"Of course, Your Excellency," said Luigi soothingly. "We all do. I am sure you understand I am only reporting H.R.H.'s words. There was another point he asked me to mention to you. As he came into the Courtyard he caught sight of something that looked distinctly like washing on a line, hanging up to dry."

"It probably was washing," answered Count Mapponyi defiantly.

"Well, H.R.H. does not like it. In fact, he objects very strongly."

"What *am* I to do?" moaned the Chamberlain. "It isn't the first time this has happened. I have spoken to the Mistress of the Wardrobe about it half a dozen times. And she asks, quite reasonably, where else can the washing be put? I am sure the garments were not obtrusive.

I ask you, Signor Pavellicini, is it fair? If we put the washing in the Gardens, His Royal Highness complains that it makes the Garden Parties look ridiculous. If we put it in the little Tiltyard—that is wrong too, because the Presence Chamber overlooks it. If we hang it in the Court of the Ladies-in-Waiting, even under the cloisters, then he tells me it can be seen from the Banqueting Hall. And now even the Grand Courtyard is forbidden! I assure you," added the Chamberlain, "that the Countess Tacora—she told me herself—has given special orders that the things must be hidden as far as possible. I am sure I have been through the Courtyard a hundred times, and I have never noticed it."

"H.R.H. did," Luigi reminded him.

The Chamberlain sighed. "Oh dear, I suppose it is disrespect-ful, but I do sometimes wish it was not the custom for our Royal Princes to go to England and come back with these new-fangled ideas. There was never any complaint about the washing from Queen Hanna when the Prince was away at school. What do you think, Professor?"

Professor Andreyi was of the opinion that none of the ancient sovereigns of Iconia would have objected. "They would probably have considered a display of linen a happy ostentation," he explained. "Few Iconians except the wealthier landowners would have been in a position to own a change of linen in those days."

"You see?" said the Chamberlain triumphantly. "After all, every-one knows things must be washed. Do you know how many table-cloths alone go to the wash here every week?"

"I don't," admitted Luigi. "Unofficially I agree with you. But H.R.H.'s wishes must be respected. Couldn't the things be sent to a laundry?"

"No," said the Chamberlain firmly. "I could never be a party to such an extravagance. It would be perfectly absurd to send our washing out with hundreds of idle hands in the servants' quarters. I will speak to H.R.H. about it myself. Where is he at the moment?"

"I left him with the Queen," answered Luigi. "Oh, and by the way," he said to Venables, "Her Majesty has been informed by the Prince of your arrival, and she has expressed a desire to see you at eleven o'clock to-morrow."

"I'll look in and see you before you go over the top," murmured Brightholme into Venables' ear.

Chapter IV

THE SILKEN CURSE

B efore he went to bed, Charles Venables ordered breakfast to be served early in his room. Brightholme had offered to show him the famous Chapel of St. Boron and the Museum in its crypt. Venables, remembering his audience with Queen Hanna at eleven next morning, was anxious to get any light he could on the background, and so he had held Brightholme to his promise and arranged to visit the Chapel before the Royal interview.

As he drank his coffee next morning and read his *Times* and *Mercury* of two days ago, Venables found his mind wandering. Was his position a sinecure? Or did a real danger menace Queen Hanna? Supposing it did, would he be justified in taking on the responsibility of shielding her—he, a stranger to Iconia and the Palace—in this huge caravanserai of utterly foreign men and motives? It was true that the six members of last night's dinner-party had individualized themselves for him, and of course he had become fairly well acquainted with Gustav, Luigi, and Rosa. But the rest of the inmates of the Palace were about as scrutable to an Englishman as ten thousand Cantonese. They all had a similar cast of features—squashy noses and narrow eyes. They all—the men at least—bowed like machines and spoke the same slurred coldly correct English. Venables had never seen so many varied uniforms in his life even at a Levee. Ladies-in-Waiting, Equerries, Masters of Horse, Secretaries, and God knows what titles untranslatable into an English equivalent—did all palaces breed this odd species of wooden-faced, soft-voiced, petty-minded people, or was it peculiar to the Milö Palace?

He supposed in time he might learn to differentiate between one and another, that eventually he might be able to distinguish the bright pink face of Warden of the Queen's Forests Count Angelef, from the bright pink face of Marshal of the Nobility Count Herreshyi, but even then he would be almost as far as ever from discovering what (if anything) went on behind those faces. It was hard to remember that a Count with a pedigree as old as Christianity had probably only two shirts and the income of a British miner.

His reflections were interrupted by the cheerful voice of his compatriot. Brightholme came in. He hung his hat on the outstretched marble leg of Cacus struggling beneath the onslaught of Hercules, and looked round the room. "Crikey, they've done you proud. Sleep all right?" he asked.

"Not too well," admitted Venables.

"Dietetic deficiency," diagnosed Brightholme cheerfully. "We'll go out and have a square meal later. I know a tavern in the town, if you don't mind Iconian cooking. Lots of saffron and fat, you know. You'll see a good deal of people from the Palace at the said tavern—those who can afford it."

"Has the food always been like this?" asked Venables.

"Only since the inflation!" explained the other. "The Iconian dracon is worth fivepence instead of tenpence now, but the Civil List allowance hasn't been increased. Demetrior, the Chancellor, you know, simply daren't while agriculture is doing so badly. There's the revenue from oil royalties, of course, but by an odd coincidence," Brightholme winked, "it exactly equals the interest and amortization on the British loans to Iconia.

"In the old days the Royal House was the landlord of half Iconia. In 1904 the Crown lands were all broken up and given to the peasants by the Distribution Act. So the Palace is run almost entirely on the Civil List and a few petty prerogatives. We all grumble at Mapponyi, but really the old boy does absolute wonders. He's devoted to Queen Hanna, and himself exists on nothing. In fact, I think he helps balance the accounts out of his own pocket. Lord knows how the Palace will run when he's dead!"

"It may be indelicate to mention it," said Venables reflectively, "but I hope I shall have no difficulty in collecting my fee. I'm on holiday without salary, you see, and I didn't bargain on having to pay for drinks."

"I think that will be all right," said Brightholme. "They were discussing last night how you would figure in the accounts. You must have some official status, you see; but unfortunately all the Court appointments are filled at the moment except for a Lady-in-Waiting or two. Professor Andreyi suggested reviving for you the important office of Lord Protector, which has been in abeyance for three centuries."

"Really. What were the duties of the Lord Protector?" asked Venables curiously.

"Comparatively simple. The office was instituted by King Maximilian the Second, who was scared of witches—rather like our King James I, you know. The witches of his period were apparently helpless unless they could get hold of a lock of your hair or your nail parings. So Maximilian appointed a really trustworthy Iconian noble to attend him when he was being trimmed by his barber. It was the Lord Protector's duty to make sure that all the royal hair and nail parings were burnt on the spot in a golden crucible which, by the way, is in the Royal Museum."

"I don't fancy the job, but I like the title," said Venables. "By the way, talking about titles, you are Dr. Brightholme, aren't you?"

"I am an M.D.," admitted the other; "but I'm also a surgeon, and so prefer the 'Mr.' Absurdly vain we surgeons, aren't we? Dr. Robor imagines himself a bit weak on surgery—many of these first-rate physicians do. That's why I'm here."

"I suppose you're M.R.C.S. as well. You look extraordinarily young to have all these honours heaped on your head," commented Venables, looking at him curiously. "How do you manage to keep the schoolboy complexion?"

"Oh, fasting and hard work," answered Brightholme vaguely. "Look here, we'd better be going along to the Museum if we're to get back in time for your appointment. Queen Hanna is very punctual. She's the only person in Iconia who is, I should imagine."

Venables followed Brightholme through the maze of passages which, thanks to a retentive memory for this kind of thing, he was already beginning to place. A little plan of the Palace was slowly taking shape in his notebook. In succeeding days he added largely to it, with the aid of some eighteenth-century engravings in the Royal Library.

To reach the Museum they crossed the Tiltyard, passed through a wicket gate into a neglected walled garden, at the end of which was a crumbling grey stone Romanesque chapel—a chapel in name, but a church in size.

The two soldiers on duty at the gate evidently knew Brightholme. They saluted him, but looked more closely at Venables. Once inside, the two stood for a moment silent by the red sandstone font.

The Chapel of St. Boron was charming—more intimate than awe-inspiring. The walls were covered with mosaic saints, as stiff and conventional as the severest Byzantine tradition could make them. But their colouring was as vivid as an advertisement, glowing with defiant richness beneath the misty breath of time.

The heavily coffered barrel vaulting, sprinkled with gilt-plate stars, met in a dome, round the base of which ran a text. It was uncomfortably apposite in view of the dubious history of the Herzvogin line. It read: "The man of blood shall not live out half his days." On the inner surface of the dome was a design of angels, evidently belonging to a later period than the mosaic on the walls, for, in contrast to those rigid saints, they used their wings freely and rollicked like birds, a cheerful squadron of looping and gliding spirits.

A gilt communion rail divided the Chapel almost exactly into halves, and the sides of the huge sanctuary thus shut off were occupied by two facing rows of carved wooden thrones, above each of which hung a coloured banner and a glowing coat-of-arms. In the centre, in front of the altar steps, and between the rows of thrones, a life-size recumbent stone figure of a man lay on a granite sepulchre. His face and flowing robes were painted in bright natural colours, giving him the odd and repulsive appearance of being a real but dead human being.

"Those are the thrones of members of the Iconian Order of Chivalry," explained Brightholme. "The Order was founded by King Boron the Good—who became the St. Boron to whom this Chapel is dedicated. After his death he was discovered to have worn under his robes, as a mortification, a heavy iron collar with spikes, which pressed continually into his flesh.

"His successor founded the Order whose members are known as Knights of the Collar. The Knights' ceremonial insignia includes an iron collar, but, I need hardly say, without the spikes. That inscription round the dome is the motto of the Order. Queer, isn't it? The ceremonial of investiture is rather fine. I saw one a month ago. That tomb in the middle holds the body of St. Boron. All the Iconian peasants invoke St. Boron for diseases of the throat. But let's go down to the crypt."

After the impressive Chapel above, Venables expected something awe-inspiring from the burying-place of the Herzvogin line. Here, since the eleventh century, every Herzvogin monarch had been entombed except during that troubled fifteenth century when the Turks, like an evil flood, had swept over Iconia, and for a time blotted out its guttering candle-flame of civilization.

But the crypt was of a primitive simplicity. It reminded Venables of nothing so much as a wine cellar. No sculpture adorned the walls, and the only inscriptions were on the six-feet-long brass plates, some almost effaced, others new and shining, which in long rows on the floor marked the resting-places of the dead monarchs.

"The brass plates are all supposed to be engraved with full-length portraits of the monarch they commemorate," explained

Brightholme, as Venables stooped over a brass depicting in black *niello* some crowned warrior. "But actually there is hardly any difference between the portraits. All the men are knights in armour, even the nineteenth-century chappies. And the women—all beautiful and young, and dressed in coifs and long robes. What happened was that each engraver copied the portrait of the preceding king, with just a few touches and inventions of his own. That's why even the newest looks four centuries old. Rather a charming idea, isn't it?"

"I think it's a pity," commented Venables. "It would have been interesting to have real likenesses of some of these fellows."

"We have got them for the kings after the sixteenth century," remarked Brightholme. "Come into the next room."

The next room, reached through a descending tunnel, was lined with glass-fronted alcoves. Behind these, each lit by an electric bulb, like something in a shop window, horribly alive and banal, sat the wax effigies of the later monarchs of Iconia, dressed in faded clothes which had been worn by the originals themselves.

An inheritance of realism, as strong in its opposite sense as the tradition of conventionality which inspired the engravers of the brass portraits, was behind these wax figures. Here were real human beings. Sad faces, soft faces, mad faces, weak faces, artists' faces, heroes' faces—all stared from their shop windows at the casual passers-by. And like a chime of bells ringing its changes, a lip, or nose, or lift of the eyebrow could be followed zigzagging its hereditary path down the ages, linking with a common touch sinner and saint, warrior and clerk.

Brightholme halted before the last effigy—a man, apparently in the early thirties, whose bushy Victorian side-whiskers contrasted oddly with his ceremonial robes of state.

"That's Francis II," he said, "the father of 'poor little Max,' whom Naomi was gassing about last night. He reigned a month, and he was succeeded by his sister, Queen Hanna. The two loathed each other like poison, and for a long time she refused to put up his effigy here, although it had been made before he died, like that of every Iconian monarch. I believe the Patriarch of Iconia (His Beatitude Dr. Igor) eventually persuaded her to do the right thing by Crispin."

"She loathed him, did she?" said Venables reflectively. King Francis looked quite a nice young man—a little weak perhaps, but amiable. "Why did they quarrel?"

"I don't know," confessed Brightholme. "Robor would know. He's been at Court as long as the Chamberlain."

"There was nothing fishy about his death, I suppose, was there?" asked Venables. "Perhaps I have an unduly suspicious mind, but what with the lurid history of the Herzvogins one can't help wondering."

"Sorry to disappoint you," answered Brightholme, looking at Venables with an odd expression; "but I don't think Queen Anne can be held responsible. King Francis was shot by Nicolet Burgin, the leader of the Iconian Peasant Party, during the agrarian troubles which were pacified by the Distribution Act. Burgin was executed, of course."

Venables turned away from the effigy and its amiable and ineffective simper. "Who was Gustav's father, by the way? Did he die before his wife came to the throne?"

"No, about a year after," Brightholme told him. "I gather he was a pretty weak sort of fellow. He was Prince John-Boris-Erich—one of the Varangian princelings. You know all the Varangians are a bit inclined towards T.B. John-Boris-Erich wasn't very popular, particularly as he died apparently without ensuring the succession to the throne. Of course everyone started talking about the Curse. But people had misjudged him. Gustav was born posthumously, six months after the Prince-Consort's death. Luckily the T.B. has overlooked Gustav. Robor says he's as sound as a bell. You could guess it from looking at him, I imagine."

They passed on to the Museum itself. After the bizarre vitality of the waxworks, the historical collection seemed flat and tame. The authentic Imperial diadem of Constantine, brought to Iconia by the

Palæologue princess... The patent of the Most Peaceable Order of the Collar... The black Fatimate banner wrenched by Maximilian the Great from a Saracen... The Iconian Regalia, hardly visible behind the triple barring and heavy glass which protected it... The veritable Iron Collar of St. Boron...

"And here," exclaimed Brightholme, "we have the oldest relic of all. If it's authentic... The silken cord with which Augustus the Clerk and his five children were throttled." Brightholme's jaw dropped. The blood left his face for a moment. "Good God!"

The glass case, the two hooks, the blue plush background, and the neat label in Andreyi's archaistic script were all there.

But the silken Curse itself was gone...

Chapter V

THE PLEASANT PRINCESS

"**P**inched!" breathed Brightholme. "Somebody's snaffled the Curse."

The two men stared at the rifled case.

"Mightn't Professor Andreyi have taken it out?" suggested Venables.

The surgeon shook his head. "No, old Andreyi would never dream of doing such a thing. He examines everything on the spot. He'd never dare to take the Curse out. The Queen will have ten fits when she hears." He gave Venables an odd smile. "You'd better tell her about this business yourself."

They turned as they heard the echo of voices in the next room. Then the footsteps came near—a heavier tread and a scampering.

"My God, those pests!" groaned Brightholme.

A boy and a girl walked in. With them was a woman who held the girl by the hand. Venables judged the children to be about ten years old. Both wore sailor suits, the boy's with white trousers and the girl's with a white skirt, but the likeness between their faces was more arresting. Obviously these were Gustav's twins, Petro and Petra.

The woman was an unusual figure. For the moment Venables was unable to place her. She was tall and massively built—not in any way fat, but with the sturdy frame of a woman athlete. Her hair was startlingly red, and was set off by the clear white of her brows and neck. She moved quickly and a little clumsily. About twenty-five years old, Venables judged. Although she was physically a little alarming, the open good-nature of her face made up for everything. It was not perhaps a beautiful face, although the features had a marked distinction, but it was a cheerful, extremely prepossessing face. It smiled at Brightholme familiarly, and then inquiringly at Venables.

Brightholme presented him, but the girl had obviously guessed who he was. "Princess Vera," explained Brightholme to Venables.

So this was Princess Vera of Kossovia, Gustav's bride to be! They certainly would make a magnificent pair; both were built on the same Homeric scale.

Venables smiled propitiatingly at the royal twins who were standing opposite him, watching him in the inscrutable manner of children. They were pleasant snub-nosed beings, with the blue eyes and fair hair of their father. The boy was clasping a half-grown tabby cat.

"Would you like to stroke Kitty?" he asked Venables, with a confiding smile. Meanwhile Brightholme, taking the Princess a little to one side so that the children should not hear, told her of the disappearance of the Curse of the Herzvogins. The Princess evidently refused to believe it was anything but a joke.

Venables, rather touched, accepted the boy's offer. Petro stuffed the animal into his arms. Instantly it became a screeching tornado of furs and claw. It gashed open the back of his hand and made a frantic attempt to get at his eyes, before he dropped it hurriedly. Then it raced round the Museum swearing like a devil, with all its fur erect. Princess Vera turned just in time to see the incident. She made two enormous strides towards Petro, swung him off the ground by the slack of his collar, and cuffed him vigorously. The boy remained dumb, but Petra, horrified at her brother's fate, emitted the most appalling scream Venables had ever heard. This, however, had not the slightest effect on the Princess.

"I am so sorry," said Princess Vera, after the boy had been made to apologize to the injured investigator. "That dreadful little animal is half an Iconian wildcat. Only the children can do anything with it. They are devoted to animals. I'm afraid," she added, "they're half animals themselves."

"They won't allow you wildcats at Eton, Petro," Venables warned him.

"I'm going to Marlborough," answered Petro.

"Or there," Venables added.

"Would they allow a goat?" he asked hopefully, and seemed to lose interest in education when he was told it was unlikely.

"They've been allowed to run wild," went on Princess Vera, in her rich voice with its faintly German inflexions. "Miss Fotheringay is afraid to punish them because if she does they put snakes in her bed. They tried it on me the first night I was here." Princess Vera smiled at the recollection. "They made the mistake of hanging round to see the fun. They've never done anything like that since. I smacked them so hard that the officer on duty turned out the guard in my wing, thinking someone was being murdered!"

Petra had wandered back into the room of the wax figures. She returned shortly afterwards, an interested look on her face.

"When will they stuff father?" she asked curiously.

Princess Vera frowned. "You mustn't say that sort of thing. Poor father!"

"I think it would be rather amusing," said Petro animatedly. "He'd be quite the biggest there, wouldn't he?"

"Ow, there you are, yer Rile 'Ighness!" said an unmistakably Cockney voice. There was a wheezing noise, and in came an old woman with a wrinkled moon-like face and an extraordinary dress of starched linen and ample petticoats which only remotely suggested a servant and was faintly reminiscent of a nurse. "Miss Fotheringay 'as sent me to look for their Rile 'Ighnesses."

"Oh yes, of course, Mutch. I was forgetting," answered Princess Vera. "Come along, children. And don't take that animal into lessons with you, or I shall be annoyed."

Venables and Brightholme were left alone again.

"Rather a dear, isn't she?" said Brightholme, looking after her with a smile. "She's the only one who keeps those two brats in order, and yet they absolutely adore her. Mutch would be good with them too, but she daren't spank them. The Princess has an advantage there. By the way, did you hear that odd thing Petra said about her father?"

"I did. Callous little brutes children are sometimes, aren't they? Of course they never realize what they are saying."

"I'm not so sure," said Brightholme reflectively, as they walked up from the crypt. Back in the open air he filled and lit a pipe. "I'm not so sure. You know they don't get on with their father. I don't like to say it, but I think it's their grandmother's fault. I honestly believe the Queen's jealous of Gustav and tries to put them against him."

"Against her own son! Good Lord, what a family!"

"Yes, I know it takes some believing. Princess Vera hinted that she heard the Queen telling them Gustav had been unkind to their mother. An absolute slander, of course. They worship her memory, and I believe she was a darling. The trouble is they don't see much of Gustav, who spends nine months in the year abroad—I don't blame him—and so the Queen has a good deal of influence over them. It's a bit diabolical, isn't it? Of course Princess Vera will stop all that as soon as she marries Gustav. She's about the only woman who could take on Queen Hanna."

They walked back together to Venables' room. "By the way," asked Brightholme, "what are you going to wear for your audience?"

"Is there a sort of Windsor uniform or anything?" asked Venables. "I have always wanted to wear knee-breeches."

Brightholme shook his head. "No. Everyone in Iconia seems to belong to some regiment or other, and they wear uniform here."

"I was in the Boy Scouts," answered Venables hopefully. "Or perhaps I could wear evening dress, as they do at the Vatican?"

His problem, however, was soon settled. When Venables opened the door of his room, Warden of the Queen's Forests Count Angelef (or was it Marshal of the Nobility Count Herreshyi?) was waiting for him. The Count bowed.

"You are commanded to attend on Her Majesty in twenty minutes in the Silver Drawing-room. Morning dress: black frock coat, striped trousers, white slip and spats, grey tie, white shirt, no hat, gloves to be carried." He bowed again. "In twenty minutes."

Chapter VI

THE FRIGHTENED QUEEN

The Silver Drawing-room was an octagonal room in a turret which balanced the belfry tower of the Milö Palace. Its eight windows surveyed the straggling roofs of Isorb, the knotted cloud-caped shoulders of the distant Alps, the glittering ribbon of the Iranyi River, and the golden wheat-fields of the encircling plains.

Whether such was the Iconian etiquette of audience, or whether it was some feminine caprice of the Queen, Venables found himself left alone in the Silver Drawing-room. He stood uneasily in the centre of the white carpet, where his mentor had abandoned him, and stared idly out of the windows...

"The Most High and Mighty Princess Hanna, by the Grace of God Queen of the Territories of Isorb, Duchess of Iconia, Most Exalted Augusta of Constantinople, Sovereign Prior of the Royal and Peaceable Order of the Collar..."

This pompous and ridiculous description of Queen Hanna, which he had seen on an illuminated genealogical tree in the Museum, flitted through his mind as he waited in the Drawing-room... A door opened behind him, and there was a rustle of skirts. He turned to meet the reality behind the magniloquent style. The Queen...

Tall, angular, thin-faced, with green eyes and a fox-like inquis-itive nose, Queen Hanna leaned in the doorway on a stick and looked at Venables with silent attention. She was dressed in a long full-sleeved gown of scarlet silk, embroidered with beaded designs of a barbaric splendour. As she leaned there, her head a little on one side, she reminded Venables of nothing so much as a parrot about to speak.

Her face was repulsive and yet impressive. Deep wrinkles scored the pendulous cheeks, which were grained and thickly covered with cosmetics. Her reddened lower lip was hanging loosely with the laxness of age. Her eyes had been empurpled and their sparse lashes blackened to brighten their tired gaze. A towering red wig was perched on her yellow brows and added to her already formidable height.

Queen Hanna made some inarticulate exclamation of approval, and her watchful expression became a coquettish simper. The green eyes softened and fell. She extended her hand for Venables to kiss.

"So, so," she murmured. Her English was correct, but the familiar Iconian slurring of the stressed syllables made it a monotonous sing-song. "Young, distinguished-looking, clever. My son has chosen admirably. And you have come to help me, I thank you."

Queen Hanna walked slowly to the carved armchair which was placed unceremoniously beside the fireplace. In spite of her ill-shapen body and the infirmity in her gait, which needed a stick, she managed to move with unembarrassed dignity.

"You are comfortable, is it so?" she asked after a pause.

Venables assured her that he had never been more comfortable.

"Good. I told them to put you in the Blue Room. That woman is always talking about the draughts," muttered Queen Hanna a little obscurely. "A thoughtless fool, but devoted."

There was a pause. Queen Hanna seemed to draw into herself. Her eyes grew cloudy. "And now you will want to know why I sent for you." She motioned Venables to fetch an embroidered stool and sit down in front of her. Then with one gnarled and beringed hand she sought in some pocket in the capacious folds of her scarlet skirts and produced a letter. She handed it to Venables, who read it aloud:

"Give up your foolish plan. If not you die. The only Doom of the Herzvogins is that of all indiscreet monarchs who have passed the age when they can be trusted with affairs of state. Remember Maximilian!"

Queen Hanna nodded her head as he finished. "Now, Mr. Venables, your frank opinion? Do not concern yourself with etiquette now. I am consulting you as I would consult a doctor."

Venables examined the writing through his pocket glass. "A clumsily disguised handwriting. A man's."

Queen Hanna tapped her foot irritably. "Obviously! Don't talk like my Chief of Police." Venables accepted the rebuke meekly. "The Maximilian referred to is, I suppose, your nephew?" Queen Hanna's lips parted to show her long yellow teeth. "So, you have heard all the Court gossip already? No doubt they have told you that I poisoned my nephew?"

"I have heard a great many silly rumours, Your Majesty," admitted Venables, "which I imagine are common to all palaces."

"Do not apologize. I admire your shrewdness in having learned so much already. Go on."

"This cannot be the first threatening letter Your Majesty has had?" he went on. "A person in your exalted position must get thousands which your secretaries would not trouble to show you. There is some reason why you attach particular importance to this?"

"There is. As you say, my secretaries deal with the other silly letters. But this I find in my pocket when I am dressed, so." Queen Hanna plunged her hand into her skirts again and pantomimed an expression of surprise. "That is not silly."

Venables' eyebrows rose. "Someone near you, eh? Have you made any investigations?"

Queen Hanna nodded moodily. "I have examined personally every one of my servants. I have frightened them so that some were sick." She showed her yellow teeth again. "But it was no good. They are fools. There can be no danger from them. It is someone else. You must find who."

"Let us try from another angle. Can you tell me what the plan is to which this letter refers, and which you must not carry out? Has Your Majesty some particular project in mind?"

The Queen was silent for a moment. Her tired eyes looked past Venables into space like those of an old eagle. "You have heard of our legendary Curse perhaps?" she said at last.

He nodded. "Yes, ma'am. I was in the Chapel this morning, and—" The Queen interrupted as he was about to tell her of the theft.

"No matter! You know, then, that no Herzvogin monarch of true blood and descent may reign for more than thirty years." The Queen's voice dropped to a whisper. "To-morrow is the eve of the thirtieth anniversary of my accession to the throne." She smiled reminiscently to herself. "Thirty years, Mr. Venables. It found me little more than a girl. It has left me what you see." She raised a bony finger as Venables was about to speak, and tapped his cheek. "No! do not flatter an ugly old woman. But remember this: I found my country torn with civil war, distracted, impoverished. To-day it is rich as we value money, and above all, peaceful. But the art of rule is eternal vigilance, Mr. Venables. So simple it seems to hold a country quiet in prosperity and peace." She clenched a bony fist. "But no. Relax your grip." She unclosed her hand. "A tiny crack appears. The crack spreads. And look, everything explodes, blows to fragments." Her vigorous gesture overturned her stick, which clattered on the silver fireguard. Venables picked it up.

"Thank you. Well, if the Curse is true, I die to-morrow." Her head sank on her chest. "I do not care. It is not for that I call you. Indeed it would be childish of me to try to outwit Fate with the help of a detective—ridiculous and unworthy. It is time another took my place." The Queen paused, drifted into reverie. "Gustav is a dear boy," she muttered, "but he is not interested in ruling. He wants nothing but to be away—in Paris or London. And he grumbles because our income is less than that of a Jew, and that out of it I maintain a thousand souls. But to give more than you get—that is the duty of a king. Perhaps the Crown will sober my successor as it sobered me…"

Queen Hanna seemed to have forgotten entirely the object about which she had called in Venables. She was embarked on one of the easy reveries of the old. "If Petro now were to succeed me! He has the real Herzvogin spirit."

Then she picked up the letter again and seemed to come to herself. "No doubt, with your English common sense, you laugh at this Curse. We all pretend to, here, Mr. Venables. When I was your age, newly come to the throne, I laughed at it. But lately one knows differently." She pressed her tired old eyes with her beringed hands. "I have such dreadful dreams—if indeed they are dreams, for I have only to cover my eyes so, and I see these awful things." She stared at Venables. "Do you know, I have felt a dagger at my breast in the night and woken screaming with the pain still there." She pressed her scraggy body convulsively, under her silk wrappings. "And I have felt hands stealing about my throat in broad daylight..."

There was such a strange conviction about her words and gestures that for a moment Venables was transported into her nightmare-ridden mood. He shook himself free with an effort.

"You have been in our Chapel... *The man of blood will not live out half his days*," she quoted solemnly. "You remember that? Ah, ours is a blood-stained line. But let the Curse come as it will, I shall make peace with my soul. St. Boron groaned his life long under the burden of the Collar. I have my collar, too, Mr. Venables. To-morrow, on the eve of my accession—and by a strange chance it is St. Boron's day in our calendar—the world will be shown my collar." She crumpled the letter up and threw it on the floor (whence Venables later recovered it). "I am not to be frightened by that kind of thing. I was wrong to take it so seriously—a Herzvogin and afraid of anonymous letters!"

"Is anyone in your confidence?" asked Venables.

"No; but two people know enough to guess. The writer of this letter, it seems," answered Queen Hanna. "And one other man."

"Might they not be the same?" he pressed.

Her eyes blazed. "If I thought that! But no, it is impossible. There is too much for him to lose and too little to gain. He would never dare to threaten me, for I hold his reputation and his life in my hands. I could extinguish him—like that!" She snapped her fingers.

"Can you tell me who the man is?"

"Mr. Venables, you are not to interfere in any matter beyond that on which I have called you in. I have been threatened. You are to protect me, and find who it is who has threatened me. For the rest, complete discretion, you understand?" She had again become a straightforward and business-like queen.

"You may rely on my discretion, ma'am—particularly if you honour me with your confidence."

She smiled. "I do rely on it. And so I shall tell you the man who knows enough to guess my intention—it is my physician, Dr. Robor. But I tell you this merely to show my confidence. I do not believe—I know it is impossible—that he wrote this letter."

Venables bowed. "I will remember that. May I ask another question? Are you adequately guarded? You came in here unaccompanied."

"I need no guard; I am a Constitutional Monarch," she said coldly. "My confidence is in the love and loyalty of my people."

"Including the writer of this letter, Your Majesty? There was a Judas among twelve apostles, and you have half a million subjects."

"I see you have familiarized yourself with my little kingdom." She smiled. "What do you suggest?"

"If I may advise Your Majesty, since the essence of this threat is to prevent some act you are to carry out to-morrow, the next twenty-four hours are dangerous. You should go back to your room, and take care to have with you—sleep in the same room at night—at least two people whom you trust. Again—I know it sounds melodramatic—be careful about your food. Finally, have a double guard on the door of your suite to admit no one in without your spoken permission."

"I have never had a guard..." repeated Queen Hanna wearily. "Still..." she hesitated, and got slowly to her feet. Venables helped her. The arms in their flowing sleeves were as thin as sticks.

"Only for twenty-four hours!" urged Venables. He searched round for something to emphasize his plea. "I feel I ought to tell Your Majesty a discovery that was made in the Museum this morning. The cord which is known as the Curse has been stolen!"

The effect on the Queen was alarming, and not at all what he had expected. The blood rushed into her face, and her eyes seemed about to burst with the stored-up fury behind them. She stamped impotently on the floor with her stick.

"I am surrounded by villains and traitors," she screamed. "Not one of all of you would lift a finger to save a weak old woman from the hand of an assassin. The very soldiers on guard allow my sacred family relics to be snatched from under their noses." She relapsed into a stream of fluent Iconian unintelligible to Venables, and began pacing the octagonal room like a beast. Suddenly she stopped dead and pointed with her stick to the Courtyard below. A sentry, his rifle propped up against the wall, was talking to a servant girl with a basket of fruit over her arm. "God damn the villain!" she screeched, and before Venables grasped her intention she had fished into the depths of her skirts and produced a huge pistol of antique design. There was an ear-shattering report and a tinkle of falling glass. The sentry snatched up his rifle and then looked round bewildered.

"An old woman..." muttered Queen Hanna, stuffing the weapon into her pocket again with a malicious grin. "But still a Herzvogin!"

A minute afterwards two men burst into the Silver Drawing-room with uncourtly haste. One was Marshal of the Nobility Count Herreshyi; the other was an older man whom Venables had not seen before. Both were frightened, and panting with haste.

Queen Hanna looked at them with a contemptuous smile. "Too late! I should have been dead by now," she said, and hobbled from the room.

Chapter VII

THE PUZZLED DETECTIVE

"Mr. Charles Venables—His Excellency the Chancellor, Count Demetrior," introduced the Marshal of the Nobility as soon as he had sufficiently recovered from the effect of the Queen's dramatic exit from the Silver Drawing-room. Venables was struck favourably by the appearance of the Chancellor. An elderly man, with wise eyes, firm chin, and the wrinkles of benevolent toleration round mouth and forehead. "Excuse me, gentlemen," added the Marshal, and fled like a scared rabbit after his Royal mistress.

"I had an audience at eleven-thirty," said the Chancellor to Venables. "I was chatting to Herreshyi when I heard the shot. Naturally we were worried. What happened?"

"Her Majesty saw a sentry neglecting his duty and took a pot-shot at him," explained Venables.

The Chancellor smiled. "What a woman! This is your first audience?"

Venables nodded.

"And what do you think of our Queen? I am not a courtier, so you see I can ask these indiscreet questions."

"A very powerful personality!" admitted Charles guardedly. "I wish I knew how seriously to take all she said."

"She spoke to you about this gesture of hers to-morrow? What has she got up her sleeve? It worries me. She is capable of anything. This project: I ask myself, is it political? She is quite equal to announcing her abdication or an alteration of the Constitution. But she refuses to tell me. She says, with that queer metaphor of hers: 'In a few days you will see the collar I have been wearing so long.'" The Chancellor sighed.

"Is she popular in the country—if I also may ask indiscreet questions?"

"Adored, Mr. Venables. I choose the word advisedly. Ah, you see her now an old woman—crotchety even, if I may say it without disrespect—and cannot understand. But when she came to the throne! Picture her. Little more than a girl—a useless, sickly husband; her predecessor assassinated; the whole country in a turmoil; mobs running at large through Isorb; the Balkan Powers, like wolves, waiting to 'intervene.' You should have seen her, on the day of dreadful riots, after her Coronation, sitting on a white charger, addressing the Palace Guard. After that speech they would have died for her to a man. The party in power wanted her to put down the risings with a firm hand. They were all landowners, you see. That would have been the end. She had the political wisdom to summon our great predecessor (whose monument you doubtless saw on the Vio Victorio), then an almost unknown man." Demetrior saw a twinkle in Venables' eye, and laughed himself. "I see someone has been telling you that malicious story about the Arch of Memory. But he was a great statesman all the same. She empowered him to carry out the new agrarian policy which resulted in the Distribution Act, and has pacified this country. Since then Iconia has gone on from strength to strength. She has even succeeded in entering into commercial agreements with Britain," added the Chancellor, with an ironical smile, "and yet maintained autonomy in all but strictly financial matters."

"If what she told me just now is true, she really may be in some danger," said Venables seriously. "I have warned her to make sure she is adequately guarded during the next twenty-four hours. She has neither agreed nor disagreed. Can you use your influence? I have no standing here, you see, and I can do no more than recommend."

"We none of us can do no more than that with Her Majesty," said Count Demetrior ruefully. "I shall do my best. I had better have a word with Herreshyi. She occasionally listens to him—God knows why."

Venables returned slowly to his room. He felt a great need of putting his puzzled thoughts in order. Finally he set out his leading queries haphazard on paper. In view of their subsequent importance, we record them below:

QUEEN HANNA

1. *Is the Queen really scared, or was she acting a part when she spoke to Venables?*
2. *If the former, what revelation is the Queen about to make?*
3. *If the latter, did she forge the letter she showed him?*
4. *And was her interview with Venables to-day merely to make an ass of him?*
5. *Is she really a little mad (hallucinations, etc.), or is she putting it on? (See 4.)*
6. *Is there anything in the rumours about young Prince Maximilian's death, and if so, was there anything fishy about the death of his father, King Francis (Brightholme says no)?*
7. *What was the ground of her feud with King Francis?*
8. *What is the secret she shares with Robor? N.B.—Dr. Robor attended Prince Maximilian.*
9. *Why does a well-qualified medical man like Brightholme come out to such a dead place as Isorb, and why has he taken the trouble to learn so much about the Herzvogin history?*
10. *Why does Queen Hanna try to set the children against a decent chap like Gustav?*
11. *Why does the Queen allow her Mistress of the Wardrobe to retain her important position, knowing she drinks?*
12. *How does Luigi view the approaching retirement of his relative, Rosa, to whom doubtless he owes some of his influence with the Prince?*
13. *What are the Prince's real views about his very odd mother?*

14. *What does Princess Vera think about the bunch she is marrying into?*

15. *Is the Chamberlain so devoted to his Royal mistress as he is reputed to be?*

"A nasty and suspicious nature," Venables commented to himself as he read his questions.

Venables, be it noted, made no attempt to answer them there and then. For obvious reasons. Indeed, had he been able to do so, the whole of the tangled skein of the Milö Palace's intrigues would have been apparent to him. This, at least, shows that he had interrogated himself with perspicacity, even if he as yet lacked sufficient information for the answers.

Chapter VIII

THE INEXPLICABLE DEATH

"So you think," said Prince Augustus, "that her fears are justified?"

"I do," answered Venables. "At least, sir, I should not like to take the responsibility of saying they are not."

"Neither should I," said the Chancellor, and the Chamberlain groaned.

They spoke with lowered voices in an anteroom. On the other side of the carved door, with its gilt Royal arms, was the Queen's private office. She had sent, by Luigi, a summons to the three men to attend her and Prince Augustus there.

Gustav, fresh from one of the reviews which seemed the almost endless occupation of his life at the Palace, flung his white sheepskin head-dress on one end of an embroidered sofa and flung himself heavily down on the other. For a moment he moodily regarded the toes of his well-cut riding-boots. Then he looked questioningly at the Chancellor. "We can't leave it like that," he said. "Not if she is in any danger."

The Chancellor sighed. "I cannot persuade her to be guarded," he said. "Of course eventually the responsibility is thrown on us.

"Perhaps the Chamberlain will lie across her threshold," he added, with a mischievous smile at that official.

The Chamberlain smiled in reply, but somewhat sourly. "I would willingly do it, if I thought she would permit me. She has, however, already expressed her opinion of our well-meaning attempts to protect her. Why she ever brought Mr. Venables here I do not know."

"Confound this Palace life," ejaculated Prince Gustav suddenly, jumping to his feet. "Its intrigues and endless gossip sicken me. The Palace is crawling with people who live on my mother, and yet I sometimes believe there is hardly one who would not be ready to betray her for a ten-dracon note."

It was impossible for Venables not to sympathize with the straightforward young giant stifling in an environment strange to him by nature and education. No wonder he lived abroad most of the year.

The Chamberlain flushed at the insult to the Royal Household, but he said nothing.

"Do you know what Her Majesty has called us to her office for?" asked the Chancellor, as he indicated the door.

Gustav shook his head. "No, but she is writing something in there. You know, of course, to-morrow is the day about which she has talked so much. I imagine she is at work on some kind of proclamation which she wants you to approve and perhaps issue. She would hardly have asked you to come to the Palace otherwise, Your Excellency, the day before Budget Day, unless it was something of vital importance."

"Ought she to be left alone there?" queried the Chancellor, with a significant glance.

Prince Augustus looked disconcerted. "Of course not!" he exclaimed. "Excuse me, I will find Luigi."

He returned smiling. "There is only one other door to her room besides this," he said, "and I have told Luigi to hang round."

Gustav paced the room uneasily for a moment, and then halted opposite them, his booted legs apart, his back to the fireplace.

"We must not shirk the issue, gentlemen," he said. "The Queen is in danger, however slight it may be. It is our duty to see she is properly guarded. She has refused to give the order herself. It seems that now I alone am in a position to act. I know, of course, that I am legally as much a subject of my Royal mother as Your Excellencies, but my position as Heir Apparent gives me certain rights. I propose to exercise them with your approval. You know that since the fifteenth century the Crown Prince of Iconia has had at his disposal a personal bodyguard of twelve men, whom he is entitled to choose himself and set on duty wherever he wishes in the Royal precincts? You may even remember that one Crown Prince exercised his prerogative, one troublous time, to the extent of being surrounded by these guards in the Chapel of St. Boron itself, where otherwise no arms may be carried. I shall detail six of those men to guard, as unostentatiously as may be, the Queen's suite when she retires to-night, and I myself will make a point of being beside her to-morrow."

Without, in fact, waiting for their approval Gustav immediately left the room. The Chamberlain made a wry face when he had gone. "Goodness knows how the Queen will take it!"

"Probably quite well," answered the Chancellor shrewdly. "You know she is rather fond of forbidding a thing she is ashamed to order, and expecting other people to disobey her and do it for her. It has always been her pride not to fear assassins, and she is probably ashamed to advertise her apprehension by ordering a guard now. But she may be quite glad when she finds one there, and can blame Gustav."

Prince Augustus returned ten minutes later. "Well, I've done it," he said. He looked at his watch. "No word from the Queen? Perhaps I had better go in."

The Prince knocked on the massive oak door, but there was no answer. He opened it, and then hesitated on the threshold. He frowned inquiringly, and then a slow smile spread over his face. He motioned to the Chamberlain and the Chancellor to approach him quietly. The two joined him for a moment, and then they all three returned, closing the door carefully after them.

"She has fallen asleep at her desk!" said the Prince to Venables. "She has done that so often lately. Age, I am afraid. And she hates to be discovered asleep. We must pretend we have not been in and let her wake herself."

An hour passed. The Prince proved himself an excellent raconteur, and told them some of his adventures as "Mr. Shillingford" in

Paris and Berlin. Gustav certainly had an appealing personality and none of the humourless egoism usual in the nobly-born.

Then he cautiously opened the door again. But Queen Hanna had gone.

"Doubtless Her Majesty was too tired to see us," said the Chamberlain, seeing an expression of irritation on the Chancellor's face. "She has had an exhausting day. More than twenty audiences! It is too much at her age. There is no need to remain at the Palace, Your Excellency," he added. "Either she has forgotten the appointment or has changed her mind. Her memory seems a little weaker," he added reluctantly. "Pray God it gets no worse."

"Good-bye, Your Royal Highness," said the Chancellor. "So we are not to be enlightened after all as to what is in Her Majesty's mind. If she changes it again to-morrow, I have a telephone at my bedside."

He went out, looking worried.

Venables returned to his room. He slept deeply that night, but long before his normal rising hour he woke with a jerk. His whole room seemed filled with the jangling vibration of some supernatural chatter. Then he recollected that the belfry tower was just above his room. But why was the bell ringing at this hour? he wondered sleepily. But of course it was the feast of St. Boron, and this was some celebration, though it sounded dismal enough. He was about to sleep again when the sounds of movement in the Courtyard below aroused his curiosity. He jumped out of bed and walked to the window.

Dawn had as yet hardly tinged the eastern sky, but the Palace was astir. One after another the windows of the Palace flamed with light. He heard a clatter below him in the Courtyard, and five soldiers crossed it at the double. With a grinding of brakes a car precipitated itself into the Courtyard. Then quite suddenly, as the bells paused for a moment, he heard a forced barbaric wailing. He leaned further out of the window. It came from three women below him. The bell resumed its tolling.

There was a knock on his door and he turned hurriedly.

It was Brightholme, a dressing-gown over his pyjamas, his hair tousled. "Come quickly, old chap," he said. "The Chamberlain sent me to call you. The Queen is dead! That is the passing bell."

On the Vigil of the Feast of St. Boron, the Sovereign Prior of the Most Peaceable Order of the Collar is by rule enjoined to keep knightly vigil fully robed, and thus kneel in prayer throughout the night. It was the sort of obsolete rule most Iconian monarchs considered best honoured in the breach. But Queen Hanna it seemed, on this night at least, though tired out with audiences, old, and a woman, had yet decided to keep the vigil. For they had found her, lying athwart the prie-dieu in her huge bedroom, before a painting of St. Boron, dressed in the scarlet and white ceremonial robes of the Order, in which at break of day she would go forth to the Chapel, where even at this early hour the members were already gathering. The hood, slipping back from her head, had carried with it the red wig, and left exposed an uncomely pate, sparsely covered with grey hair.

Round her neck was clasped the broad iron collar of the Order. And above the collar was another necklace, thin and silken. Dr. Robor untied it and held it up. A slow murmur of horror rose from the Iconian men and women in the room, and even Venables felt the cold breath of legend.

Queen Hanna had been strangled by the same silken cord which, in the dawn of Iconian history, had first stained the Herzvogin blood with a fratricidal crime. The monotonous peal of the passing bell seemed to announce the execution of a judicial act.

The Curse of the Herzvogins had come back full circle.

Chapter IX

THE ECCENTRIC MURDERER

"How long?" asked Venables of Dr. Robor.

The Doctor had completed his examination of the dead Queen, who had been reverently laid on the great crimson four-poster bed.

"Ten or eleven hours," said the Doctor. "Eh, Brightholme?"

Brightholme nodded. "About that. Killed instantly, without much of a struggle."

Venables looked grave. "That means she must have been killed soon after she left us last night. Who discovered her?"

The Mistress of the Wardrobe looked up from the corpse, above whose face she had drawn the hood of the robes. The Countess was sober now and frightened. "I did. I came to call Her Majesty in case she forgot about the service at the Chapel this morning. Her memory has been so bad lately... And I found her—like this."

"But the Queen was guarded!" moaned the Chamberlain. Tremblingly he folded the frail hands of his dead mistress across her breast. His lips quivered and he hid his face in his hands, dropping on his knees beside the bed. "Forgive me... The household over which you set me..." Venables heard him mutter. His bony old shoulders shook beneath the rough woollen dressing-gown he was wearing.

Prince Augustus bent over him and put one giant hand on his shoulder. "Come, Mapponyi," he said soothingly. "It is in no way your fault. It is I who am responsible. I set these guards on the doors." He looked round and motioned to Venables. "Come with me while I speak to these fellows," he said in a voice which sounded ominous for the guard.

The six young soldiers, two of whom had been posted at each of the three doors to the suite, were white with apprehension. The Prince furiously, Venables gently—but perhaps more searchingly—interrogated them.

They stood stoutly to their story. They had watched the doors from 6 p.m. until midnight, and had then been relieved by their comrades. At six in the morning they had again gone on duty. At half-past seven the Wardrobe Mistress had entered and made the ghastly discovery. Neither they nor their comrades could report any untoward incident of any kind, most certainly no unauthorized entry.

The interrogation continued. No, simply no one had entered, not even someone familiar to them, like the Chamberlain. The Corporal burst into tears, and with Iconian ardour proffered the Prince his revolver. "Shoot me if you wish, Your Royal Highness, I deserve it. But I still swear no human being could have passed in or out to-night."

Gustav turned from him with a groan. "Either they have all decided to hang together or they are telling the truth, God knows!" he said helplessly. "I had better dismiss them, I suppose. They can do nothing now."

"On the contrary," pointed out Venables, "they must watch out more carefully than ever."

Prince Augustus looked startled. "My dear fellow, why on earth—?"

"They swear that no one passed through those doors to-night, sir," said Venables quietly. "But Her Majesty was killed. The presumption is that the murderer is still in there!"

Gustav looked round uneasily.

"Good God, you mean hiding in the room?"

The soldiers murmured.

Venables shrugged his shoulders. "Alternatively, as there are half a dozen people in there with the Chamberlain, he might be one of them!"

"This is awful! I see what you mean," admitted Gustav. "But how can one suspect people like the Chamberlain, or the Countess Naomi, or poor old Mutch?"

"We must act as if we suspect all," pointed out Venables, "in fairness to each. I propose, sir, that these men now note everyone who comes out. In the same way they must put their heads together, and let us have a list of the names and approximate times when anyone entered or left the suite, starting with the Wardrobe Mistress at 7.30 a.m. If anyone came in and out more than once, as I have done for instance, that must be recorded too. You realize I am guarding against the possibility of the murderer waiting in there and relying on being sufficiently well known to slip out openly with the rest of us. But if anyone comes out whom the soldiers did not positively see go in, then our task is done. Meanwhile I suggest the relieved guard should make a search of the four rooms and the corridors of Her Majesty's suite, in case the assassin is in hiding."

"Yes, of course, Venables." Prince Augustus pressed his brow. "Thank God you can keep a clear head in all this. I confess mine is spinning. This dreadful business will set Iconia by the ears. I hope to God we find the murderer before he can get away."

"Your Royal Highness," said a distracted voice at his elbow. Marshal of the Nobility Count Herreshyi had come hurriedly up the stairs. "The Chancellor is here. He is coming up at once."

Indeed, the Chancellor was following hard on the Count. He took Prince Augustus by the hand and pressed it silently. "You have lost your mother, Your Royal Highness," he said with some emotion, "and so has Iconia—for she was her country's mother too. She has left us her tradition of duty first—first whatever our personal feelings. We have two duties now—to discover and punish this dastardly murder, and to settle the succession and the affairs of State involved. I am, of course, entirely in your hands," he added.

Prince Augustus smiled. "You had my mother's complete confidence, Count. Therefore you have mine. As long as you consent to head my Ministry I shall be content to leave affairs of State to your discretion." The Chancellor bowed. "As to the discovery of this murderer, that is a more immediate problem. Come into the anteroom and we will discuss it. We must make some announcement to-day, I take it."

"I passed the Chief of Police in the Courtyard," said the Chancellor significantly. "He should be with us any moment."

"I don't want that old charlatan!" exclaimed the Prince angrily. "Good Lord, Demetrior, you know well enough that he is an absolute dummy!"

"He is not gifted with brains," admitted the Chancellor equably, "but he is a good soldier. The public like him—he looks magnificent sitting on a large horse at police reviews. It is essential that the public think he is supervising the investigation.

"After all," added the Chancellor, "he has the reputation of being incorruptible, which makes him both popular and unusual."

"You are right," admitted the Prince. "I rush into these decisions without thinking. I am grateful for your steadying hand. If Mr. Venables here would be ready to work in co-operation with him..."

Venables smiled. "He sounds rather like one of our own Chief Constables. You will find me tactful enough. All that is necessary is that he gets the credit. I'll do the work."

"Here he is," whispered the Chancellor.

Magnificent in gold-braided scarlet uniform and white-plumed cocked hat, the Chief of Police drew himself up before the Prince and bowed deeply.

"May I respectfully commiserate Your Majesty. God rest your sainted mother's soul. Have no fear. We shall lay her murderer by the heels before another day dawns."

"I am sure you will, General," said Gustav amicably. "This is Mr. Venables—General the Chief of Police Count Georgico-Maria Millitranyi." The Chief of Police bowed slightly. "My mother called him in, on the recommendation of Scotland Yard." The Chief of

Police started, and looked at Venables with a new interest. "But before he could begin his investigation this tragedy happened."

"I regret Her Majesty did not see fit to confide in me," said the Chief of Police a little stiffly.

"I am afraid at that date she underestimated the gravity of the affair, General," returned Prince Augustus smoothly. "Shall we go into the anteroom?"

The four seated themselves in the little sitting-room, sparsely furnished, still bearing in such trifles as an opened book or a pile of papers the personal touches of the dead monarch who had used it.

Venables explained the measures they had already taken. Red-faced, goggle-eyed, and with a set expression of unbending severity, the Chief of Police nodded vigorously. "I was about to suggest that myself," he said.

"I think," said Venables, rising, "if you will excuse me, I will go and make sure that the search is thorough. Not that it is easy to overlook a man, but one wants to be certain."

Quarter of an hour later he returned, a puzzled frown on his face, and a brown-paper parcel under his arm. "There is no one in hiding in the apartments. Of course, I did not expect anything so crude. But I also have the lists prepared by the guards, in which everyone who has been in and out of the suite to-day is named. I have checked them over carefully, and have every reason to suppose they are correct, as the guard corroborated them independently."

Venables paused while the three men looked at him expectantly.

"If this evidence is to be believed," he went on, "the murderer was invisible. He came and went through guarded doors and thick walls, without a sign or trace of his presence or his passage."

The Chief of Police turned a shade less red, and plucked at his moustache. The Chancellor smiled unbelievingly.

"Have you any idea how that could be done?" he asked.

"None, at the moment," admitted Venables. "But I have had to ask myself a queer question. If I could find the answer it might help us."

"And the question is?" asked the Chancellor.

"Why did the murderer, after killing the Queen, dress her in the robes of the Order?"

"But what makes you think he did?" said Prince Augustus, startled.

"Because she could never have dressed herself in them alone. I pointed it out to Doctor Robor, and he agrees with me. Even the most athletic young woman would have needed assistance to lace up the corselet at the back. And the Queen was old and feeble."

"But her maids?" expostulated the Prince.

"They both swear, sir, that Her Majesty never called on their services at all that night, but told them not to disturb her because she wished to work. As she did not ring for them, they went to bed. She had done this before apparently. I understand ceremony rather irked her, and she often undressed, and sometimes even dressed by herself. She was then still wearing a scarlet dress with beaded embroideries."

"She was wearing that in her Office yesterday night," commented the Chancellor.

"And for her audience with me this morning." Venables placed the brown-paper parcel on the table. He carefully opened it and shook out the silken folds of a scarlet dress.

"Why, it was that very dress!" exclaimed the Prince.

"Exactly. The murderer removed it, clothed her in the robes of the Order, packed it up in a brown-paper parcel, and threw the parcel under the bed, where I found it. Why?"

"A madman?" suggested the Chancellor.

"I think not," answered Venables. "Not that kind of a madman, anyway. A man of intelligence. He has set us these riddles. Unless we can answer them he will prove himself more intelligent than us."

The Chief of Police surreptitiously crossed himself. Whether this was in pious memory of the Queen or a tribute to the apparently supernatural traits of her murderer, Venables did not know.

But it was certain that throughout the Palace the members of the Royal Household shiveringly repeated the words of the Curse, and speculated as to what blood-freezing form the avenging apparition had taken.

"No flesh and blood walked past six boys of the Prince's Own," declared a fat corporal in the guardroom. "It was Augustus the Clerk himself, mark my words, carrying his head under his arm and followed by his five little children. I believe the Chief of Police knows it too, and that little Englishman who thinks he's so clever will find it himself before long."

Meanwhile the Chancellor and the King-designate put the finishing touches to the proclamation which was tacked on to the official bulletin of the Queen's death published that morning. The material paragraphs read somewhat as follows:

"We Augustus, by the Grace of God, etc., do hereby appoint General the Chief of Police Count Georgico-Maria Millitranyi head of the Extraordinary Commission of Inquiry into the dastardly murder of our beloved Mother the Queen Hanna, to investigate with all diligence and dispatch the circumstances of this crime, and to question and detain all manner of witnesses thereto, and to suspend and override all sort of graces and privileges otherwise permitted in judicial process, and we do enjoin every one of our subjects to assist the members of the Commission and their duly appointed agents, and to withhold no information or evidence likely to assist the Commission in their task."

(Here followed the nobodies who constituted the Commission.)

"And for the better prosecution of their investigations we have appointed Charles Venables, Esq., of London, to advise and assist the said Commission.

"Given under our hand and seal at our Court of Milö, etc., etc."

"There is nothing in it," explained the Chancellor, "except that it will prevent anybody about your person who might plead prerogative doing so, which they are not likely to do anyway. But the Commission shows the right spirit. We don't want the public to think we are trying to hush anything up."

Venables was less interested in the proclamation than in a warrant which King Augustus had given him, and which read as follows:

"This is to enjoin every one of our subjects to give Charles Venables, Esq., all manner of aid and information he may require, and access to all places as he may demand.

"Augustus, R."

"It's all very fine," Venables said to himself, "but no amount of warrants tells one how a murderer makes himself invisible or accounts for his morbid fondness for dressing and undressing Royal corpses."

Chapter X

THE SHOT GHOST

The Affair of the Ghost might have been dismissed as the natural superstition of the ignorant Iconian peasantry, from which even the Palace guards were drawn, if it had not been for certain odd features in the apparition.

Night had fallen, and the Palace rooms and corridors had looked bleared and eerie in the dim light filtering through the crape swathed round the chandeliers. All day long, it seemed, the bells of Isorb had tolled a monotonous tribute to the departed soul of Hanna of Herzvogin, and like pairs of spectres Orthodox monks or nuns flitted through the Palace, their eyes downcast, their heads bent.

The ceremonial anniversary of the Order had been postponed until after the Coronation of the new Monarch and the obsequies of the old. The Chapel of St. Boron, which should have been the scene of the colourful pageant of the Order, was also in mourning. The statues of the saints and the crucifixes were wound in black coverings, like corpses in their cerecloths. Black curtains hid the flying angels of the dome and the rigid saints of the frescoed walls. A dull hammering reverberated from the crypt, where a new resting-place was being added to those of so many centuries. In an atmosphere sickly with the fragrance of piled-up heaps of waxen lilies, Queen Hanna lay in her gilded coffin, her face veiled to hide the unpleasant distortion of her features. Her hands loosely clasped a gilt crucifix.

On that evening, when the ancient Palace seemed to rustle with whispers of its infamous history, anyone might have been excused for being nervous. Even Venables felt a little keyed up as he walked round the Chapel in the moonlight, passed through the wicket gate, and was about to enter the Palace. And it was then that the whispering stillness was torn by a shot, and—mingled with its echoes—a scream, and a clatter of running feet. A man in the green uniform of the Palace guard shot out of the doorway into the arms of Venables.

"*Lefik!*" muttered Venables soothingly, as the man stared at him, trembling, with bulging eyes. It was one of the few Iconian words he knew. It was used indifferently as an equivalent for the English "Steady the Buffs!" "Pull yourself together!" "Don't lose your temper!" But the guard could apparently speak English, as indeed could most Palace inmates, however humble their position, and he plunged into an explanation as soon as he recognized Venables.

"God forgive me, I saw her!" he groaned.

"Saw whom?" asked Venables.

"Her Majesty herself, God rest her soul, walking down the stairs with St. Boron!"

"Don't talk nonsense!" said Venables. The man did not seem to have been drinking. "Her Majesty will never walk again, and I doubt if St. Boron comes here often."

"I saw her!" reiterated the sentry. "With these eyes."

"You saw two people in the dark," said Venables patiently. "Don't jump to conclusions."

"It was not in the dark," answered the sentry. "At least it was dark there, but I flashed a lamp in her face." He produced an electric torch.

This began to grow interesting. Venables pressed him further. It seemed that the sentry had heard footsteps, and had seen two dim figures creeping down the corridor. He had challenged them, and they had stopped without answering. Then he had flashed his torch on one, and at once it had—clearly and distinctly—lit up Queen Hanna's face.

"Like a corpse's," he said with a grimace. "Horrible; but her eyes were empty—so." As for the other figure, he had not stopped to investigate. It was either the devil or St. Boron—he didn't know which—and he had thought it politer to assume it was St. Boron.

"And then?" queried Venables.

"Then I said, 'I will shoot.' And she just stared at me. *Ouf!* it was horrible. Dead, and she stared at me! I drew my revolver and fired—so!"

"Good God!" exclaimed Venables, who had not credited the scared young man with such drastic measures. "What happened?"

"It hit her in the chest, so!" He struck himself. "And the chest caved in as if she were dry—like a corpse." He shuddered violently. "And then they glided away down the passage, and I shouted and ran—for help," he added.

Venables succeeded in persuading the sentry to return and show him the place. But there was not a trace of blood, ghostly or otherwise. In the wall, sunken deeply, Venables found the bullet. The sentry seemed to take this as proof of his whole story. In any case he refused to be shaken in his account of the incident.

"Just as I said, I saw her. I fired. It hit her so; she was like a corpse," he insisted. "But her eyes were empty... horrible!"

And there, for the moment, the matter rested.

Chapter XI

THE OFFENDING COUNTESS

In certain of its features the murder of Queen Hanna reminded Venables of his first case in Kensington. There, too, had been the same difficulty of finding how the murderer had got to the victim. The problem was complicated in this murder, however, by the fact that no one could have entered the Queen's suite by the windows. Like all the windows on that wall of the Palace which overlooked the public road, they were heavily barred. According to Professor Andreyi, these bars had been put up in the troubled weeks preceding the passing of the Distribution Act, when mobs and demonstrations before the Palace had caused King Francis to strengthen its defences.

Therefore the Queen's murderer must have entered by the guarded doors. There was, it was true, the possibility that one of the two maids might have been the murderer. But after examining the badly scared girls, Venables felt it was unlikely. Rightly or wrongly, Venables eliminated them on psychological grounds.

Returning to the purely physical problem as to how the murderer got in, Venables was driven back to the hypothesis that the guards must have been mistaken. He was not happy about this; it was a little too easy. There was only one other possibility, on the surface. The Wardrobe Mistress, still an enigmatic character, might have strangled the Queen, and then pretended to find her dead. That possibility was, however, eliminated by the doctors' evidence. The Queen had been killed the preceding evening, Robor and Brightholme had agreed, and the guards stated that the Countess Naomi had not entered until seven-thirty next morning.

Venables now tried to find out the exact time of the Queen's return. The Chancellor, the Prince, and he himself had seen her in the State Office shortly after 6 p.m. She had gone when the Prince looked into the Office an hour later. Did she then go straight back to her room, or did she have some other interview before retiring for the night? Venables, after putting the point to the Chief of Police, sent for the Corporal who had so dramatically proffered his pistol to Gustav, and put the question to him.

The Corporal stared in astonishment at Venables' question. "What time did Her Majesty retire?" he repeated. "But she had already done so when we were put on guard!"

Venables consulted his notes. "That is not so. His Majesty has told me that you were put on guard outside the suite at six o'clock."

"That is so, sir," answered the Corporal.

"Well, a few minutes after that time the Queen was seen by the Chancellor and the Prince in the State Office," said Venables.

The Corporal's mouth opened and closed silently. "It is impossible, sir," he faltered at last. "If I may say so with all respect."

"Why, my man?" barked the Chief of Police. His finger shot out threateningly. "Keep nothing back!"

The Corporal licked his lips nervously. "There is nothing to keep back, Your Excellency. We never saw Her Majesty that night. We knew nothing till Her Excellency went in and screamed for us. There she was, dead!" He crossed himself. "She must have been in her rooms before we came on duty."

Venables did not at first believe the man's statement. But when he pressed him, and examined the other soldiers, he reluctantly came to the conclusion that they were telling the truth.

"I ask you, sir, could we have overlooked Her Majesty?" remonstrated the Corporal. "Naturally we are on the watch. We have to present arms. It would have been impossible!"

The Chief of Police waved the men out of the room and goggled at Venables. "If one were superstitious, one would say there was something of the supernatural in this!" He laughed nervously.

Venables gave him a slightly contemptuous look. "Certainly, my dear General; but since we are sceptical policemen, several perfectly natural explanations occur to us."

"Of course," echoed the Chief of Police unsurely.

"Which do you think the most likely?" went on Venables a little cruelly.

The Chief of Police pulled fiercely at his moustache. "H'm! The matter requires consideration."

"A secret passage," said Venables, "seems to me to need no further consideration. In a palace as old as this... It would also, of course, explain the murderer's entrance."

The Chief of Police's eyes gleamed. "A secret passage! Of course! My dear Venables, I will at once locate that secret passage. Before the day is out! Positively! I have a man in my department who was trained at the Sûreté, and who is expert beyond words in the discovery of such matters! To watch him at work is a pleasure. I have seen him search a Communist, thus"—the General gave a pantomime of hasty fumbling—"and look! in a second he has drawn a letter from the sole of the wretch's boot."

The Chief of Police rose and left the room, as delighted as a terrier with a rat. Venables settled down with a sigh of relief to read the pile of notes he had accumulated.

Venables called on the Chamberlain later that day. He seemed still more stooped, to have passed from being elderly to being aged. Perhaps it was the blackness of his suit of mourning contrasting with the pallor of his face and his prophetic beard.

"Ah, Mr. Venables, have you discovered how this dreadful outrage was committed?" asked the Chamberlain. He was standing in front of a sheet of paper, pinned to the wall, on which letters in red and black ink showed the order of precedence of the funeral cortège.

"Not yet. In fact, we have so far only discovered in how many ways it could not be carried out." To the Chamberlain Venables looked depressed, though in fact he was only puzzled. The depression reacted on the Count's opinion of Venables. Never very high, it fell lower. Venables heard him sigh gently.

"I am afraid you must find it very difficult, coming from outside into this little world of ours," said the Chamberlain, the polite phraseology barely concealing his opinion of Venables' ignorance of Iconian Court politics.

"I do," admitted Venables. "Therefore I propose to ask you a few questions. I am afraid you may find them—shall we say indiscreet?" The Chamberlain's eyebrows rose. "But His Majesty has assured me that this matter must be cleared up at any price."

"Naturally," said the Chamberlain a little stiffly. He motioned to his secretary to leave the room.

"It is impossible not to be personal," went on Venables.

"Of course," agreed His Excellency, adding a final touch to the funeral cortège.

Having felt that he had done all the fencing the situation required of him, Venables now plunged into his investigation with a suddenness which made the Chamberlain drop his pen.

"How long," asked Venables, "has the Countess Naomi been drinking—I mean drinking heavily?"

Count Mapponyi went a little red about the cheekbones. The question reflected on his conduct of the Household. However, he answered it straightly enough.

"For ten years at least. Of course it has been getting worse lately."

"Her Majesty knew?"

"Yes," said the Chamberlain quietly. "I complained—in the early days."

"But later it was no use?"

The Chamberlain was silent. Venables pressed him.

"Why did not Her Majesty dismiss her?"

"She had known the Countess so long..." faltered the Chamberlain. "She hoped, perhaps, she would reform. A friend of her childhood..."

Venables' unenthusiastic face showed to the full his scepticism.

"Was Her Majesty in the habit of putting private obligations before public duties?"

"No, she was not," admitted Count Mapponyi miserably.

"Supposing," went on Venables, "you had been asked whether Her Majesty would appoint a drunkard—to the most important post any lady can have at this Court, I believe—because she was an old friend, what would you have said twelve years ago?"

The Chamberlain wriggled. "The question is hypothetical."

"Naturally, Your Excellency. And all I ask for is a hypothetical answer."

"I should have said it was absolutely impossible," answered the Chamberlain defiantly.

"Was the Countess genuinely devoted to Her Majesty, do you think?" said Venables, looking at him sharply.

"Heart and soul!" exclaimed the other with sincerity. "She worshipped her. When, five years ago, at the opening of our Diet, a man rushed from the crowd and attempted to shoot at the Queen, the Countess immediately flung herself in front of them. Had the revolver not misfired, she would certainly have been killed.

"In fact," went on the Chamberlain happily, "it was probably because of that incident that the Queen was so lenient with her."

Venables punctured him. "This was five years ago!" he reminded him. "The Countess's failing, you tell me, dates from ten years ago." The Chamberlain was silent.

"Her devotion to the Queen mystifies me," went on Venables, "because, of course, the obvious assumption a detective would make is that the Countess was blackmailing Her Majesty into leaving her in her position." The Chamberlain opened his mouth in horrified protest, but Venables went calmly on. "Of course all this is hypothetical.

We will not labour the point. Do you know anything about the death of the Prince Maximilian?"

It was at this point of the interview that Mapponyi revised his opinion of Charles Venables. The question, delivered with apparent absence of sequence—an absence only apparent—transfixed the Chamberlain in his most sensitive spot.

"I was not then Chamberlain," he said in a low voice. "I was appointed by Her Majesty on her accession. The Prince died while his father, King Francis, was on the throne."

"But Your Excellency was at Court?"

The Chamberlain nodded.

"And Dr. Robor attended the child?"

Count Mapponyi started.

"Er—yes. Indeed Dr. Robor could tell you far more than I can about the Prince's death. It was from meningitis, I think."

"He could, but he might not want to," pointed out the detective.

"I do not follow you?" asked the Chamberlain, who obviously followed Venables very well.

"No matter. Leaving aside the absurd rumour that Prince Maximilian was poisoned by Her Majesty's command," said Venables, who obviously did not leave it aside, "do you think Dr. Robor might have been at all—er—negligent?"

"He is a brilliant physician!" said Count Mapponyi defensively.

"I did not mean that kind of negligence," explained the detective.

"I cannot believe it!" exclaimed the Chamberlain indignantly. Venables decided to touch him on the flanks again.

"Dr. Robor attended the Countess Naomi's son, I believe?" he said innocently.

"I suppose he would have done. Yes, he did," answered the Count.

"H'm! Of course the supposition that Dr. Robor was negligent in this case also, and that as a result Her Majesty felt under a debt to the Countess—such a supposition would be too fantastic, would it not?"

"It would!" said Count Mapponyi warmly, with an unpleasant awareness that the shrewd young Englishman with the feline green eyes felt nothing of the kind.

"I suppose His Majesty—then Prince Augustus—would have known nothing of these unpleasant rumours?"

"No!" answered the Chamberlain positively. "He had too much respect for his Royal mother ever to permit anyone to breathe a word against her."

Venables, remembering how Rosa had been abruptly squashed in London for such an impertinence, was inclined to agree. He thought for a minute.

"What was the reason for Her Majesty's quarrel with her brother?" he asked suddenly.

The Chamberlain had by now reconciled himself to the fact that this acute young Englishman was prepared to stir up an unlimited quantity of mud, and he answered candidly without any prodding.

"They quarrelled dreadfully as children. Her Majesty was the first-born, and as a precocious and ambitious child looked forward to reigning herself. Then Francis was born. Perhaps that was the start of it—childish jealousy. Certainly the Princess Hanna had brains and character enough for two men. And as they grew up the contrast became more marked. Now Francis might have made it easy for her, even leaned a little on her acute brain. Instead the young fool continually emphasized the fact that he would be the sovereign and she the useless woman. He teased her cruelly. Once she made the mistake of pointing out that he might die childless, and then her children would come to the throne. He swore that he would use his power to forbid her marriage, and make her die an old maid. What things children argue about! And in fact, when he came to the throne, he did put obstacles in the way of her marriage. But what most pained her was that she saw the country misgoverned. She tried to make him follow the only possible line, and all the thanks she got was that he accused her of treason. Indeed he had actually been pressing his

Chancellor to indict her when he was shot. Some months before, his heir Prince Maximilian had died. She came to the throne; married; and then, soon after the Consort's death, Augustus was born, as you doubtless know."

Venables was thoughtful for a long time. At last he said, "Have you any idea what Queen Hanna would have done to-day had she not been murdered?"

"No," said the Chamberlain obstinately. "It is a mystery to me."

Venables looked him straight in the face. The old man's eyes dropped after a time. He mumbled something in his beard.

"I beg your pardon, Your Excellency," said Venables softly. "I should not have asked you that." He had seen tears in the old man's eyes. The Chamberlain could guess shrewdly what act of expiation the Queen prepared, but his loyalty endured beyond the grave.

"What do you know about Brightholme?" asked Venables. The question sounded as if it were a forced change of subject, and the Chamberlain took it at that. He could hardly know that when Venables' lean nose was once sniffing at a trail, his doubling, however sinuous, merely meant that the trail doubled too.

"Nothing," he said in astonishment. "It was entirely Dr. Robor's idea to engage him. The Doctor pays his salary, you know, so it is hardly in my province to interfere at all. He seems a very pleasant young man," he added.

"Thank you; then, Your Excellency, that is all," said Venables, and gathered up his papers. The Chamberlain stayed him with one white and bony hand.

"One moment... if I may say a word. You are very clever, Mr. Venables, with that keen and ruthless young brain of yours. But there is something in experience after all, and I have been at this Court for forty years... My mistress was a woman, but she was above all a ruler, such a ruler as we shall never see again. Oh, I know this is an age of republics and constitutions, and Monarchy has become an empty symbol, a show. But it will be my delight and pride that I have been permitted to serve, in however humble a way, a Queen who understood that the Crown can still demand and enforce the privileges of bygone days, if it gives in return as generously of strength and service. And this Queen Hanna did for Iconia. Remember that, Mr. Venables, and you will understand and overlook a lot."

Venables was touched by the old man's earnestness. And indeed there was something romantic, something historic, in a voice uttering sentiments that echoed the first stammerings of feudalism. The speech had one positive result. In his list of questions Venables crossed out: "Is the Chamberlain so devoted to his Royal Mistress as he appears?" Of that, at least, there could be no doubt.

The Chancellor, whom he saw later, expressed the politician's point of view, more cynical and realistic than that of the courtier. "A tartar of a woman—a real Machiavellian prince. But, by God, she knew her job! I do hope things are looking a little clearer, my dear fellow?"

"According to the newspaper," said Venables slyly, "the police expect to make an arrest at any moment."

The Chancellor looked a little embarrassed. "We simply had to say that, Venables. I hope you will forgive me. The people must be soothed with the idea that we are on the job."

"Of course. I really came to ask you something about your last sight of the Queen. You remember?"

"When she was asleep. Yes, I remember," said the Chancellor gravely. "Poor old lady—so tired and old. And then, a little later, that brutal death."

"But are you sure it was her?" asked Venables.

The Chancellor's jaw dropped. "My God, do you mean—?"

"That it might have been someone else—dressed in her clothes."

The Chancellor pressed his hands to his eyes. "Let me recall it!" He dropped them and looked at Venables. "I am sure," he said with finality. "The light from the lamp fell clearly on her face, and

I remember thinking how young she looked while she slept. I could never mistake her features."

"And are you sure she was only asleep?" said Venables significantly.

The Chancellor looked slightly sick as he grasped the significance of the remark.

Chapter XII

THE MYSTIFIED KING

"What the devil," asked King Augustus X, "is that old fool Millitranyi doing? I found him crawling all over the floor in my mother's old room, with two other equally fat idiots."

"They are looking for a secret passage, sir," answered Venables with some relish.

"A secret passage, good God!" the King snorted. "A nice —— fool I'll look when next the English Ambassador asks me how the search is getting on—and I have to say my Chief of Police is looking for secret passages! He'll be playing at Red Indians next. Who on earth gave him that idea?"

"I did, sir," said Venables meekly.

"You! Really, Venables, I should have thought you had more sense. Do you suppose this is a Ruritanian Palace, all honeycombed with dungeons and trap-doors and God knows what?"

"I have never supposed it, sir. If I had I should have looked for the secret passage myself."

A slow grin of enlightenment dawned on the King's face. "Oh, I see! Something to keep him busy, eh? An excellent idea, Venables; but for heaven's sake stop him sawing up at the panelling. He talked about doing that this morning."

"I will certainly stop that," Venables promised. There was a silence, and Venables noticed that Gustav looked worried.

"I wish you had something positive to report, Venables," he said. "This blasted Palace is buzzing with gossip. Not that that's anything new. But in the old days I could cut and run, but now I'm stuck here. Twelve months of reviews and other damn fooleries a year instead of three." He ran his hands through his hair. "Why did they kill her?" he asked suddenly.

Venables wondered how much the King really knew. Surely he could not have missed *all* the gossip that floated round the Palace?

Venables temporized. "It was because of something she was going to reveal the next day," he said. "We do not know precisely what, for the murderer has been successful. If we could discover what it was, we should discover the murderer."

"Then there is no reason why I should be attacked?" asked Gustav, with evident relief. "That sounds cowardly possibly," he added, "but I do not mean to make the same mistake as my mother."

"You stand in no immediate danger, sir," Venables assured him; "but you may do so when we have discovered more—when we are pressing the fellow hard. I shall give you ample warning. Until then, if I may advise you, you should appear to know as little as possible."

"That will not be very difficult," said Gustav sardonically. "Listen. I have been thinking the matter over, and I distinctly remember that my mother was writing some important document in the State Office. It was on the stamped vellum that we only use for final drafts of official Acts. Luigi and I have since turned out her Office without finding it, and the Chancellor cannot suggest what it might have been. I should recognize it at once if I saw it. I have since wondered if it could have had something to do with the murder? I suppose nothing of the kind was found in her room?"

"No. And it was carefully searched. But you are undoubtedly right, sir. This document would have been some kind of declaration which at all costs the murderer would have wished to suppress. By this time, unless the murderer is very foolish, it no longer exists."

"What on earth could it have been?" asked the King innocently. If he was unable to imagine what it might have been, thought Venables, he would be the only person at Court in that position. "I feel conscience-stricken to think of the way in which I laughed at my mother's fears," went on Gustav. "So far from being nervous, she was too rash!"

"Might I have a word with Luigi, sir?" said Venables. "Her Majesty's movements on the night of the murder are proving oddly difficult to place."

"Certainly, my dear fellow. I'll ring for him."

While the King waited for Luigi to appear, he turned over the papers with which the desk was littered. He did so with an expression of distaste. It is a pity, thought Venables, that anyone with physique and mien so magnificently royal should have so little taste for the merely humdrum, the administrative side of ruling.

Luigi came in cheerfully. His cheerfulness was not surprising. He was now favourite for the succession to the Chamberlainship. Already he had taken over much of the business which in Queen Hanna's time devolved upon the Chamberlain. And, to do him justice, he did it efficiently. Nothing seemed to disturb his dapper unhurried air.

"I wanted to find out what time the Queen left the Office, Pavellicini. If you remember, His Majesty asked you that evening to remain outside the door to prevent any suspicious customers barging in?"

"Yes, I remember," said Luigi. "I stayed there until His Majesty told me to go. The Chancellor had left the Palace then."

"And how long after that did Her Majesty retire?"

Luigi looked surprised. "I don't know," he said. "She did not go out by my door."

"*What!*" exclaimed the King, looking up. "She must have done so. The only other door leads into the anteroom, and we were in there all the time."

"If Your Majesty will pardon me... I am positive. I never left the door."

The King banged the palm of one giant hand furiously on the desk. "Upon my soul, I am almost beginning to agree with the old women and think the devil is behind it all. How else did my mother and her murderer make themselves invisible?"

"Millitranyi would take that as another proof of his secret passage!" said Venables with a smile.

"Pshaw!" exclaimed the King. "There are no secret passages."

"Yes, I think the murderer has too many marks of intelligence to use so crude a device."

"Still, how did she vanish from the Office under our eyes? Give me an explanation," pressed the King.

"I do not want to be a bore, sir," said Venables seriously, "but may I say, here and now, that it is not the detective's business to produce by pure induction the explanation of a set of facts? Given certain physical facts, there are a thousand possible hypotheses. The more imaginative you are, the more you can think of, and the more useless it is. In this case, for instance, Her Majesty may not have gone when you thought she had gone. She may have been in hiding, and left later. The murderer may have been in the room all the time, may have killed her there, and hidden her body there, until he could move it to her bedroom. I will not bother you with further possible explanations. The point I wish to make is that this is the wrong method of attack. It is from the psychological point we must tackle this problem. Once we know the motive, we know the murderer. Once we know the murderer, there will be no difficulty in establishing *how* the thing was done. The right explanation will grow spontaneously from the character of the man. It will be dictated by his known movements and the means at his disposal at the time."

Luigi's eyes sparkled with interest. "That's really excellent, Venables! I had never realized before that there was a metaphysics of detection."

"Don't be misled," Venables warned him. "In the last resort it's an art—a flair—and we invent the scientific explanation for our success afterwards. It's not so different from the savage way of smelling out witches. I have generally found the murderer whiffed of brimstone slightly to my nostrils."

"And can you smell this murderer?" said Luigi. "If he were in this room, for instance?"

"I can smell something fishy here," said Venables with a laugh. "But we are boring His Majesty."

"Luigi loves talking!" said King Augustus gloomily. "The only fault in an otherwise admirable secretary. By the way, Luigi," he added testily, "I don't know what the devil to do with these Cabinet minutes." He pushed a sheaf of papers disconsolately across the table.

"If you will permit me, sir, I will make the necessary comments," said Luigi, sweeping up the papers.

Gustav gave a sigh of relief. "Yes, do! No criticism, you know! You can imitate my handwriting all right." He said something to Luigi in a low voice as he bent over the desk, and Luigi nodded.

Gustav turned to Venables. "Well, Venables, you seem to have matters well in hand. I am so busy I don't know where to turn, I must confess, and I rely on you entirely to pull this off all right. Otherwise I shall be the most unpopular person in Iconia. I don't think there was anything else I wanted to ask you." He looked at his watch. "I have a high official coming to see me in a moment."

Venables withdrew. His unusually keen hearing had caught a word or two of Gustav's whisper to Luigi, and he was not surprised therefore when in the corridor outside he met the "high official." It was Rosa, still classical, but depressingly draped in quantities of black material...

Venables frowned thoughtfully as he tactfully turned off the corridor without greeting her.

Chapter XIII

THE OBVIOUS CULPRIT

An Extract from the Notebook of Mr. Charles Venables

(Reproduced by permission of Mr. Venables
and the publishers of the *Art of Criminal Investigation*.)

"It is fairly obvious that the Queen was murdered because she was going to publish a confession that thirty years ago she procured Dr. Robor to dispose of Prince Maximilian, either by poison or simple wrong treatment of a real illness. Was she also responsible for King Francis's death? I am inclined to think not. It was probably a fortunate accident, but I doubt if his life would have been worth much once the bother about Maximilian's taking-off had died down. She was obviously determined to wipe out her hated brother's line.

"Presumably the Countess was in the know. Did the death of her son have anything to do with the matter? It is difficult to see how there can have been any relation between the two, but it is a possibility. Anyway, it is obvious the Queen would never have stood for Naomi's tricks unless Naomi had some hold on her.

"Who killed Queen Hanna? The obvious answer is—Dr. Robor. But it is not certain. There may be someone who might suffer still more from the exposure of the crime, although I cannot see who it is at the moment.

"What did the Queen mean by an act of expiation? Not a simple confession surely? And since her brother's line is extinct, she cannot make any reparation. Perhaps, therefore, she proposed to abdicate. I suspect she had the dramatic idea of making the formal announcement to the Knights of the Collar gathered in the Chapel. It appears that it is the duty of the Sovereign Prior to make a short address. That would have given her her opportunity.

"Where did the letter of warning come from? The Mistress-of-the-Wardrobe had fairly free access to her person. Was the Countess Naomi in league with Robor?

"The astonishing thing is that the Queen did not appear to suspect Dr. Robor of writing the warning. Surely it ought to have occurred to her at once?

"I think it can be definitely taken that the murder was premeditated. It seems a bit theatrical to use the Curse of the Herzvogins to do the deed, and also risky. I imagine the murderer's aim was to give the crime a supernatural air in the hope that the public might regard the murder as an Act of God—or the devil. It has certainly succeeded with the superstitious.

"Things look black for Dr. Robor on the whole. Meanwhile it is galling for us to leave a murderer at large, particularly as the Royal Physician. But before we can do anything we must at least have some plausible suggestion as to how he strangled the Queen without being seen. And also why he changed the Queen's clothes.

"Whatever the explanation, it must also account for the Queen's mysterious evanishment from the State Office. One is rather inclined to the theory of an impersonation, particularly after the odd incident of the 'ghost' who was shot. I fancy the sentry only imagined he hit the 'ghost.' There would have been at least some blood if he had, and the corpse should surely have turned up sooner or later, even if her companion had whisked the dead or wounded ghost out of sight before I got to the spot. Even so, how on earth could the impersonation have been good enough to deceive both the Chancellor and Gustav, with the features clearly revealed by the light of a lamp?

"Another person who asks for investigation is Brightholme. Any pal of Robor's is bound to be a suspect anyway, and it seems curious that nobody quite knows why Brightholme was ever engaged at all. Brightholme seems oddly well informed about Iconian affairs, and the other day I saw him conversing in fluent Iconian with a servant. Queer that—to have picked up the language so quickly. I am loath to think ill of him—a nice lad—but these points must be explained. By the way, he seems to spend an unnecessary amount of his time with Princess Vera; but that is all to his credit.

"As I expected, Millitranyi found no secret passages. Gustav chaffed him a great deal—rather cruelly, I thought. Millitranyi blames it all on me.

"I am disappointed in Gustav. Rosa has moved into the Palace! Considering we are still in mourning, and that Princess Vera is also in the Palace, this seems to me the height of impropriety. The Chamberlain is almost in tears. Gustav, oddly enough, seems ashamed of it. Why did he do it? Is it Luigi's idea? Somehow I don't think so. It may have been imagination, but I thought I saw him giving his cousin a dirty look. If he has the intelligence I credit him with, he should be all against Rosa's arrival. How did Rosa work it? I got the impression in London that she was well under Gustav's thumb. Princess Vera seems to be taking it very sportingly, but I think she will have a good show-down with the young man in a few days. I detected the light of battle in her eyes when the twins thoughtlessly mentioned 'father's friend.' A bad show.

"The Coronation was a very splendid affair. I got quite a thrill when the dried-up Saracen's head was produced. The genuine article. What a barbarous people our ancestors were! The King looked a splendid figure, vowing to let no Saracen pass the frontier. The Turkish Ambassador grinned. But the Chancellor is right about Gustav's unpopularity. Unless we get someone for the murder soon he is in for a sticky time. Some of the remarks along the route were quite audible in spite of quantities of mounted police with fierce moustaches and sharp swords. I detected the Chamberlain looking longingly at Dr. Robor's head…

"The Chamberlain, by the way, still appears to be in charge of the Palace budget. The food is as bad as ever. And Miss Fotheringay was right about the draughts…

"I don't as a rule like to handle two cases at once, but I have had a most interesting letter from the little Delfinage girl on the Fairview Estate, which has set me thinking. It is possible that something exceedingly queer and unpleasant went on down there… I always did distrust that perfect alibi.

"I found two frogs in my pyjamas this morning. I can't imagine what I have done to annoy the Herzvogin kids. However, I told the Princess, who very kindly walloped the Crown Prince for me. Petra confessed that she had been against the frog idea, but had given in to her brother. Well, I am glad the girl at least has a spark of humanity. Frogs in the middle of an Iconian winter! I pity Miss Fotheringay. It must need all the blood of the Stuarts to cope with the twins!"

Venables encountered the twins shortly after he had made the entries in his notebook quoted above. They were walking hand in hand across the Tiltyard. Hopping beside them was a hunched little figure with a tail.

"Hallo, Mr. Venables," said the Crown Prince distantly. "This is Pongo."

Pongo was as unattractive as most monkeys. He clawed at Venables' trouser-legs and gabbled.

"He likes you!" exclaimed Petro in some surprise.

"He certainly seems to," replied Venables gravely. "Odd, isn't it?"

Petro hesitated. "I'm sorry about those frogs," he said at last, with a scowl at Petra, who had been whispering in his ear.

"That's all right," answered Venables. "You might warm them in future."

Petra giggled.

"You're fond of the Princess, aren't you?" Venables went on.

The twins nodded enthusiastically.

"Well, then, if you want to help her, stop playing tricks on your father's friends. *Any* of his friends, do you understand me?"

"Yes, Mr. Venables," said the Crown Prince with an obstinate glower.

"What on earth is that round your neck?" exclaimed Venables suddenly. "I thought I saw it move."

Petra looked embarrassed. "Oh, that's only Rosa," she said. Venables recoiled a pace as she unwound a snake from her neck, a striped reptile about three feet long. It hung from her hand, lax and motionless, and then slowly reared itself and curled round her hand. Venables shuddered.

"It's quite harmless," Petro assured him. "Mutch got it for us from a sailor on the Danube. It's had the fangs taken out, see?" He clutched the head and opened the gaping jaws. "We have to feed it on bread and milk."

Venables looked stern. "Have you told the Princess what you have called this reptile?"

"No," confessed the boy guiltily.

"Well, you'd better tell her. Or, better still, take my advice and change it."

Petra, looking a little ashamed, rewound the unpleasant object round her neck and took her brother's hand.

"Mr. Venables, has father said anything to you about my going to school?" asked Petro, exchanging his air of sullen obstinacy for one of winning affability.

"I remember his mentioning it," answered Venables, "but he didn't say when you would go. Why?"

"Because I don't want to go," said the Crown Prince decisively. "I don't want to leave Tirra." Petra herself showed every sign of being about to cry.

Venables cleared his throat and endeavoured to look magisterial. "You can't be together always," he said.

"Why not?" asked the boy.

"Well, you'll have to be the King one day. And perhaps Petra will become a queen somewhere else. And you'll marry, too."

"I shouldn't mind marrying the Princess," admitted Petro. Then, seeing Petra's face fall, he added, "But I couldn't possibly leave Tirra. Besides, I don't want to be a King. It's a —— awful job, if you ask me."

"Here, I say, you mustn't use that word!" exclaimed Venables. "Where on earth did you pick it up? Miss Fotheringay would be horrified!"

"Mutch is always saying it," said Petro. "Aren't kings supposed to use it?"

"No," said Venables, not very truthfully.

Petro repeated it several times under his breath with relish. "I don't want to be a king anyway. I want to keep a Zoo. I say, Mr. Venables, do speak to father for me. He never listens to us. I don't want to go to England, you see. I don't mind going to school, but I want to go to school with Tirra, here in Iconia."

Venables sighed. "All right. I'll speak to the King about it."

Petro smiled at him winningly. "Oh, thank you. Here, Pongo, take your hat off to the gentleman." He thrust his fingers in his mouth and gave a piercing street-urchin's whistle. The monkey, gabbling to itself, raised the tiny head-dress and ducked several times. Then Petro picked it up, slung it on his shoulder, and raced round the corner, followed by his sister.

Venables felt a little conscience-stricken about the children. They had, of course, been kept in ignorance of the dreadful end of their grandmother, and had accepted her disappearance with the blissful serenity of children. All the same, the Palace was no sort of place for youngsters to live in at present. Both possessed uncomfortable quantities of temperament, the boy particularly. If Gustav really carried out his plan of sending the boy to an English school, the twins would be miserable. It was late to effect a drastic alteration in a child's habits. The lack of discipline of the Palace had been bad in its effect, but it did not follow that a reaction to the opposite extreme might not be more harmful.

He might venture to put that point of view to Gustav, to whom it possibly had not occurred. It was extraordinarily fortunate for the twins that Vera was marrying Gustav, as the Princess could give them the necessary combination of discipline and sympathy.

Venables wondered, incidentally, why the betrothal had not yet been announced. Gustav's accession to the throne made his marriage really urgent, yet nothing was said. Although Venables was not familiar with the domestic arrangements of sub-Balkan palaces, he would not have been surprised if after the new Rosa development the Princess had refused to proceed with the match. But in that case she would surely have returned to Kossovia. The fact that she had not done so seemed to prove that the betrothal was still on the cards. He had not heard any of the Palace gossips discuss the betrothal, but perhaps this was due to the fact that the Princess's suite, from her chief equerry to her youngest maid, were reserved, large-boned Kosserbs who spoke nothing but German and Kossovian, with neither of which languages were Iconians familiar. This no doubt stopped rumour at its usual source.

It was not till the next day that the Great Row started. Before it began Venables had been summoned by the King, who no doubt wished to make his customary mild complaint at the slow progress of the investigation. It was eleven o'clock in the morning. Venables had hardly had time to say a few words when he heard Rosa's imperious voice in the anteroom, demanding admission. Luigi's low tones could be heard denying it. Venables talked on, endeavouring not to notice the altercation, but it was impossible not to do so when Rosa's voice rose to a shrill scream and there were sounds painfully like those of a physical struggle.

Gustav turned pink with embarrassment. "Come in, Rosa!" he roared. The door was flung dramatically open and Rosa stood on the threshold.

She was dressed in an ivory *peignoir*, the edge of which was embroidered in a purple Grecian key pattern. Her hair hung in two plaits—plaits which later would be dressed to fall on her nape in her customary classical coiffure. Her cheeks were scarlet with temper.

"Am I to be insulted with impunity?" she asked shrilly, with conscious or unconscious recollection of the phraseology of melodrama.

"Of course not, Rosa," said Gustav mildly. "I am sure no one would insult you. I am very busy now, and if later..."

"Later," Rosa laughed scornfully. "And so they can insult me as much as they like when you are busy." She stamped her foot and advanced two paces. "Gustav, cannot you see that in insulting me they insult you?"

The King sighed. "My dear, I am sure you must be mistaken. What exactly *has* happened?"

"Oh, nothing," she said with withering irony. "Nothing. A mere trifle. Only that I might have been stretched dead at your feet this moment."

"Good God, my dear Rosa, surely you are not serious?"

"I am perfectly serious. There was a poisonous snake in my dressing-gown this morning. I nearly died with shock. And what is more, I know who put it there. Your children!"

"Really that is too bad of them," said Gustav angrily. "Miss Fotheringay has no control over them whatever."

"Specially to insult me," went on Rosa. "If not to murder me!"

Venables ventured to soothe the storm. "I think it was only a little joke. They put frogs in my pyjamas. This particular snake has had its fangs removed, by the way, so it is quite harmless."

Rosa turned her large eyes on Venables and gave him a glance of utter scorn. She did not vouchsafe him an answer.

"What is more, they have named the vile reptile Rosa!" she said furiously. "I know what it is. That woman has put them up to it."

Gustav ran a worried hand through his hair. "It *is* abominable, Rosa. I am sorry. I will not let the matter rest there. I will continue our discussion later," added the King to Venables, who accordingly went away.

Venables speculated frequently and also a little anxiously about the fate of the twins. When he saw Gustav that morning he had hoped to put in the promised word for Petro. No worse moment could, of course, have been found to do so, and he now intended to let the storm blow over. All the same, he could not help thinking about them. Gustav's annoyance and Rosa's rage looked bad for the pair. He had suspected they were up to mischief. Unfortunately they had ignored his friendly warning.

Next day Princess Vera's equerry came with a message from the Princess, asking him to tea in her apartments that afternoon.

There were several other guests—the Chamberlain, Brightholme, two visitors from Kossovia—a soldier and his wife—and Venables thought at first that the invitation was merely a formal courtesy. Perhaps it was etiquette for the Princess to work steadily through the list of the Royal Household and offer all some kind of hospitality. But as Venables was rising to leave she detained him with a quiet word, and he remained on after the other guests had gone.

"I wanted to have a word with you, Mr. Venables," she said, "because I believe you have some influence with the King. More perhaps than I have," she added a trifle bitterly.

Venables disclaimed it. Everyone at the Palace appeared to credit him with being Gustav's friend and adviser. Even the twins seemed to be prepared to blame him for everything that Gustav did.

"Ah, you may not realize it, but the King really does listen to what you say. And I do feel so sorry for those poor children. He does not understand their natures. Petro will never, never settle down in an English school. He will die first."

Venables was inclined to agree. "White mice might be permitted, but not monkeys. I was going to speak to the King about them, Your Royal Highness, when a favourable opportunity occurred."

"You must speak to the King at once," insisted the Princess. "He has sworn that he will send Petro off to England to-morrow, and Petra down to a convent school in Theria. It is so dreadfully sudden. The children are almost mad with grief. Nothing I can say to the King seems to make any difference. It makes it so difficult for me, because he seems to think that in some way I am to blame for the bother. I still don't quite know," added the Princess helplessly, "what it is all about. But the whole business seems nasty and sordid, and so unsettling for the children. Can't you persuade the King to change his mind?"

"I'll try," promised Venables. "But I don't think for a moment I will get any result beyond a telling-off for my impertinence."

"I think I have only made things worse by sticking up for the children," went on Princess Vera. She muttered something which sounded singularly like a Kossovian imprecation upon Rosa's head. Venables was about to go when he realized that there was something else the Princess wished to speak about, but that she had some difficulty in leading up to it. Her methods were normally direct, in harmony with her forthright personality and open face. Finally, after an awkward silence, she burst out without any pretence at maidenly delicacy.

"What on earth has come over Gustav? I simply cannot believe he is the same person. Oh, it's no use my pretending to you to be ignorant about what is happening here, Mr. Venables. You know I feel somehow that as you are a stranger here—as I am—I can speak a little more freely... What in heaven's name *has* possessed Gustav to bring that woman into the Palace?"

Venables murmured something to the effect that it was a great pity.

"Oh, I wouldn't mind if he were genuinely in love with the girl," exclaimed Princess Vera, blushing slightly, "but I'm quite sure he isn't. In fact, when I spoke to him to-day about the children, I sensed that he was almost as fed up with her as we are. You see, Mr. Venables, I've known Gustav since he was quite young, and he is not at all the type to be ruled by women. Quite the contrary, in fact. He can look after himself very well. Yet this woman has installed herself in the Palace at the worst possible time and is upsetting all our plans. Now there's no nonsense about me. I know Gustav's pretty well *got* to marry me—I'm about the only eligible woman at the moment, for the Hohenzollerns and the Bernadottes and the Savoys would not marry a Herzvogin, not even a reigning one. And I'm quite sure we'd get along very well together. But I'm not the sort to be made a fool of, and until Gustav has dismissed this wretched woman properly, with a pension and so forth, I am not going to have our betrothal announced. And what is more, I know that Gustav is too much of a gentleman to ask it of me. As a matter of fact he is so ashamed, he hates meeting me nowadays. But if he knows he is making an exhibition of himself, why does he go on doing it?"

Venables smiled. "I hope to know in a day or two. One can guess, but I should like to be sure before I do anything."

"I see," said the Princess with relief. "Well, I think you ought to be able to get the better of her. She hasn't much sense. Poor Augustus! But meanwhile things are in a turmoil. Almost everyone is involved in the row. The Chancellor won't see the King again until His Majesty has apologized for what he said to Demetrior when he quite respectfully raised the question of our marriage. Then the same afternoon poor Mapponyi ventured to suggest that Rosa's presence in a mourning Court was a little open to criticism. Gustav bit his head off. The Chamberlain has had to take to his bed until the thing blows over. The King certainly has a lot of his mother in him. I feel so guilty about it all, because I really am the cause of the trouble. I ought to return to Kossovia at once, of course, but then there are the twins. The poor children have absolutely no one else to keep an eye on them if I go. Oh dear, it is just like them to barge right into the middle of this row and stir everything up!"

Venables was leaving when the Princess's equerry entered. He said something to the Princess in a low voice. She turned a little pale and called Venables back.

"Mr. Venables, this is awful. The twins have disappeared!"

"The whole Palace is now being searched," said the equerry. "They cannot be found anywhere!"

Chapter XV

THE IMPERIAL TOKAY

"It's the devil succeeding to the Crown just at this time!" groaned the King to Venables. "First of all, these quarrels among the Household! Then on top of that my children run away! Confound that old fool Millitranyi, he still hasn't found a trace of them. I can't even rely on my ministers. My Chancellor suddenly decides to get a fit of sulks, and old Mapponyi insults me to my face!" Gustav growled, and glared out of his study window at the bleak Alps on the skyline.

"If I might have a word with Millitranyi," suggested Venables, "I think I could suggest where he ought to look for the twins."

"Excellent, Venables! I'll get him to see you next time he comes over to the Palace. It's very worrying. I don't think they'll come to any harm, of course."

"Charming children, sir!" ventured Venables. "And devoted to each other! I don't think Petro will take very kindly to school discipline."

The King glowered. "Look here, Venables, if you start on that game, I'm damned if I'll have you in the Palace, investigation or no investigation. You're worse than the blasted women! What the hell do you mean?"

Venables hesitated between his natural desire to pursue the case to the end and stay at the Palace, and his equally natural desire to tell a monarch to go to hell, and leave. The King apparently read the struggle in his expression, for Gustav's face softened, and he made what was in effect an apology.

"I'm so badgered by one thing and another I don't know where I am!" he confessed. "The fact of the matter is, I'm in a mess. Confound my mother! What did she think she was getting up to?"

"If only Your Majesty would be good enough to be frank..." said Venables, still smarting a little from the earlier remark.

"Frank, frank, frank!" groaned Gustav. "It's easy enough to talk about it, but not so easy when you're pulled twenty different ways. I wish to God I'd guessed what I would have to take on while I was still Crown Prince. I should have taken care to marry someone like Rosa, and get debarred from the succession."

"I understand, sir, and I regret I can be of no assistance," said Venables stubbornly.

"What do you think of Princess Vera?" asked Gustav suddenly, after the silence which necessarily followed Venables' unhelpful response.

"Very likeable," said Venables, a little surprised at the question.

"Damned likeable," muttered Gustav enigmatically. "She's got too good a heart, that's her trouble." He relapsed into a gloomy silence.

Venables drew his chair a little closer to the King. "Your Majesty," he said in a low voice, "when you sent for me, and I came in here, I found you alone, with no one in the anteroom, and your back to the door. Was that wise?"

The King started, and looked distressed. "Why, good Lord, what do you mean?"

"Only that I shall be surprised if someone does not make an attempt on your life within the next few hours."

Gustav gave Venables a curious look. The green eyes did not falter, but were uncommunicative.

"Why the devil do you say that? Are you trying to frighten me?"

"No, sir, merely to prepare you."

"But who do you expect will attack me?"

Venables' eyes wandered. He was silent for a little. "I might be wrong. It would be better not to tell you at the moment. Treat

everyone as if he were a potential enemy." He smiled. "Even myself—
or Luigi!"

"I see." King Augustus X stared straight in front of him, at his
gold and quartz inkwell. He looked as if he saw very unpleasant
things therein. Then he looked up. "I would be obliged if you would
come and dine with me to-night, Venables. An informal little dinner.
You know how I detest ceremony. I have an announcement of some
importance to make. You will probably be able to guess its nature
from the company you meet there." He nodded, and Venables
withdrew.

Venables suppressed a grin that evening when he saw the invited
guests as they took their places at the table. At the foot of the table
sat Rosa, her magnificent bust rising proudly from a glittering black
corsage. Venables was placed next to Dr. Benedict Robor, whom
he had not seen for some time. Dr. Robor stared at Venables with
an enigmatic smile, and drew his hands rapidly from his wrinkled
forehead to his mouth with a nervous gesture. He seemed worried.

Opposite Venables were Luigi and Brightholme. Brightholme
winked at Venables. Luigi, thought Venables, looked a trifle pale,
and not his usual unconcerned self.

Rosa, however, was in magnificent form. Indeed, anyone might
have been excused for taking her for the First Lady of Iconia, instead
of someone holding the rather notorious office of Ballet Mistress. She
sparkled at Venables, chaffed Robor, was sweetly maternal to her
cousin, patronizing to Brightholme, and affectionate—with just a hint
of wayward imperiousness—to the King. Gustav said little, looked
at her wearily, and only occasionally made some pleasant remark of
a kind which showed that his thoughts were elsewhere. Concerned,
no doubt, with the real object of the dinner, diagnosed Venables.

Whatever that object, it was obviously impossible for the King
to broach it until the servants had left the room. The meal was finished at last, however, Rosa pushing the conversation by main force
through one or two stiff patches.

The poor quality of the food, and the wine that accompanied it, still betrayed the stewardship of the Chamberlain, active even when, as now, he sulked in his bedroom.

Dinner ended. They all left the table together, and the King led the way into the next room—a small white-walled library hung with modern paintings. When they were seated Gustav gave a schoolboy-ish smile and went to the desk. He opened one of the deep drawers and pulled out a set of glasses. They were wide-mouthed and lustrous, with interlaced stems in which colours flitted like imprisoned butterflies. The King held them up to the light before proffering them to his guests, and made the most of their exquisite colouring. "Given to Augustus II by the Doge of Venice as an acknowledgment of the part Iconia played in the battle of Lepanto," he explained. "Iconia was not a sea-power, of course, as our only port is on the Danube, but we paid for one galley which rammed a Turkish ship and sank it."

He turned to the drawer again and pulled out a huge bottle festooned with cobwebs. The cork was sealed with a coat of arms surmounted by an Imperial crown. "Luigi brought this up from the cellars himself!" the King said with a wink. "The Chamberlain mustn't know! It's our precious Imperial Tokay, given by the Emperor to my grandfather, who married a Hapsburg. We have only a dozen left. There will be still less after this evening."

He drew the cork himself, but Dr. Robor and Brightholme started forward. "Allow me, Your Majesty," offered Dr. Robor smoothly.

"Let me act as wine-waiter, sir!" said Brightholme.

Gustav surrendered the menial task to Robor with a smile.

"Good Lord, is that a Picasso?" asked Brightholme suddenly, as the wine was being poured out. He walked up to the wall and stared at a picture.

"It may be. My mother was very fond of modern painters," said Gustav indifferently. "I confess I find that golden fluid more lovely at the moment than any painting."

Somewhat abashed, Brightholme turned from the picture, and the rest of the company guiltily looked at their wineglasses again. Venables at any other time would have been interested by this new revelation of Queen Hanna's intelligence. But at the moment his mind was grappling hard with a problem.

Gustav lifted his glass. The company elevated theirs. It was at this moment that Venables came to a conclusion. Since he had come to it by rational methods and with tolerable certainty, he acted on it. He knocked down Rosa's arm before the glass touched her lips. She screamed, and as she dropped her arm there was a tinkle. The stem had been knocked off her glass and half the liquid spilled on her skirt. Venables snatched the remains of the glass out of her hand. "Stop drinking, all of you!" he shouted. He dipped his finger in the dregs of Rosa's wine and sniffed.

There was a dead silence as the astonished guests stared at him.

"Enough prussic acid to kill an ostrich," he announced calmly. He walked slowly over to the King and took his glass out of his hand.

Venables put it down gravely after a brief inspection. "That would have been your last drink, sir," he said.

Gustav went white.

"It is fortunate," went on Charles quietly, "that my sense of smell is unusually keen."

The company accepted his explanation without remark, although it happened to be untrue.

The other glasses, including Venables' own, were harmless.

Rosa had not said anything, up to this point, beyond her first scream. But as she understood how narrow had been her escape the blood fled from her lips and cheeks. Even her nose seemed to become suddenly pinched as the blood ebbed away.

And then, quite suddenly, she went into hysterics. She laughed shrilly, and this dissolved into a wheezing cackle, while she drummed her heels violently on the floor. It was all very upsetting. Dr. Robor and the King advanced simultaneously to soothe her. She recoiled spasmodically as the Doctor, the nearest of the two, reached her chair. The chair itself tumbled over. She retreated still farther and stood facing them, trembling.

"Get away, everyone!" she screamed. Her eyes roamed the astonished company and fell on Venables. He was sitting on the sofa dipping a thin sheet of blue paper in a glass of wine, without showing any trace of interest in her conduct. Rosa tottered over to him and collapsed on to his shoulders. He put the glass on one side, supported her, not very gently, and placed her back against the sofa head. Then he picked up the glass again.

"Don't leave me!" she groaned. "Save me, Mr. Venables!"

Venables sighed, and said something encouraging.

It was then that Dr. Robor, looking extremely frightened, glanced unsteadily round him.

"This excitement is very bad for me," he said. "I am not so young as I was. I may say I feel distinctly unwell. With your permission, sir, I will retire, and go to bed."

"You may retire," said the King dryly. "And Luigi will go with you to look after you. Take care," Gustav added, "that you do not get up from bed too soon, Robor. In fact, Luigi or someone else had better stay with you to make perfectly certain that you do not expose yourself to that risk."

Dr. Robor grinned mirthlessly, bowed, and retired.

When they had gone Venables turned to the King. "You were about to make some announcement to us, I believe, sir?"

The King nodded. "I was. I have changed my mind," he said slowly. "You may all go."

"For God's sake," moaned Rosa in Venables' ear, "go with me as far as my rooms."

Venables turned to look at the King before he went. Gustav's face was that peculiar mottled colour assumed by a tanned face when it pales. He was staring fixedly at his glass, whose contents, as Venables knew, would speedily have accounted for Augustus's giant frame, in fact for the frame of an elephant. Then he went to his desk, and before Venables closed the door behind himself and Brightholme he saw the King take from it a revolver and slip it into his pocket.

Once Rosa got to her apartments, her colour returned, and she became more like herself. She spoke shrilly to her maid as the latter came to answer her bell.

"Quick, Maria, pack up all my things this very instant!"

"Pack up your things?" repeated the maid with a flabbergasted air.

"Yes. Are you deaf? Pack and be quick. Hurry!" Rosa sank into a couch and let her arms droop forlornly along the back. "God help me to get alive out of this den of assassins. Heavens, what is that fool of a girl dawdling for?"

She jumped to her feet and ran into her bedroom. Venables heard her urging on her maid at the top of her voice. "Quick, Maria! You goose, I tell you our lives are at stake! No matter about the folds. My God! what does the woman think she is doing? Here, I will close it. Call Jan and send him downstairs to get a taxi. Quickly!"

A moment later Rosa came back and started to sweep together such of her things as were in the sitting-room. Venables helped her. She snatched a small flat jewel case out of his hands and thrust it in her handbag. She allowed him to help her pack the rest.

"May I help madam to change into a travelling dress?" said the little maid, returning a moment later.

Rosa gave a groan. "Change? Do you think I change into travelling dresses while murderers wait round the corner with bared knives? We must be out of the Palace in five minutes!"

At last the trunks were filled with Rosa's miscellaneous belongings and the lids closed. A pile of articles still remained over. "They can send those on," she said.

Rosa's frenzied haste had disarranged her hair, and her black evening gown was creased. Her cheeks were red with exertion. This was no longer the classically posed Rosa of Venables' first acquaintance. She clasped Venables' hand and shuddered.

"See me to the Courtyard," she begged. "I dare not go alone."

Directly she left her rooms her fears seemed to return. Venables had never seen a woman so suddenly and ludicrously frightened. When someone passed her in the long corridors of the Palace, she gripped his arm and pressed against him as if she feared to feel a knife between her shoulders at any moment.

"My dear Rosa," protested Venables. "It is not so dangerous as all that!"

"I never realized how dangerous it was till to-night," breathed Rosa. "What a fool I have been!"

"I am afraid you have been a little unwise," admitted Venables.

"Bah! You do not know the truth. You cannot know it!" exclaimed Rosa passionately. "You think you do, but you don't. I was like you once. I have had my lesson! You saved my life, Mr. Venables. In return I say—get away while there is time!"

Venables did not point out that he had, after all, known enough to save her.

Out in the Courtyard a bleary moon lit the nymphs and gods of the fountains. He handed her into the carriage. She sat among trunks and bags, with bowed head, as might a goddess ejected from Olympus, with her divine emblems and trappings hurled after her. She carried off her retreat well, Venables admitted. Now she was in the open air, clear of the corridors, in a car that was bearing her to safety, she lost her nervous fears. Once again she posed, sinuous, impressive, classical.

She pressed his hand. "God bless you!" she said. "I thank you from the bottom of my heart. Come and see me sometimes at the villa."

As the door closed she leaned forward a little and looked into his eyes. He saw her white shoulders gleaming in the dusk as the car backed. Rosa kissed her hands to him, he waved, and the car shot away. Rosa turned and glanced up at the impressive façade of the Milö Palace. It was her last sight of it.

"Is Rosa really grateful to me?" reflected Venables, "or was that last burning look the first shot in a campaign? A damned attractive female. It is just as well that I never could fall in love with large women."

Chapter XVI

THE INDIGNANT CHIEF OF POLICE

"You might take charge of this inquiry, Finch," said Superintendent Manciple. He passed over to his subordinate a letter written on thick blue notepaper and headed "Milö Palace, Isorb." With it was a photograph. "We have unofficially promised to help Mr. Venables over this Iconian business," he explained. "He seems to have made rather a mess of things," added Superintendent Manciple uncharitably. "That Queen was killed under his nose, and he still doesn't seem to know who did it."

The letter read as follows:

"Dear Manciple,

"Can you have some inquiries made for me about the man in the enclosed photograph? I am sorry the wooden statue of St. Boron—the bearded cove—fills up most of the photo. I had to take the man's photograph without his knowing it, and so I made a pretence of photographing St. Boron. However, there's quite a large piece of him in the lower left-hand corner, complete with grin. Sorry I couldn't get his legs in. They're rather long.

"He goes by the name of Brightholme—Valentine Brightholme. He is qualified as a doctor and member of the R.C.S., and claims to have been at Bart's. You could start there. He was educated at W———. He is assisting the Household Physician here—Dr. Robor. Robor's name may crop up in the investigations. Naturally, I am particularly interested in any Iconian link-up.

"Yours very sincerely,

"Charles Venables."

Soon after this letter had reached Manciple, hastened as it was by air-mail, the writer was collaborating with General the Chief of Police Count Georgico-Maria Millitranyi in the examination of Dr. Robor. The examination was according to the somewhat elastic rules of Iconian police procedure. His Majesty, King Augustus X, had signified his intention of being present, and available, if need be, as a witness. He had suggested that the examination take place in the same white library in which the unpleasant affair of the poisoned Tokay had been transacted.

Dr. Robor's remark about feeling unwell may have had more of truth in it than appeared at the time. For when he entered the room, ostentatiously escorted by Luigi, he certainly looked ill. There were baggy pouches under his eyes. He was dressed as usual in frock-coat and grey trousers, but his usually neat stock was creased and untidy. His sparse grey hairs were unbrushed instead of being carefully arranged to cover his bald head.

He bowed to the King, and after standing for a few minutes was offered a seat.

One must explain in fairness to Venables that he was there under protest. He had told the King that he considered the examination of Robor at this stage a mistake. Their evidence was still incomplete. Millitranyi, however, was convinced that under his searching examination the Doctor would collapse and further evidence would be unnecessary. Gustav, after some hesitation, had sided with Millitranyi. Which showed, thought Venables, how much his influence with the King was really worth.

The Chief of Police goggled at the Doctor.

"Dr. Benedict Robor! You are charged with an attempt on the life of His Majesty the King, and of one Signorina Pavellicini, by the administration of a poison, to wit hydrocyanic acid, on the evening of yesterday."

"No," whispered Dr. Robor through bloodless lips. "I deny it!"

General Millitranyi blew out his cheeks and stared piercingly at the Doctor. "It is useless to deny it! There were six witnesses. You yourself took the bottle and poured it into the glasses, only two of which contained the poison. You alone had the opportunity to poison the wine."

"I deny it!" shrilled Dr. Robor, his simian little face screwed up with terror. "Tell me who saw me!"

"No one saw you!" roared General Millitranyi, thumping the desk. "Because you chose a moment when the attention of the company was distracted by your assistant, Brightholme, who had pointed to a painting on the wall. That," added the Chief of Police, puffing out his cheeks again, "is a point that will demand further investigation. But at the moment we are concerned with you."

"I repeat that I deny everything," announced Robor with more assurance.

"Well, we will soon change your tone," said Millitranyi ominously. "A few weeks' solitary confinement..."

"You cannot do that," replied the Physician indignantly. "It is not legal." He turned to the King. "Under the Habeas Corpus Act, introduced in imitation of England by your illustrious grandfather—"

"Which does not apply to cases of high treason," interrupted the Chief of Police with relish. "This is an alleged crime against His Majesty's person. In such cases we are permitted to put you to the question."

"To the question?" faltered Dr. Robor.

"Yes," answered Millitranyi. "The use of the rack would, I am advised by the Attorney-General, be permissible in this case. Also the thumbscrews. Both implements of investigation are still extant in the crypt, and could doubtless be lubricated... and whatever else is necessary."

Dr. Robor turned white. His lips trembled. "You would never dare! I appeal to the conscience of civilized man..."

"That's enough, Millitranyi," interrupted the King curtly. "As I have already told you, I wish the ordinary methods of police procedure, as applicable to private persons, to be kept to. Ignore the fact that the crime, if proven, is high treason."

"God bless you, sire!" exclaimed the Doctor with emotion.

"My action," replied the King coldly, "is dictated solely by considerations of political expediency. I have no personal objection to seeing you made uncomfortable. Please proceed, Millitranyi, bearing in mind what I have told you."

"As you will, sire," replied Millitranyi with an undercurrent of protest in his voice. He continued: "If you expect us to take your denial seriously, Robor, explain how the wine could have been poisoned by anyone other than yourself."

Dr. Robor gave a scared glance in the direction of the King. "It might have already been in the two wineglasses," he suggested.

Millitranyi went purple and jumped to his feet with a roar. "Scoundrel! Are you suggesting that His Majesty—besides, why should he wish to poison himself?" Shaking with passion, he strode over to the unfortunate Doctor, who shrunk back into his chair.

"There is no need to lose your temper, Millitranyi," interrupted the King mildly, "though I appreciate the loyalty you show. Dr. Robor has made a perfectly fair answer, in fact the only possible answer, to your question. I might have carefully poured the poison in the two glasses first. Would it have been colourless, Venables, by the way, and how much would have been needed?"

"It is not quite colourless, but it would not have shown in the glasses," answered Venables. "I estimated there was about a teaspoonful."

"It is perhaps odd," went on the King, "that I should have wanted to poison myself, but this might have been explicable by a kind of suicidal impulse. A sort of love pact." He smiled sardonically. "Now, Robor, in order to substantiate this suggestion of yours, will you explain exactly how the glasses were, and how you filled them?"

Dr. Robor screwed up his eyes in an effort to remember. "Each glass was standing on the little table in front of the person it was intended for. I took each up, so," he made a gesture, "and filled it. Then I put the bottle back——"

The King interrupted him. "You picked it up so." He mimicked the Doctor's gesture. "Now answer the truth, and remember there were witnesses. Did you have to invert the glass to fill it?"

Dr. Robor turned white. He stared about him, his eyes like those of a cornered hare. "Yes," he admitted at last.

The King and Venables exchanged amused glances. "So the glasses were upside down on the table before you poured the wine in? Then the poison I had carefully put in ought to have run out on to the table?"

Dr. Robor nodded miserably.

Millitranyi rubbed his hands. "Excellent, sire. You have trapped him very neatly. Ah, Dr. Robor, so you were a poisoner all the time, were you? And how many other people have you got rid of? What wonderful opportunities you have had to poison your enemies and then give your own death certificates for them. It might be worth while to investigate all the deaths which have occurred under your treatment." Millitranyi's voice gradually harshened, and he rose menacingly to his feet. His purple face and goggle-eyes stared fixedly at the miserable figure of the Doctor. Next moment, Venables guessed, he would have accused Robor of the murder of Prince Maximilian. But the King's deep voice cut into his denunciation.

"Sit down and shut up, Millitranyi!" he said coldly. "We are not concerned at the moment with any but the present accusation. You had better take Dr. Robor into custody."

Dr. Robor had been watching the King intently, his eyes like stones behind their thick-lensed spectacles. Now he rose slowly to his feet, still staring intently at the King.

"Very well, General," he said. "Arrest me if you will! I declare I am as innocent of any attempt on His Majesty's life as a babe unborn. And, further, I warn you that if you proceed with this wicked business I shall feel myself no longer bound by any confidences that I may have been given by Her Majesty, Queen Hanna, or her illustrious predecessors, or any members of this Household. In order to save my life from a false accusation I shall bring in evidence that will clear me, no matter whom it touches."

King Augustus X looked thoughtfully at the pale and harassed face of his Royal Physician. He looked a little quizzically at the moon-like and beetroot-coloured visage of his Chief of Police, preparing itself for a final explosion. He even glanced for a moment at the long, uncommunicative, and disapproving countenance of Venables. Then he got up.

"I have come to the conclusion that your evidence against Dr. Robor is insufficient," said the King coldly. "Dr. Robor will be kept under house arrest in the Palace until the matter has been cleared up. Meanwhile he can consider himself relieved of his duties, which will be taken over by Brightholme. By the way, Millitranyi, I am surprised not to have had some definite news of my children by now. With the whole country in a turmoil looking for them, it seems incredible that you have found no trace. Good-morning."

The King left the room. Millitranyi made three attempts to speak. Each time he stopped, apparently finding language inadequate to express his feelings. Dr. Robor took advantage of the silence to creep inconspicuously from the room.

Millitranyi turned to Venables, who appeared to find it amusing, and glared. The harassed Chief of Police muttered something under his breath.

"We are all up against the same difficulties," said Venables soothingly. "Have you heard anything about the children, by the way?"

"Nothing," admitted Millitranyi. "I hope before the day is out to have them in my hands." He said this loudly, as if to reassure himself.

"H'm!" mused Venables. "There can't have been many circuses in Isorb at the time."

"Circuses?" queried Millitranyi.

"Yes," said Venables. "I think you would be well advised to find out what circuses were in Isorb at the time of the children's disappearance. I fancy that would be where they would gravitate."

"I will certainly try it," exclaimed the General.

"I am very grateful——"

"Would you telephone me directly you learn what circuses were in town at the time?" asked Venables. "*Directly*," he emphasized, having by this time learned by bitter experience that minute hands were a luxury on Iconia's clocks.

The General promised.

Chapter XVII

THE UNQUALIFIED DOCTOR

"Just arrived for you by air-mail, sir," said the waiter, handing Venables a letter as he sat at lunch.

The letter looked important. It was marked in large letters, "URGENT, O.H.M.S." Venables asked permission from the Chamberlain to open it, and Brightholme, his neighbour, commented on the impressive look of the communication.

"Have they made you a Cabinet Minister? Or is it an invitation from Buckingham Palace?"

"It is neither," said Venables quietly. "I am afraid it is only an income tax summons." In point of fact, however, the enclosure read as follows:

"My Dear Venables,

"We have now made inquiries as to the identity and history of the man Brightholme whose photograph you sent us. We have some information about him which I think will interest you.

"First of all, I should be cautious about taking any of Brightholme's pills. He is not on the Medical Register. It is true that he was a medical student at Bart's for some time, but he was unable to pass the examinations. 'Constitutional lightheartedness' was the reason given by one friend of his. 'Brightholme was intelligent enough, but simply would not take the trouble to learn his job.' By the way, he has been through our hands several times. Medical 'rags,' you know. He appears to have been a leader of all the roughest and most irresponsible ones.

He was a popular figure during his time at Bart's. But no one was surprised that he failed in his examinations repeatedly and then left.

"The second point is that he is a ward of Dr. Robor and is Iconian by nationality. We have established this from the records at W———. Dr. Robor paid for Brightholme's education. It has always been supposed by the master we interviewed that Robor was in a somewhat *closer* relationship than that of guardian to the youth, and that this explained the Iconian nationality of the boy in spite of his English name. In other words, the mother's name was Brightholme…

"However, the boy lived in England all his life, and during the holidays he used to stay with the Earl of Grotrick, who is a personal friend of Dr. Robor. We have made judicious inquiries from the Earl, who has told us to go to hell, and stay there. So I am afraid this is all the information we can get this end.

"Yours sincerely,

"John Manciple, Supt."

"I always think it is unsettling to have anything to do with the police," said Venables to Brightholme with a sigh, as he folded the letter and replaced it in his pocket. "Your chief, no doubt, has come to the same conclusion?"

"Yes," admitted Brightholme. "I do think it is a bit unfair on Robor. They ought either to charge him or clear him. As it is, the poor old soul simply lurks in his room, never dares go out, and is frightened that at any moment he may be thrown into the Palace dungeons and garotted."

"An odd business altogether," commented Venables, with apparent carelessness.

"Deuced odd!" Brightholme looked at Venables with a knowing grin. "I say, wasn't something said about my calling attention to that painting at the very moment Robor was supposed to be lacing the Tokay with hydrocyanic? I've been expecting a visit from old Beetroot-face any time these last few hours."

"There was quite a lot said about it," answered Venables, "by our friend Millitranyi. I may say it was I who finally cleared your wounded name."

"Thanks a lot. But how?"

"I pointed out that if your remark had been merely a device to distract attention, you would have made some less intelligent comment. But to recognize the thing at once as a Picasso—it was one, as I found after considerable research—argued a genuine interest in painting—argued therefore that the remark was spontaneous."

"So that is how a great deductive brain works!" exclaimed Brightholme. "One is awestruck! But seriously I am awfully grateful to you!"

"Then you can show your gratitude in a very practical fashion."

"How?" asked Brightholme with interest.

Venables looked at him searchingly. "If I or anyone else becomes ill, kindly refrain from prescribing for us. If anyone insists on your doing so, I should, if I were you, fall down in a fit and let them send for one of the local men. Dr. Grobin is quite good, I believe. Otherwise we may be having some more unexplained tragedies."

Brightholme's grin vanished suddenly from his face. "Oh, I see," he answered uncertainly. "That sounds ominous for little Brightholme."

"I think it does," candidly admitted Venables.

"Are you telling me to Fly, All is Discovered?" went on Brightholme.

"There is no need to Fly—as yet," answered Venables. "I imagine you have various pressing matters to attend to before you go."

"Yes, I have, thanks very much. I'm grateful. You are a discerning blighter," said Brightholme thoughtfully. "By the way, how did you discover it?"

Venables threw over the photograph of St. Boron and Brightholme. "Does that explain it? Perhaps it doesn't. Anyway I sent that photograph to Scotland Yard and they did some research work. I have been wondering, though, why 'Brightholme' in particular, rather than Smith, or Jones, or Robinson?"

"Why not?" answered Brightholme defensively.

"The police, who have low minds, had quite the worst possible explanation for it," said Venables reflectively.

Brightholme laughed.

At this point Venables was called to the telephone. He returned a few minutes later looking thoughtful. "Will you be seeing the Princess to-day?" he asked the other.

Brightholme stared at him a little suspiciously. "Yes. As a matter of fact, I shall be seeing her immediately after lunch."

"The sooner the better," murmured Venables. "I have just been speaking to Millitranyi, who is still searching for the twins. I suggested to him, you know, that he ought to find what circuses were in town at the time they disappeared. It appears there was only one— Borromeo's. He has just learned that it is now at Catrin, which is a lonely little place about twenty miles from here, at the foot of the Alps. He is sending some of his men down by train right away. The train service to Catrin is very bad," added Venables.

"Oh, thanks!" said Brightholme with a wondering stare. "Thanks very much. Well, I'll be going along now." After an apology to the Chamberlain, he fled.

With a sigh and a shake of his head Venables resumed the consumption of his much-interrupted lunch.

The Chamberlain was once again in evidence at the meals of their section of the Royal Household. Apart from an extra line or two of worry on his fine forehead, he looked as if nothing out of the usual had occurred. The removal of Rosa to her old villa had healed his wounded sense of propriety, and he was apparently once more on good terms with his Royal Master. Meanwhile there had been a strange silence from Rosa. The King had refrained from visiting her, and no one at the Court had seen her since her abrupt departure.

Altogether, the Household thought, it was very odd. The sudden disgrace of Dr. Robor was equally odd. The affair of the poisoned Tokay had so far been kept a secret, thanks to the discretion of the participants. All that was known was that Dr. Robor, apparently under orders from the King, was keeping to his room, and had sent out a message that he was too ill to see anyone or to be seen. It was even rumoured that the Palace sentries had been instructed not to allow him outside.

No wonder, therefore, that the Court was puzzled—a state of mind which annoyed the Court, but which did not restrain its imagination. There is no need to record here the varied rumours, which explained Rosa's departure and Robor's disgrace on lines that gave the Doctor an undeserved reputation for gallantry.

If the Chamberlain looked well, the opposite must be said of the Countess Naomi. To everybody's surprise, she continued to keep her post at Court. It is true that it had not the same importance now that there was, for the moment, no Queen. But still the ladies-in-waiting remained, and her position as their head gave her, under Iconian Court etiquette, precedence over all ladies of the land except those of the blood Royal and the wives of the Chancellor and the Chamberlain, both of whom, however, happened at the moment to be bachelors.

Before Queen Hanna's death (pointed out Professor Andreyi to Venables) the Countess had at least never been seen drunk before the evening. But now—he shrugged his shoulders significantly, and Venables followed his glance to where the Countess sat. Her dank-looking hair was disarranged, and untidy curls strayed forlornly over her perspiring face. She was staring in front of her at nothing, in a stupor. From time to time she was shaken with some internal convulsion of mirth.

Her pasty face was bloated into puffy folds and made her look extremely repulsive. Undoubtedly she had become worse in the last few days. It was true that, on ceremonial occasions, the practice of years and some effort of will enabled her to play her part without any too obvious shortcomings. Later on in the proceedings she lost her grip, but by that time Mutch had swooped on her and hurried her off to her room with its wardrobe full of empty bottles, while the Deputy Mistress of the Wardrobe took her place. But apart from these ceremonial occasions, the Countess's life seemed to alternate between the maudlin exhilaration of intoxication and the dull torpor of recovery.

"I cannot understand how His Majesty permits it!" exclaimed the Professor. "He is much more considerate of her than ever the Queen was. The Chamberlain simply dare not mention her name to the King, he told me. His Majesty at once construes it as a complaint against the Countess, a thing he has told Mapponyi he will not tolerate."

Indeed the Chamberlain had evidently come to the conclusion that he would do far better to ignore altogether his co-official. He stared through her when she giggled at him feebly. When she addressed a remark to him he bowed with an expression of distaste and neither answered her nor looked at her.

"Unless I am much mistaken," said Venables, "she will have D.T.'s soon. The lavender rhinoceros stage cannot be far off."

"Oh, she always manages to pull herself up in time," answered the Professor indifferently. "She must have a constitution like a rhinoceros herself."

Later a message arrived asking Mr. Venables to be so good as to look in on the Chancellor at Government Buildings, in the Vio Victorio, that evening.

The Chancellor received Venables cordially, and plunged at once into his business.

"My dear Venables, I believe you are the only man who can give me the truth about this Dr. Robor business. Was the wine really poisoned?"

"Most certainly!" answered Venables emphatically.

"Then why does the King shield Dr. Robor?"

"Perhaps he thinks he is innocent?" suggested Venables.

"Bah! Of course he is guilty," answered Demetrior impatiently. "Personally, I have always thought Robor capable of anything!"

"Is that fair? After all, he has a reputation—even abroad."

"There was something fishy about the death of Prince Maximilian," answered the Chancellor firmly. "Oh, don't think I'm influenced by the gossip of the bunch of ne'er-do-wells and tailor's dummies who make up our illustrious Court! But when I came into office—you remember my predecessor had to resign because of an illness from which he subsequently died—he gave me a very strong hint about Maximilian's death, and advised me to leave the topic of Prince Maximilian severely alone in discussing the Royal Family with Queen Hanna."

"Oh, quite," said Venables. "I have never doubted for a moment that Queen Hanna instructed Dr. Robor to poison Prince Maximilian. We may as well be frank," he added, seeing the Chancellor's eyebrows go up. "But this affair of the Tokay is a different thing. In any case I don't think you quite realize how little His Majesty knows of the Court gossip about Maximilian and so forth... All I can say—if it is any comfort to you—is that it is my opinion Dr. Robor is not likely to be any danger to anyone at the Palace for the moment."

"It is a comfort," agreed the Chancellor.

"After all," pointed out Venables, "the affair has given Rosa the deuce of a fright and made her leave the Palace. I should have thought you would have been grateful to anyone who ended Rosa's influence over the King."

"I am, certainly."

"That reminds me," Venables went on, "once Rosa had left the Palace, I expected to see the betrothal announced. What is holding it up?"

The Chancellor threw up his hands. "What indeed? This betrothal is turning my grey hairs white, my dear Venables. Picture to yourself: We at last get rid of Rosa. We rejoice. We attend His Majesty, who gives me his gracious permission to make a formal declaration to the Princess Vera. I make the formal declaration to the Princess Vera—"

The Chancellor paused dramatically.

"And Her Royal Highness refuses!"

"Refuses?" questioned Venables, a little taken aback.

"*Temporizes* would be more correct," said Count Demetrior. "One can, I suppose, hardly expect a woman to do anything so definite as refuse... The Princess demands time. She will give a definite answer in a few days. And so on. What can we do? It is useless at this stage referring the matter to our Ambassador in Kossovia. All that part has been settled. We can hardly request King Wilhelm to bring pressure to bear on his daughter... Gustav is furious. Can one blame him? I have had some difficulty in keeping him to his side of the bargain. In a few days I am afraid he will insist on throwing the whole thing up."

The Chancellor gloomily stabbed his cigar butt into his silver ash-tray.

"I wish to heaven I were the Prime Minister of a republic," he went on angrily. "This confounded Palace costs me more trouble these days than the whole business of governing the country. And then there is the expense... But there. The Herzvogins appeal to our Iconian imagination! Impossible to deny it. There is something stable, something magic about a crown. Any Iconian peasant would have died for Queen Hanna or King Francis. They would as soon as not throw bad tomatoes at me, particularly after Budget Day!" He sighed. "If only we could settle this accursed business, and also marry Gustav off, he would be more popular even than his mother. He is a romantic figure, and no one need know how much he detests Iconia as long as we employ a Press Agent so skilful as little Obvogor."

There was a knock on the door and a secretary came quietly in. He spoke to the Chancellor.

"Millitranyi wants you on the telephone," said the Chancellor to Venables. "They will put the call through here."

Venables held the receiver at a safe distance from his ear drums as he heard the General's roar.

"Hallo, Venables," said the Chief of Police. "I say, old chap, I'm in the devil of a fix! My men got down there, to that blasted circus of Borromeo's. Well, it seems Petro and Petra had joined it, complete with a snake and a performing monkey. They told some wicked lie about being English children kidnapped by gipsies who wished to work their way home to England, and Borromeo, being a soft-hearted fellow, believed them. They pretended not to speak Iconian. The troupe are all Italian, of course, and don't read our papers, so they knew nothing about the disappearance of the Prince and Princess. At least they said they didn't. It's my belief they knew quite well, and had taken to the children, who seem to be fond of animals or something. Borromeo kept on saying they would have made wonderful lion tamers."

"Congratulations!" said Venables smoothly. "The King will be pleased!"

"Wait!" moaned the General. "Here comes the awful part of it—unspeakable! An hour before our men arrived, there came a man who spoke English and also Italian, and claimed to be the father of the children. As the children seemed to know him, Borromeo let them go. The man appears to have had a fast car, and so far we have found no trace of them. I ask you, Mr. Venables, who could possibly have perpetrated this unspeakable outrage?"

"I have no idea, General," said Venables, with a regrettable lack of truth.

Chapter XVIII

THE LONELY MONARCH

The King had sent for Venables. But when Venables had got there Gustav seemed reluctant to come down to the reason for the summons.

Gustav was in the State Office, that dark but lofty room, panelled in oak and furnished rather abominably in mahogany, in which Queen Hanna had spent so much of her time. Her son, it was certain, spent considerably less time there. However, at the moment he was seated at its huge mahogany desk, which rose in a pagoda of pigeon-holes halfway up the high wall, and was surmounted by a carved and gilded coat of arms. The desk was covered with papers. Most of them were dusty and faded, Venables noticed.

"I don't think you are much good, Venables," the King suddenly mumbled. This was after a halting succession of irrelevant remarks, mainly about the weather. "Here you have had the run of the Palace, and all the help you want from Millitranyi, and still you have got no nearer finding who killed my mother."

"At least," said Venables, "I have had the good fortune, sir, to prevent two additional murders."

"Oh, no doubt. I don't deny it," answered Gustav. "But you must realize how unsatisfactory it all is. And then there are my children!"

"I don't think you need worry about them, Your Majesty! They have the gift of falling on their feet, as the circus incident showed. You may be sure they are quite safe wherever they are. We shall soon discover what lies behind that disappearance from the circus."

"You seem curiously sure that they are safe," exclaimed Gustav, giving Venables a distrustful look. "Anyway, what are you going to do about it? Stay here, with that air of bland reassurance, for ever?"

"Until you tell me to go, sir," said Venables stubbornly, refusing to be ruffled by the King's offensive manner. "I can assure you I am exerting myself to the utmost. No one can do more, I am sure." He stated the platitude with a tone of admirable sincerity.

Gustav suddenly changed his manner. He sank his massive chin in his hands and stared gloomily ahead. "The whole business is getting me down! I suppose you realize there must have been something behind that attempt to poison me—that it was part of a settled plan, following on my mother's murder?"

"I realize it very well," admitted Venables.

"First my nephew—dead of meningitis certainly, but still dead. Then my uncle Franceo—killed by a political assassin, *they say*. Then my mother—strangled. And had it not been for you—dash it all, Venables, though I may seem short-tempered sometimes, I am infernally grateful for that—had it not been for you I should have been dead—poisoned. In my despondent moods I get like one of the old women of the Palace, and wonder whether, after all, there is not some evil power working." His eyes clouded. "As if the Curse had gained power and now had as its object the destruction of the Herzvogin family. Even my children——"

"But they ran away, sir, of their own accord."

"Yes, so it seemed. And it seemed as if Maximilian and my uncle died by accident. But they died. And now we three are the last of the Herzvogins—a family not without honour in their time. My mother was very much loved here, you know, Venables!"

"And you too, sir, surely."

Gustav shook his head and smiled wryly. "Don't flatter me, old chap. I was brought up in your country, and I've got out of the way of being flattered. I know perfectly well that the people here don't trust me. They think I've lived abroad too much. The Chancellor thinks I'm a brainless fool whom he has to suffer gladly. Really he'd prefer a republic." Venables winced a little at this unconscious echo of Demetrior's actual remarks. "The Chamberlain thinks how inferior I am to my mother. Princess Vera——" Gustav jerked his chin up angrily. "Well, don't let's talk of *that*. Even my own children have been turned against me by their grandmother. The Palace itself is full of half-educated popinjays who batten on my revenue and hope with a kind of malicious thrill that the Curse of the Herzvogins will fulfil itself." His voice rose, and he clenched his hands. "Can you wonder that I get to a stage where the food tastes queer, where I almost wait to feel a knife or a bullet in my back? There are only two people in Iconia who care a damn if the knife or the bullet did find its mark," he finished forlornly.

Venables waited to hear the names of the devoted pair. They were hardly the two he would have selected.

"And they are Luigi and Naomi Tacora," said Gustav.

A bit hard on Rosa, thought Venables. After all, she had been selected for destruction in company with Gustav.

The King might almost have guessed his thoughts, for he went on to speak of Rosa.

"Have you seen anything of the Signorina lately? You saved her life, and she ought to be grateful."

"No, I haven't seen her," admitted Venables.

"Neither have I," said Augustus thoughtfully. He cleared his throat self-consciously, and then looked up at Venables with a naïve expression of ingenuousness.

"I can't very well approach her myself. But if she does happen to get into touch with you, you might hint to her that I am surprised not to have heard from her. It would be sufficient if you told her I often asked you if you had seen her." Gustav grinned. "Look here, Venables, I leave it to your tact! She's easy enough to handle if you understand women."

"I don't," confessed Venables; "but I will do my best."

He left with the firm conviction that the King had seen him

neither to reproach him for his lack of results nor to bemoan his own isolation in the Palace, but to make sure that Rosa was informed of his tender interest.

Now this, bearing in mind Rosa's precipitate retreat from the Palace, and Gustav's obvious restiveness under her influence, was somewhat odd...

So Gustav only trusted Luigi and the Countess Naomi, did he? thought Venables. Luigi was understandable enough; but why, out of the whole population of the Palace, did he select that gin-sodden old woman? Certainly Queen Hanna had trusted her, shown at least a curious reluctance to get rid of her. There was, of course, the incident when the Countess had thrown herself between the Queen and an assassin's bullet. Was that the cause of Gustav's trust in her? Or was there some secret tie known only to Hanna, and her son, and the Mistress of the Wardrobe? She was a Tacora, and according to Brightholme the Tacoras were the oldest of Iconia's noble families, always ranking immediately after the blood royal, claiming indeed to be older than the Herzvogins themselves. Perhaps, therefore, there was a tradition of loyalty of the Tacoras to the Throne which gave Naomi, almost the last living representative of her line, a special trustworthiness in the eyes of any Herzvogin.

Venables was not surprised, when he returned to his room, to find a note waiting for him:

"Dear Mr. Venables,
    "I should like to thank you. Could you possibly come over and see me this afternoon?

                                                    "Vera, P."

He went over to the Princess's suite. Of late her usually open face had worn a worried, slightly secretive air. It brightened now when she saw him.

"You magician! Thank you sincerely. How much you must have guessed!"

"I don't think there is anything to thank me for," said Venables evasively.

Princess Vera smiled. "Just as you like. Naturally, you have to be discreet. But even if there is nothing to thank you for, I thank you."

"Are they over the frontier now?"

"By now they are in Kossovia!"

"I say, that's a bit risky, isn't it?"

Princess Vera shook her head. "As Princess Royal of Kossovia, I own a little *Schloss* right in the mountains, miles from even a village. Everyone there is devoted to me. I have sent the children there."

"But will they really want to stay there? I mean running away is one thing, and staying away is another."

"The *Schloss* has a small private zoo," answered the Princess with a smile.

"Well, that certainly settles it. All the same I feel a little guilty," went on Venables, a worried frown on his face. "After all, in spite of their danger here, am I really entitled to take them away from their father? And ought we not to tell him?"

"No," said Princess Vera firmly. "Once we tell him, we cannot refuse to give them back."

"I think you might get them both to write him a letter, explaining that they are all right. Have the letters posted over the border, of course."

"I have already arranged for that. But after all you cannot say that he is very worried about them!"

"Poor Gustav, he has other worries enough! But you are right. It is no use my getting frightened now. Those children mustn't be in the Palace, or even Iconia. There is no doubt about that. Only I feel a little guilty about it when I speak to the King."

"Well, I feel proud," said Princess Vera quietly.

"You are an enigmatic person," remarked Venables with a smile. "Why do you take this interest in the children?"

"I adore them both," she said simply. "You almost seem surprised that one is human!"

"I do," admitted Venables. "It is like a breath of fresh air to find somebody human in this confounded place!"

"Oh, come," she remonstrated. "There are some very human people. Old Mutch, the Chamberlain, Mr. Brightholme, Professor Andreyi, Miss Fotheringay——"

"Surely not Miss Fotheringay," he interrupted.

"But yes. You will see. How can one help loving the twins?" Venables thought ruefully about the frogs in his pyjamas, but did not interrupt. "They have all Gustav's good qualities without——" She broke off, momentarily embarrassed.

"Quite," answered Venables. "By the way," he went on, apparently disconnectedly, "I had an interview with the Chancellor this morning."

"I suppose he was complaining about me?"

Venables was silent.

The Princess was kind enough to volunteer an explanation. "As you will have gathered, the marriage is one of convenience." She stopped short. "I may appear to be very free with my confidence. But I am not." Venables bowed. "We are already partners in one enterprise, Mr. Venables, so I find myself speaking freely to you. Naturally I have always expected a marriage of that sort. I have no complaint to make. There are many good qualities in Augustus. It would, of course, be foolish to pretend I should have chosen in that way. Gustav and I are too like each other, perhaps. Or else we have known each other too long. But I have a great respect for him. Yet now I hesitate... Mr. Venables, what on earth has come over him during the last few days?"

"That is not easy to answer, Your Royal Highness," said Venables gravely.

"Do you know this latest idea of his—to be always accompanied by two armed plain-clothes men wherever he goes, even in the Palace? It is dreadful. What would the Queen have thought—who could not even bear to be followed by a detective when she went out? Why is he so afraid? He never lacked courage before."

Venables did not answer.

"Do you think I am wrong, then?" she asked.

"No," answered Venables earnestly, "I think you are right! You seem to have got as far with your intuition as I with my detection. Poor Gustav! I am afraid his armed bodyguard won't be able to protect him from the kind of danger he fears."

Venables had a visitor himself that evening. It was Professor Andreyi. Some secret trouble appeared to have been unsettling him. His long hair was untidier than ever.

"I am a very worried man," proclaimed Professor Andreyi, dropping his pince-nez as he said it, and retrieving them with a short-sighted scrabbling. Venables assisted him.

The Professor blinked. "I have come to the conclusion that I have a duty to perform. To be brief, Mr. Venables, I must tell you that I know who is the murderer of Queen Hanna."

"Quite a lot of people do," Venables warned him. "Dr. Robor appears to be quite the most disliked man at Court."

"I am not thinking of Dr. Robor," answered the Professor reproachfully. "I consider him a much-maligned man. No, the murderer is a very different person. I know—I have long known—that there can be but one murderer at this Court, and that is the Countess Naomi!"

"Good Lord! But she was devoted to the Queen!" protested Venables.

"No matter," answered Andreyi. "I now feel it my duty to tell you what I know about the Tacora family. It is perhaps the noblest in Iconia, and certainly the most exclusive. As a result it has interbred a good deal. Now as a man of intelligence you will know that there is nothing in the popular fallacy that interbreeding weakens. But if there does happen to be a bad recessive strain in a family, interbreeding will cause it to emerge in one or two generations. There is such a taint in the Tacora family. It is a form of insanity, of homicidal paranoia. Often it lies dormant for many years. The Tacora who suffers from it appears a normal, even a fine specimen, perhaps devoted to his family. Then suddenly the mania manifests itself. All springs of human affection seem to dry up within him. He believes himself persecuted and betrayed. He murders a wife or a faithful servant. These facts are not generally known. Naturally the Tacoras themselves have always tried to hush these cases up, and only a student of Iconian history like myself knows how many there have been."

"But is it fair," suggested Venables, "to assume that the Countess suffers from this taint just because she is a Tacora?"

"I have always considered the possibility of its showing itself," explained Andreyi, "for her father married a second cousin. She herself married a third cousin, so perhaps it was as well her child died. Indeed it was the death of that child which first made me suspect the mad streak in her."

"How?"

"When the boy died some thirty years ago, she showed none of the sorrow a mother would feel. I realized that either the shock had upset her reason, or the egoistic indifference to other beings of the paranoiac had already manifested itself. I have watched her ever since. I have wondered sometimes if she guessed it herself, and that was why she took to drink. I do not know. But it is obvious that, at the last, she turned against the being she loved best in the world—the Queen."

Venables was silent for a long time. At last he spoke. "I am grateful to you, Professor. I believe you have told me who the murderer is. But not quite in the simple way you think... Still, we cannot accuse her on mere suspicion. We are driven back to one inescapable fact—how was the Queen murdered when no one entered her room?"

"It was the Countess who found her," pointed out the Professor.

"Certainly. But she had then been dead, according to the Doctor, twelve hours."

"Could the Doctor have been mistaken?"

Venables shook his head. "No, it was glaringly obvious that the Queen had been dead many hours. Her body was as cold as ice and rigor had already set in. So you see we can only watch and hope."

"For how long?" said the Professor, getting wearily to his feet.

"Not very long now," said Venables grimly.

Chapter XIX

THE REBELLIOUS FLY

"My Dear Mr. Venables,

"When are you coming to see me? It is embarrassing for me, who owe you so great a debt of gratitude, not to be able to thank you. I cannot count as thanks those few hurried words when I was, I must confess, so terrified that I hardly knew what I was saying.

"Could you call on me to-morrow afternoon?

"Rosa Pavellicini."

"Here comes the second shot! I might have known that that last lingering look at the Palace gates had some ulterior motive," was Venables' modest thought. None the less he dressed himself with great care. Remembering Rosa's taste in shirts and ties, he even chose a combination which gave him a momentary shudder when he looked at it in the glass. "And now," he said to himself, "for the spider's parlour."

The official residence of the Ballet Mistress was the middle of a row of three little stucco houses—charming little buildings huddling together in a poverty-stricken street with an air of forlorn and decayed gentility. The neighbouring houses had formerly been the official residences of the Royal Bear Warden and the Master of the Royal Music. Both these offices had sunk into desuetude, however, and the houses were now Government offices. One was used by the Ministry of Agriculture and Fisheries, and the other by the War Office.

Rosa was looking well. Hers was the type of beauty that was at its most effective in the afternoon of an Iconian winter. The dusk was particularly kind to Rosa's mellow beauty, but the early hour made it possible to wear a gracefully draped gown from which her splendid throat emerged like a swan's. Her arms hovered over the tea apparatus with conscious grace yet without affectation. Rosa was in one of her softest moods. For a moment Venables felt himself sliding—becoming sorry for her...

He pulled himself up with a jerk. Danton, no weakness! he told himself. "Two pieces of sugar," he said aloud, as Rosa poised the tongs in the air with the mien of a goddess offering a mortal his choice of worlds.

Rosa had inquired politely after the Chamberlain, coldly after His Majesty. The conversation, in other words, had been general. But as it grew a little darker, and the carefully shaded lights of the room threw a soft glow on Rosa's classic features, it became more personal. They discussed the curious affair of the poisoned Tokay.

"It was wonderful, your presence of mind that day!" said Rosa a little tremulously. "How did you guess?"

Wants to find out how much I know, reflected Venables. Aloud he said, "Oh, just luck. I happened to get a sniff of it as I leaned forward to pick up my own wine."

Rosa's eyes widened. "But how fortunate! And have they found who did it?"

"Dr. Robor is under house arrest," said Venables, watching her closely.

Her eyelids flickered. "Really. Fancy, I should never have suspected him! May I have a light from your cigarette?"

Rosa leaned forward, her face a foot from Venables'. Their eyes met. "Would *you* have suspected it, Mr. Venables?" pressed Rosa.

"I was astonished," said Venables, without moving a muscle of his face.

Rosa leaned backwards and puffed at her cigarette in silence for a few moments. "If only I had your brains..." reflected Rosa softly.

"The gods have endowed you so richly as it is…" said Venables gallantly.

Rosa ignored the compliment. "I suppose you know everything," she mused sadly. "I ought to have guessed you did. You sit there so quietly, it is difficult to realize you are taking everything in."

"My game is essentially a waiting one," pointed out Venables.

"I suppose I was a rash fool," she went on.

"You were unwise, Signorina," corrected Venables, "if I may say so. Had I been in your position I should have handled the matter with the greatest care."

Rosa's face became suddenly watchful. She looked intently at Venables. "So *you* would have known how to handle it, Mr. Venables?"

Venables nodded.

Rosa gave a happy smile. "I understand. It is necessary for all of us to live."

"Naturally, I could not be disloyal to an employer…" began Venables.

"But of course not—Charles…" said Rosa sweetly. "But your employer is dead, is she not? And we must live."

"Very true, Rosa," remarked Venables impassively. "And how hard it is."

Rosa placed her snowy arms on the table and leaned forward. "Advise me, Charles," she said. "I am so frightened after that incident! Yet I know there is money to be made."

"You should have been content with money," Venables reminded her. "You could have got quite a lot of it. Instead, you made the mistake of insisting on being in the foreground. You can't have both the cash and the credit."

"I should be content with the cash now," said Rosa firmly. "What shall we do? I assure you that I would not go in that Palace again for a million pounds."

"There is no need to. But are you sure you are as strong as ever?"

"What do you mean?" asked the woman.

"I don't want to alarm you," replied Venables, "but have you the evidence in a safe place? And have you looked there recently? A burglary seems such an obvious thing..."

Rosa's face went quite white. "He wouldn't dare!" she breathed. She stood up and went to a safe concealed by a mirror on the wall. In a few moments she had opened it. She removed a flat jewel case and laid it on the table. From it she pulled out a sealed envelope. She glanced at the seal hastily and put one hand on her heart.

"Good heavens, what a fright you gave me! But here it is!" She waved the envelope triumphantly.

Venables advanced quietly and snatched the envelope from her. "I was always taught that it was rude to grab," he said calmly, "but if one is going to be a cad one may as well do it thoroughly. And after all you have been very naughty, Rosa. Blackmail is bad enough at the best of times, but when you try to seduce clean upstanding young Englishmen from their duty it must be stopped. My employer may be dead, poor creature, but her murderer isn't, and so I consider myself still under obligation. However, let us not be sanctimonious... I have not always been too scrupulous myself—whoa there!"

At first Rosa had made no protest when the document was snatched out of her grasp. She had, in fact, been astounded. As the full significance of Venables' action dawned on her, she gave a shrill cry of rage. For a moment she stood there, cursing him fluently in Italian, and he made no attempt to interrupt her. Then quite suddenly she snatched up a knife from the table and tried to slash his face.

Venables' lean white hands shot out and grasped her wrists. He disarmed her without much apparent effort. "Steady, Rosa," he counselled her. "I'm certain to win in a free fight! I'm sorry," he added, after she had dropped, pale and trembling, into a chair. "I sympathize with you quite a lot. If circumstances had permitted I should have been delighted to advise you on the correct technique of blackmail.

But you must see now that it is impossible. Anyway, my dear soul, nobody with your looks and personality need do this kind of thing. Why not leave this one-horse town and go somewhere where you will be appreciated?"

Rosa made no reply beyond a strangled imprecation. Then she began to sob violently on the chair arm. Venables walked hurriedly out.

"Very unpleasant," he reflected. "Really I could get to like Rosa. What a pity she is so elementary! It is no use being spider if you get taken in by the fly..."

Once in his room Venables carefully opened the envelope, lifting the seal with a hot knife. In it, as he had suspected, was the document on which Queen Hanna had been working in the State Office on the day of her death. How had Rosa got hold of it? Venables wondered. He read it carefully—thirty or forty lines in the elegant if slightly crabbed penmanship of the dead Queen. It contained nothing he had not already guessed.

Venables spread out the parchment on the table and produced from a drawer a sheet of identical parchment but blank. This, it must be admitted, he had stolen from the State Office. He took off his coat, shaded a light carefully on to the table, and began to write, slowly and painfully, more like a person drawing than one writing... It was noticeable that he referred frequently to the Queen's parchment.

This done, he placed the original parchment in his pocket and sealed up his own production carefully in the envelope. He then placed it on the top left-hand corner of his bed canopy behind the valance.

That evening he sent a message in to Gustav by Luigi, and the King told him to attend on him immediately.

"I have called on Signorina Pavellicini, Your Majesty," explained Venables. "I bore in mind your message, but was unable to give it."

"No matter," said Gustav crossly.

"The fact is, sir, the Signorina revealed to me that she was in possession of a certain document belonging to the Queen, your mother. A very important document."

"Really!" exclaimed Gustav. "Surely not the one she drew up before she died, the paper Luigi and I hunted for everywhere?"

Venables nodded. "It was."

"The deceitful——!" ejaculated Gustav. "So that was her game. What did you do about it, eh?"

Venables hesitated, looking at Luigi. Gustav marked the glance and laughed.

"Oh, don't mind Luigi. He loathes his cousin like poison; don't you, Luigi? It's the one thing he can't understand in his sovereign, my partiality for Rosa, eh?"

"She is a dangerous and stupid woman, sire," answered Luigi with a flush, "as I have often ventured to tell you."

"You were right, as always, Luigi," admitted the King.

"Well, then," said Venables, "there's not much to say except that I found out where she kept that document and took it."

"Good man!" said Gustav enthusiastically. "How did you do it? Surely Rosa didn't just let you take it away?"

"She did attempt to knife me," replied Venables, "but apart from that there was no trouble at all."

The King held out his hand. "Well, let's see this precious document."

"I have not got it with me."

Gustav laughed. "Get it, then! Or stay! tell me what it said."

"It was in a sealed envelope," said Venables, "which I have not yet opened."

"Well, bring me the envelope to-night. I'll have the Chamberlain or someone trustworthy there, and we'll open it formally," said the King. "Is it in a safe place?"

"Very safe—where nobody would think of looking for it," replied Venables clearly. "It is hidden behind the valance on the top of my formidable bed. It is not likely to be disturbed any more than the dust it is lying in—if Your Majesty will pardon me."

The interview with the Chamberlain that night was somewhat shorter than might have been anticipated. The King, Luigi, and Mapponyi were waiting in the State Office—had been waiting for five minutes—when Venables appeared.

"I am almost ashamed to tell you what has happened," said Venables with the utmost calm. "I must apologize for my utter foolishness." He did not look apologetic. "I have just found that my room has been ransacked during dinner. The sealed envelope has disappeared without a trace!"

Chapter XX

THE STOLEN DOCUMENT

V enables did not try to trace the stolen document. He spent the interval instead in speculating on the psychology of the thief. On the whole his speculations proved correct, because two days later he found a sealed envelope lying casually on the edge of the carpet in his room. He picked it up and inspected it closely. It was the stolen envelope, but the original seal had been broken, and was replaced by another in which an Iconian dracon's obverse had been used to give the pattern.

"Shall I see what is inside?" he asked himself. He examined the seal carefully and came to the conclusion that it would be impossible to lift it without leaving some signs of damage. "Oh, well, I'm pretty sure of what's inside it now," he reflected.

Having decided that, Venables placed the envelope on the great carved mantelpiece and went to sleep. Next morning he saw the King.

Gustav was at first inclined to chaff him. "My dear Venables, the document obviously was not stolen at all. It dropped off the valance, and you overlooked it."

Venables shook his head. "I beg your pardon, sir, but I am afraid we must take it that it was definitely stolen."

"But why?" asked the Chamberlain, supporting his master. "Surely if it were really stolen the thieves would not go to the trouble of returning it. Otherwise why steal it?"

"May I suggest that their object was simply to inspect the document? Either they wished to get the information it contained, or else they found after stealing it that it was more harmless than they thought. In either case," he added, "they are a step ahead of us."

"Who could want to steal it?" said Mapponyi. "Is it your theory that the murder of Her Majesty, and the attempt on the King's life, and now this, are all connected? What the devil could this document have to do with it all?"

"Well, don't argue about it," exclaimed the King impatiently. "Open it and find out!"

Venables tore open the end of the envelope and pulled out the now familiar folio parchment of the State Office with its impressed coat of arms. Very deliberately he read out the contents:

"We, Hanna, Queen by the Grace of God, etc., being now come to a state wherein we regret and would expiate the wickedness of our younger days, do hereby make declaration that in the year 1902 we did procure our physician, Dr. Benedict Robor, to slay by poison the Prince Maximilian, our nephew, then Heir Apparent, which crime we now wholly detest and denounce.

"Wherefore upon this day, the Feast of our Holy Ancestor, St. Boron, we do as token of our contrition solemnly and for ever abdicate our titles as Queen and Monarch, and renounce our inviolability as Sovereign Prior, and give over all privilege or prerogative of blood or office whatsoever, having by this, our Last Act, appointed our beloved son, the Prince Augustus Crispin-Maximilian, to succeed us as King, and we now commend ourselves to the King's Justices that they may have mercy upon us.

"Given at our Court of Milö, etc."

Venables concluded the reading and looked up. The Chamberlain had buried his face in his hands. Gustav was looking as if he had been struck. He took out a handkerchief and wiped his forehead.

"My mother!" he murmured. Then he turned to the Chamberlain. His voice rang out commandingly, accusingly: "Mapponyi! Did you know of this?"

The Chamberlain answered him humbly: "I suspected it, sire!"

"But why didn't you tell me?" he raged. "Have you no duty towards me? What am I, a puppet-king, to tell what you think good? Come, answer me."

The Chamberlain strove helplessly to exculpate himself. "How could I, sire? I only suspected—and it was your mother! What would you have said had I told you a mere suspicion?"

The King was unable to answer. He was silent for a time. Then he turned to the Chamberlain again with a keen glance.

"Answer me, Mapponyi! The truth this time! Has this abominable business been suspected at Court? Did anyone besides yourself ever guess the truth?"

The Chamberlain looked for aid to Venables, who was unable to give him any. "The Palace is full of gossip," said Mapponyi defensively. "Such a suggestion, among others, has been made; but not, of course, with any real belief that it was true."

The King pressed his forehead with his fists. He rose to his feet and towered above them, almost beside himself.

"Have I been the biggest fool in Iconia, then? This sort of thing has been going on in the Palace in which I grew up. Yet not a word has been said to me, the Heir Apparent! You, Mapponyi, you who call yourself my Chamberlain! By birth and by office you are supposed to be guide and mentor to the Herzvogins. Yet you let me grow up in ignorance of this terrible slander. Not a hint—not a whisper. Picture what my dreadful situation might have been. I would have come back to Iconia on that day, and then in the Chapel of St. Boron, surrounded by the leaders of this country, I should have heard my mother confessing in public that she was a foul murderess. How could I have endured it? Mapponyi, I shall never forgive you for letting me run that danger."

The Chamberlain made no reply.

The King sat down again and sank his head in his hands. "How could she have borne to live so long with such a secret in her breast! Was she sane?"

The Chamberlain could contain himself no longer. "With your permission, sire! I will not argue that she was justified in poisoning Maximilian. It was murder. None the less it is impossible for us who have lived through Iconia's troubled times not to realize that if a youngster had been on the throne at the time of the agrarian revolt the country would have been torn asunder."

"You *are* attempting to argue that she was justified!" answered Gustav sharply.

"Sire, I was about to say that, however the deed was done, once it was done her true expiation was to keep silent. This"—he pointed to the proclamation—"would have been a second wrong, as great as the first. It is the duty of a Prince to be to his people an ideal, a symbol, the rock of stability on which the State is built. And once Hanna gained the throne, by whatever means, it was her sacred duty to remain that symbol and ideal. This talk of expiation is childishness; it is pure self-ishness. Her confession would have shaken the succession, profoundly upset the country, rallied our disaffected elements, and perhaps brought civil war. However her conscience may have tortured her, I say she was not entitled to do this. Her public duty comes first. She herself realized this well enough, but old age weakened her will. She became a moral coward, anxious to purchase salvation at any price."

Gustav groaned. "Don't, Mapponyi. You are making my head spin. You can't get away from the unescapable fact that she killed her nephew—an infant."

The Chamberlain leaned forward persuasively, tears in his eyes. "Sire, that is done with. Nothing can raise Maximilian from the dead. But Iconia and the Herzvogins remain. Our duty is not concerned with ancient curses, but living people. Let us save your mother from her second and worse mistake!"

The King looked sharply at the Chamberlain. "What the devil do you mean, Mapponyi?"

"Merely this, Your Majesty, let the thing be! Let Queen Hanna remain what she always was in the eyes of our people—a great woman, a just woman, and a most loving Queen. Only we three know of this document. We are vowed to discretion." He stretched forward a blue-veined hand. "Let Your Majesty give the paper to me, and it will be as if it had never been."

"As if it had never been! Do you believe in retribution? Do you not see anything almost fatal in the death that has stricken down my mother, that seeks for me, and the wild spirit that has made my own children run away from their home?"

"I see nothing, Your Majesty, but a plot that we shall presently unmask," answered the Chamberlain stubbornly. "Be strong, I beg of you, sire! End the matter now."

The King rose to his feet. "Your suggestion is insulting to me, Mapponyi. No considerations of that sort would persuade me to pervert the course of justice. My mother's crime and her repentance must both be known, and her accomplice must be punished. I wish you not to discuss the matter further. At a later date you may be called upon by the Commission formally to authenticate this document. The same applies to you, Venables. Dr. Robor will be accused of the murder of Prince Maximilian to-morrow. Meanwhile, you may go."

Venables and the Chamberlain left together. Mapponyi looked white and tired, but he insisted on Venables coming to his private suite. Evidently he wished to unburden himself.

"His own mother," murmured Mapponyi dismally to Venables, when they were seated in the Chamberlain's prim little sitting-room, with its plain furnishings and threadbare air. "And it is so easy. A ruler would have seen at once that the thing must never come out. This talk of expiation is school-boyish."

"My dear Machiavelli," said Venables, "the King is not such a bad ruler as you suppose. Did he deceive you with his play-acting?"

"Play-acting?" returned the Chamberlain, astonished.

"Yes. Do you really suppose he is any more anxious than you are for this dirty business to come out? His own mother, as you say, and an occupant of the throne? Obviously it will be most unpleasant, if not dangerous, for him. But, unlike you, Gustav is a realist, and he sees that this thing has gone too far to be hushed up. So he is going to make the best of it."

"But why not destroy the document?"

"Do you really suppose that would be enough to end the thing? Don't you think the King is tired of being blackmailed by Rosa, for instance?"

"Good heavens!" exclaimed Mapponyi. "Blackmailed?"

"Wasn't it obvious enough? Goodness knows how Rosa got the Queen's confession, but the fact remains she had, and was using it. I don't want to make out that Gustav is a hypocrite. No doubt he never saw the document, and his surprise on reading it was genuine. At least it may have been. But it is quite obvious that Rosa had convinced him that she had some grisly secret about his mother, and until she was frightened and ran away she had Gustav under her thumb. That shows you how afraid Gustav really was of having this business come out. Incidentally, the mysterious poisoning is explained."

"Yes," admitted the Chamberlain. "No wonder Robor wanted to get rid of the only two people who knew his secret!"

"Well, then, we have Rosa in the know. And the next thing is that I get hold of the document. Of course Gustav doesn't really trust me in a matter of this importance. Oh, don't look surprised, Your Excellency; you know it. Then on top of that someone in the Palace stole the document and read it. Well, Gustav is not a fool. He realized that the time was past for discretion and hushing-up. It was all right to hush it up when, if the thing did come out, he could pretend he had known nothing about it. But supposing it came out, and it was found he had ordered evidence to be destroyed? Our noble monarch would be in the devil of a mess! It might cost him his throne. So very wisely he prefers to appear as the champion of justice at all costs. The whole matter will be rushed before the Extraordinary Commission. The King himself will lay the information. And so, however much Hanna suffers, Augustus has a fair chance of riding out the storm."

"You are a cynic, Mr. Venables," said the Chamberlain sadly.

"Come, Your Excellency, you have already given us excellent advice on the art of being a monarch. Can you deny that Augustus is the artist? Isn't it all exactly what Hanna in her prime would have done? Isn't Augustus carrying out his task of preserving himself as a symbol and an ideal? It's true that in doing so his own mother got pretty badly blown upon, but that seems inevitable in any case!"

The Chamberlain stroked his forked beard. "You are right. Augustus is wiser than I thought. How like his mother! Queen Hanna had just the same way of apparently turning down my advice, but really acting on it."

When Venables returned to his room he found a letter awaiting him. It had arrived by hand. It was from Rosa Pavellicini, and ran as follows:

"Sir,

"Your action the other day stamped you as a cad. No gentleman would have taken advantage of a *defenceless* woman in such a manner. I could pardon your brutality, your deceit I will never pardon. I thought you were an English *gentleman*. How could I have been so mistaken! You are nothing but a *cad*, a cad of the most repellent type. I will not soil my pen with the word that fitly describes you. You were pleased to be *humorous* then at my expense. It may amuse you to know that, thanks to your action, I am in the most *dreadful* distress. The King has dismissed me from my post, without a pension. Such a thing is unheard of—abominable. My cousin does not lift a finger to help me. All men are the same. I have been told to leave the country *immediately*. And such is the *shameful* position in which I find myself, that I am unable even to lay my hands on the money to enable me to reach my home. This, no doubt, will amuse you *enormously*. I could bear that, but I cannot endure the thought of your acting with Gustav the farce of *pretending* to save me from *poisoning*! I could weep when I think of how I was taken in. But at least you may know that I now see through it all, and realize at last the despicable *depths* of which you are capable.

"I am, with frank contempt,

"Your humble servant,

"Rosa Pavellicini."

Venables read this extraordinary document with enormous delight. "What a pity Rosa is going," he said to himself. "I like her more and more each day. Where on earth does she get her amazing epistolary style? From some Victorian novelist perhaps? An odd letter. Rosa started out to write a begging letter, and then her pride got the better of her."

Venables answered as follows:

"My dear Rosa,

"I am sorry you took personally what was a necessary duty. I have to live, although you may not see the necessity. Perhaps you will take it less hardly if I assure you on my honour (however blasted it may be) that if you had drunk that wine, as you were meant to, you would have died in most unpleasant circumstances.

"I think you have been treated abominably. Could I possibly persuade you to accept the enclosed cheque? Treat it as a business loan, and do not trouble to acknowledge it. By the way, cash it as soon as possible. Credit balances at my bank are apt to be of short duration!

"With unvarying admiration of your great personal qualities,

"Believe me to be,

"Yours very sincerely,

"Charles Venables."

Chapter XXI

THE ROYAL PARDON

Venables, by virtue of his privileges, accompanied General the Chief of Police Count Georgico-Maria Millitranyi on his mission of arresting Dr. Robor. The police head was delighted. "At last," he exclaimed, "we have action! We have investigated too much as it is. Arrest first, I always say, and investigate afterwards!"

Millitranyi was honouring the occasion by one of his most impressive uniforms. He was accompanied by two policemen. Millitranyi wore a sword, and the underlings carried sidearms. Evidently the Chief of Police expected the frail old Doctor to put up a fierce struggle.

Dr. Robor was sitting in an armchair, wearing a dressing-gown. He was smoking, but he put down his pipe and got up nervously when Millitranyi came in.

"To what do I owe the honour?"

The Chief of Police stood at attention in front of the Doctor and read from a paper.

"Benedict Robor, Doctor of Medicine, I arrest you in order that you may answer with your person and property the suit of His Majesty the King."

Robor peered uncertainly at him. "What is the charge?"

"Wilful murder!" said Millitranyi.

The Doctor shrank back. "No... he wouldn't dare," he muttered. "Whom do they say I murdered? I never went near her."

"The charge has no reference to a woman," said Millitranyi coldly. He consulted the paper again.

"The charge is that on or about October 12, 1902, you did wilfully and feloniously slay by poison the Prince Maximilian, then Heir Apparent."

Dr. Robor blinked. "Good heavens, this is the most preposterous nonsense! What proof have you? I deny the charge completely. His Royal Highness died of meningitis."

"The evidence will be published in due course," said the Chief of Police severely. "You will have the goodness to get at once into respectable clothing. You are to be brought immediately before the Extraordinary Commission appointed by Order in Council to investigate the death of Queen Hanna. We propose to examine you as to the connection between her death and the murder of the Prince. You will then be brought before the judge and formally charged with your crime, and by him committed to jail."

"I must have the advice of a lawyer," protested Robor. "If I am to be examined by the Commission now, I am entitled to legal aid."

"We want no legal trickery!" said Millitranyi indignantly. "You will answer the Commission's questions like an honest man, without quibbling or splitting hairs."

"Surely you would not deny me elementary justice?" pleaded Dr. Robor. His black little eyes glittered coldly behind their glasses.

"Justice is all very well for the innocent," replied the Chief of Police magnificently. "You, a murderer, are hardly in a position to bleat about justice. What justice, I ask you, did your hapless victim have? None! Hurry up and put your trousers on."

Robor dressed quickly, and paused only to unlock a drawer in his desk and take out some papers. Then he pronounced himself ready.

"Very well," said Millitranyi, "we will take you before the Commission immediately. It is awaiting our arrival. I am, as you know, its Chairman, and I warn you that there will be no nonsense in our dealings with you. Hurry now! Anton! Franceo! The prisoner, Dr. Robor, is in your charge. March!"

The Extraordinary Commission met in a room in the office of the Bureau of Public Safety. The active members consisted of a representative from the Ministry of the Interior, the Public Prosecutor, the Professor of Law at Isorb University, a delegate from the War Office, and the Marshal of the Nobility, who represented the Royal Household. Venables was surprised when, soon after Robor had been brought in by two policemen, Gustav quietly entered. The King took a seat that had been put a few feet away from the table round which the chairs of the members of the Commission had been placed. "Be seated, gentlemen," he said. "I am here unofficially. Take no notice of me. Nothing about my presence should appear in the minutes."

The Public Prosecutor, as the most experienced in investigation, was acting as Examiner. Dr. Robor was seated in a chair opposite him, on the other side of the table. He looked furtively at the King and then stared down at his toes. Gustav had given him no sign of recognition.

"Dr. Robor," said the Examiner, "in the course of our investigations into the murder of Her late Majesty we have come across a document that implicates you in an earlier murder. It is our duty as a Commission with unlimited powers to take cognizance of this evidence so far as it might throw light on the murder we are investigating. Then, if it seems proper to us, we shall hand the whole matter over to the proper authorities, who will proceed with your prosecution in the ordinary way."

Dr. Robor bowed in acknowledgment. "I do not question your powers as a tribunal, sir," he said.

The Public Prosecutor mopped his red face and fumbled in his briefcase. He took out the document in which the Queen confessed to the murder, and read it out aloud in a low voice.

Dr. Robor pursed his lips. "I wish to inspect the document," he said.

The Examiner handed it over.

"The signature is not witnessed!" Dr. Robor pointed out.

"A proper observation!" admitted the Prosecutor. "You forget, however, that it is not necessary for the Sovereign's signature to be witnessed when attached to formal Acts such as this. You will note that it is written as from the State Office, and that the Queen has signed it in her formal style as Sovereign."

Dr. Robor returned the document. "I bow to your legal knowledge. But I solemnly swear that I did not poison Prince Maximilian. I should like to make, here and now, a statutory declaration to that effect."

"It is our duty not to let him perjure himself," exclaimed General Millitranyi heatedly, getting to his feet.

The Public Prosecutor, who was leaning across him to interrogate the prisoner, gave him an angry glance. Then he addressed Robor again. "Are you prepared to swear you had no share of responsibility in the Prince's death, either by negligence or by any deed of omission or of commission? Think carefully now!"

"I have thought, and I do swear it!" said Dr. Robor firmly. "So help me God!"

"You are prepared to swear that the Prince Maximilian died a wholly natural death?"

Dr. Robor hesitated. "I am not," he said at last.

The Prosecutor's eyebrows rose. "Indeed! You swear that you had no part in his death. Yet you admit he did not die naturally. The matter cannot rest there. Explain yourself!"

"I refuse," said the Doctor, folding his arms.

With unconscious imitation, the Public Prosecutor also folded his arms. He frowned at the Doctor. "You refuse to explain? Very well. You are entitled to make what statements you like and to refuse to incriminate yourself. We on our part are entitled to believe or disbelieve you. I regret to say we disbelieve you. You will be committed at once to prison on a warrant of this Commission. I may remind you that the Order in Council appointing this Commission exempts its committals from the Habeas Corpus Act. Of course, no bail will be allowed."

"One moment, gentlemen," said the Doctor calmly. "Before you commit me I demand that the Commission reads this Act of Indemnity."

He opened his pocket-book and held out a tattered yellow paper. The Public Prosecutor took it with an air of surprise and inspected it carefully.

"This purports to be written by Her late Majesty, Queen Hanna," he said. "It is dated thirty-two years ago. The Queen signs herself in the style of Princess Royal, as she then was. Her signature," he added, "is witnessed by one Skaya Verdrina."

"Verdrina is dead," remarked the Marshal of the Nobility. "She was the Princess Royal's close friend."

"The document undoubtedly bears on the present case," went on the Public Prosecutor, his voice, in spite of himself, shaking a little. "It reads as follows:

"'I hereby order Dr. Robor to remove the Prince Maximilian, my nephew, by any secret and convenient means, and I solemnly swear that on my accession to the Throne I shall indemnify him and hold him harmless against any manner of penalties or disabilities therefor.

"'Hanna, Princess Royal.'

"This is useless," said the Prosecutor triumphantly, "except as evidence against you. The Princess Royal has no statutory powers to indemnify or pardon."

"Have the goodness to look on the back," said Dr. Robor sulkily.

The Prosecutor turned the paper over and his face fell. "H'm. Yes. Here is more of the Queen's writing. It is dated three years later, and is signed by Her Majesty as Queen. I will read it.

"'We, Hanna, etc., etc., do hereby fully and freely pardon our beloved physician, Dr. Robor, for his felony in removing our nephew, Prince Maximilian, by poison two years ago, and hereby indemnify him against all consequences of this Act whatsoever, and furthermore command him, on his duty and loyalty to us, to keep perpetual silence touching this matter.

"'Given at our Court, etc.'"

The Public Prosecutor wiped his torrid face. "Whew! what a woman, to put a thing like that down in black and white! The risk was appalling."

"She had no alternative," pointed out the Doctor quietly. "I was already in possession of the secret."

The Prosecutor turned round to his fellow members and flung his hands dramatically into the air.

"Well, gentlemen, there appears to be little we can do. Prince Maximilian was certainly murdered by Dr. Robor, but the Sovereign, in legitimate exercise of her prerogative of pardon, has indemnified him. Therefore any warrant we make or charge we bring in this matter is automatically estopped by the production of this document." He smiled sardonically. "You leave this tribunal, sir, without a stain on your character."

Millitranyi gave a strangled snort of protest, and the representative from the War Office rose indignantly to his feet.

"But this is monstrous; the man confesses..."

"I do not confess," insisted Dr. Robor. "I did not poison Prince Maximilian."

"Bah!" protested Millitranyi. "The document is a confession. I demand that we, as Commission Extraordinary, sentence him to death. Sooner than that he should escape, I will strangle him with these bare hands!"

The Professor of Law came to the defence of the Prosecutor. "My learned friend is right, General. There is nothing we can do. The Sovereign's prerogative of pardon overrides everything. Even in England, where the monarchy is perhaps more severely limited than in any other country, any process would be estopped by an unconditional pardon over the Sovereign's signature."

The representative from the Ministry of the Interior had been comparing the two documents carefully. Now he looked up suspiciously. "What if Dr. Robor's pardon is forged? The writing seems to me to be different from that on the Queen's confession."

The Prosecutor compared the two carefully.

"Well, now, I am inclined to believe you are right."

"Look at the difference in time!" protested Dr. Robor. "The writing is bound to be different..."

"Even allowing for that... Mr. Venables, will you give us your opinion?"

Venables studied the documents carefully. "Dr. Robor's document is undoubtedly in the genuine handwriting of the Queen, gentlemen. His Majesty will know her handwriting well, and may confirm my statement." He handed the paper to the King.

"I do confirm it," said Gustav, after a careful scrutiny. "I think we should be ill-advised to contest Dr. Robor's pardon on those grounds. But are we not allowing ourselves to be victims of a mere formality? I personally have no intention of seeing Dr. Robor escape so easily. I agree that it is the prerogative of the Sovereign to grant pardons, but equally, I take it, his prerogative permits him to revoke them. Our jurists will doubtless be able to give a definite opinion on this point. If I am correct, I will at once annul my mother's pardon, and you will be in a position to commit Robor for immediate trial."

The Prosecutor rubbed his hands and gave a wolfish grin. "Most ingenious, Your Majesty. Your prerogative undoubtedly permits you to annul this pardon. Perhaps, Professor, you will be good enough to draft the necessary form, as I can at the moment recall no precedent which will help me."

Dr. Robor jumped to his feet, his teeth showing in a snarl like that of a trapped jackal. "How dare you! I warn you, sire, that if you do that I shall consider all vows of silence at an end. I shall tell the truth about your mother. I shall let the world know what—"

Gustav's voice, good-tempered yet loud, cut short Robor's tirade. Dr. Robor had advanced to within a foot of him, his face wrinkled with fury.

"I appeal to the protection of my Commission!" said the King, with a smile.

Millitranyi leaped across the table and interposed himself between them. He pushed Robor violently into his chair. "Silence, you scum!" he shouted, his face purple. "How dare you threaten your Sovereign! Unless you keep to a strict defence of yourself, you will be denied a right of reply at the trial."

Dr. Robor looked up with a sullen stare. "I shall insist on speaking. I shall—"

"Officers!" yelled Millitranyi. "Gag him and remove him!"

In response to his shouts two police officers appeared. One clapped a great red hand over the unfortunate Doctor's mouth, and the other pinioned his arms. They began to drag him out... Dr. Robor succeeded in freeing his mouth for a moment by the expedient of biting the policeman's hand.

"I apologize to the Commission!" he shouted, struggling wildly. "Allow me one last word! I withdraw my threats! Listen."

"Let's hear him," said His Majesty mildly. "If he will only keep to the point. Otherwise he becomes boring."

"Very well," said Millitranyi. "Provided you keep strictly to your defence; and this is your last chance, for which you must thank His Majesty's clemency."

"Gentlemen," said Dr. Robor earnestly, "it was a mistake on my part to produce that Act of Indemnity. I see it now. I attempted to outwit a lawyer by legal means. That is always unwise!"

"Do not be impertinent," said the Public Prosecutor, frowning.

"I had no intention of being so, sir. I wish to state once more, with the utmost solemnity, as God is my judge, that I did not poison

Prince Maximilian. And I demand an exhumation of the Prince's remains."

"An exhumation!" exclaimed the Prosecutor. "Are you serious? The child has been dead heaven knows how many years! What can an exhumation prove?"

"My innocence," insisted Dr. Robor. "Beyond all manner of doubt!"

Chapter XXII

THE FEMALE IMPERSONATOR

An Extract from the Notebook of Mr. Charles Venables

(With acknowledgments to Mr. Venables
and the publishers of the *Art of Criminal Investigation*.)

"I have arrived at the most difficult stage one can reach in an investigation. I know who the murderer is, and why he committed his crime, but I am utterly unable to account for the way in which he established his alibi. And until I have done that I might just as well not know anything about the case.

"How on earth was Queen Hanna made to appear in the State Office at a time when by all the laws of logic she ought to have been dead? For at that time the suite was guarded and the sentries are prepared to swear that nobody passed by them afterwards. Yet somehow the Queen and her murderer got back into the Royal bedchamber.

"I assume, therefore, that they were posted after she was killed, in which case she could not have visited the State Office. But she was seen there. Therefore she must have been impersonated. But who is capable of impersonating her? I myself can think of nobody who could carry off an impersonation to deceive a man who saw her almost daily, like the Chancellor.

"Until I can solve that problem there is nothing I can do. In fact, I must be outwardly friendly towards the murderer. It is the more difficult because he guesses, I think, that I have already discovered a good deal about him. If I try to hide my knowledge of this information, it will only make him suspect that I know everything, including even his murder. My only possible attitude, therefore, is one of friendly confidence and understanding. I hope my features will stand the strain of dissimulation.

"I am afraid that as long as he is at large he is a general danger. If only one could devise some harmless means of getting him out of the way!

"Meanwhile poor Robor still languishes in jail. I cannot feel altogether sorry for him. He deserves a good deal of what he is getting…"

"Fly! All is discovered!" breathed Venables into Brightholme's ear as he dropped into a chair beside him for luncheon.

"Oh!" Brightholme was silent for a moment. "All?" he said at last.

"Well, all is on the point of being discovered. It simply *must* be discovered. So my advice is, fly!"

"Very good of you, old chap," murmured Brightholme. "But I really can't! Not at this moment."

"I am quite serious," went on Venables. "I can't do more than give you a warning. I can't help you otherwise. You realize that, I hope?"

"Oh, quite. It was awfully decent of you to tell me at all. All the same, I can't go."

"The more fool you!" answered Venables. "Well, I've done my duty. How is the doctoring going?"

"Oh, don't be worried. I've managed to avoid it so far. I'm only dreading someone will have a fit at my feet. Then I shall be in a mess. One could, of course, have a fit oneself."

"You are playing a very dangerous game, you know!" Venables warned him in a more serious tone.

"I realize that, old chap. But I think it's worth it."

"I think you and the Princess and Robor have all underestimated the risks," answered Venables quietly. "Honestly, I am quite frightened sometimes when I think of the way you go on. I can do very little for any of you. I know that in theory, as a detective, I ought to be able to. But I can't."

"It's very kind of you to worry," said Brightholme carelessly; "but who's afraid of the big bad wolf?"

"I am," admitted Venables, looking at him sharply. "Quite terrified at times..."

That afternoon Venables obeyed the summons he had received to attend a meeting of the Extraordinary Commission. To everyone's surprise Miss Fotheringay had announced her desire to give evidence before the Commission. As no one attached great importance to Miss Fotheringay, the Commission consisted of a quorum of three—Millitranyi, the Public Prosecutor, and the Marshal of the Nobility, with Mr. Venables in attendance.

At three o'clock Miss Fotheringay sailed in impressively, wearing a smoke-grey dress with a high lace collar. It seemed vaguely familiar to Venables, but at first he was unable to place it. Subsequently he recognized its strong resemblance to the dress worn by Mary Queen of Scots in the famous miniature...

Miss Fotheringay bowed to the Extraordinary Commission—a bow which had a strong suggestion of a curtsy, and was so impressive that the Extraordinary Commission rose to its feet and returned it.

"Please be seated, Miss Fotheringay," begged the Public Prosecutor. "We have got your message in which you say you believe you can throw some light on this tragic affair. As we were sitting this morning to prepare an interim report we thought we would invite you to attend."

Miss Fotheringay gained possession of her seat apparently without physical effort. Leaning forward slightly, she composed her hands upon her lap.

"I have been wondering ever since Her Majesty's death whether what I saw might not have had a bearing on her dreadful end."

"We are all attention," said the Public Prosecutor benevolently. "Kindly let us know what you suspect."

"I was with Her Majesty on the day she was murdered," began Miss Fotheringay.

"At what time?" interrupted Millitranyi.

"It would be about four o'clock. I had, I must confess, come to complain strongly about the conduct of the two children. Had I known then that a few days later Her Majesty would be dead and their Royal Highnesses, poor babes, wandering homeless, who knows where?—perhaps stolen by the gipsies—had I known that—" Miss Fotheringay's voice faltered. She found difficulty in proceeding. "Poor ill-fated family! It seems almost like a curse upon the name of Herzvogin. The Stuarts were a dynasty equally unfortunate, and related, as it happens, to the Herzvogins. I myself—"

"Miss Fotheringay," interrupted the Marshal of the Nobility firmly, "we are compelled by the laws of evidence to keep strictly to the matter of the Queen's murder. Would you be so good as to give a plain narrative of the evening's happening."

Miss Fotheringay pursed her lips. "I beg your pardon. I will endeavour to keep my narrative free from adventitious comment," she said coldly. "To proceed! I found it necessary to complain to the Queen about the behaviour of Prince Petro in particular. He had insisted on having a goat in his bedroom. Obviously this could not be allowed. I begged Her Majesty to take stern measures with them. She agreed. I merely mention all this to explain why I came to be in Her Majesty's suite. Her Majesty herself looked old and tired. She was sitting in her little withdrawing-room—leading off the Royal Bedchamber—and one of the maids had brought her the Prior's robes to inspect. She wished to see if she could not dispense with some of them for the ceremony the next day. She got tired so easily—"

"Quite, quite," said the Public Prosecutor, shuffling his feet.

"You may think this detail unnecessary," said Miss Fotheringay, looking at him sourly, "but I am trying to give you an idea of the atmosphere of that fatal day. I made my complaint, and found that the Queen was distracted and could not give her mind to me. She kept on falling into a reverie. Then she would look up with a start. She would say the oddest things."

"For instance?" queried Millitranyi.

"Well, she said once, 'Miss Fotheringay, I believe I have seen a ghost. It is profoundly disturbing...' And then again she said, 'I wonder if I am going a little mad?' I could see that she was worried. There has always been an intense sympathy between us. We are in a way related. The blood——"

"I am afraid this is not getting us much farther," remarked the Marshal of the Nobility.

"I regret that you find time so pressing," said Miss Fotheringay acidly. "I have not much more to say. As I left Her Majesty, her next visitor arrived. I was interested to see to whom she had accorded the unusual privilege of an interview in her private suite. Even among members of the Household it is commonly restricted to personal servants."

"And who was it?" asked Millitranyi eagerly.

"Dr. Brightholme!" said Miss Fotheringay quietly.

"Well, well, he was doubtless visiting her professionally. You say she looked ill?" the Public Prosecutor reminded her, obviously disappointed.

"I doubt it—now," she said positively; "Dr. Robor always attended the Queen. In fact he seemed to attend everybody, and it has always been a puzzle to me why Brightholme was here at all."

"Well, go on, please," said the Public Prosecutor.

"There is only one more thing to tell. As I was going out of the suite, into the corridor, I heard through the half-open door a scrap of conversation. I heard Brightholme say, 'It will be the end of you,' and she answered, 'I can't expect mercy from you, I suppose.'"

"Good heavens!" exclaimed Millitranyi, jumping to his feet. "Brightholme threatened her! Why didn't you tell us this before?"

"I thought at the time," answered Miss Fotheringay calmly, "that it was a professional matter. I suspected her to be ill, and

I supposed that she consulted Brightholme to have a second opinion. And I thought his 'It will be the end of you,' referred to her health, and that her answer was made half in jest."

"And when did you change your mind, Miss Fotheringay?"

"Mainly as a result of Dr. Robor's arrest. But I admit I suspected Dr. Brightholme before then. Hitherto I had ruled out the possibility because Dr. Brightholme had left before the sentries were posted outside the suite."

"You know that of your own knowledge?" pressed the Public Prosecutor. "You saw him emerge before the sentries came on duty?"

Miss Fotheringay looked a little embarrassed. "Yes, I did see him leave. I—er—happened to be outside in the corridor."

The Public Prosecutor leaned back in his chair with a disappointed smile. "Your evidence is very interesting, Miss Fotheringay. But we of this Commission have in the past always been brought back by Mr. Venables to this one point: How did the murderer get to the Queen through the guards? And although the conversation you overheard is suspicious, and demands investigation, I do not see how Brightholme can be accused of the murder unless we get over the difficulty of how he did it."

"There is no difficulty, or so it seems to my humble intelligence," said Miss Fotheringay. "Horrible as it sounds, I believe the young man had killed Her Majesty before he left her."

The Public Prosecutor shook his head. "Impossible, I am afraid. She was seen in the State Office at a later time by her son and the Chancellor."

A slight smile appeared on Miss Fotheringay's face—a smile of condescension. "I am familiar with that fact, as I am with most of the details of the murder. I take a considerable interest in it, as I feel the poor Queen was in a measure a relation of mine." She looked sharply at the Marshal of the Nobility. "The answer to your difficulty is simple. Any person who takes, as I do, an interest in detective stories of the more intellectual kind—so much more healthy than these novels of passion"—Venables suppressed a start—"can guess what must have happened. It was not the Queen you saw, but an impersonator."

"But who could impersonate the Queen so as to deceive two people who knew her intimately?" asked the Public Prosecutor.

"Dr. Brightholme himself!" answered Miss Fotheringay positively.

The Public Prosecutor burst into laughter. "Come, come, Miss Fotheringay!"

Miss Fotheringay smiled thinly. "May I explain? Dr. Brightholme has several times given evidence of considerable histrionic talent of a farcical order—in the private theatricals with which members of the Household occasionally amuse themselves. But—as His Excellency the Marshal will confirm—Dr. Brightholme's great *forte* was a very vulgar imitation of Her Majesty, which I used to discourage, but which, I regret to say, other members of the Household"—here she looked hard at the Marshal—"seemed to find amusing. Vulgar as it was, I must confess that even with a handkerchief thrown over his head he had a really astonishing resemblance to the Queen. Wearing a wig, dressed in her clothes, and properly made up, I am sure that in certain lights he would deceive—at a distance—even such people as the Prince and the Chancellor."

"I had forgotten that," admitted Marshal of the Nobility Count Herreshyi a trifle shamefacedly. "His imitations of the Queen were certainly amazing. He seemed to be able to screw his features up until he was the absolute image of her!"

The Public Prosecutor looked at Miss Fotheringay with a new respect. "This grows interesting." He turned to Venables. "Have you had any suspicions of this man Brightholme?"

"I have known for a long time that he was not what he purported to be," answered Venables. "He is not, in fact, qualified as a doctor at all. He studied as one, but he failed in his examinations."

"Good heavens!" exclaimed Miss Fotheringay, turning pale. "And I have asked him for some cough mixture. I might have been poisoned! The scoundrel!"

"Not qualified!" exclaimed the Public Prosecutor. "But why on earth has Robor brought him here? What is his past history?"

"His past history is vague," said Venables, after a pause. "He is a ward of Dr. Robor's, and it was Dr. Robor who paid for his education. You may be surprised to hear that he is Iconian, and not English. I think we can assume Brightholme is not his real name."

The Public Prosecutor closed one eye. "Ha, that explains it! Now we know everything! A ward indeed! Of course, quite obviously, he is Robor's—" The Public Prosecutor stopped himself at Miss Fotheringay's reproving glance. "That is to say—he is a—er—much closer relative of the Doctor's than a mere ward."

"Well, why hesitate?" said Millitranyi, jumping to his feet. "It's obvious enough, isn't it? Robor killed Prince Maximilian. The Queen at last decided to confess to it. To save Robor's reputation, Brightholme killed her. We must commit him for trial at once!" He loosened his heavy uniform collar and sat back with a gesture of triumph.

"What do you think, Mr. Venables?" asked the Public Prosecutor doubtfully.

"I think you have an excellent *prima facie* case against Brightholme," answered Charles Venables slowly.

Chapter XXIII

THE ELOPING PRINCESS

"Valentine Brightholme, I arrest you to answer with your person and property the charge that you did wilfully, feloniously, and treasonably slay by strangling her Gracious Majesty Queen Hanna on the 5th of November of this year. God save the King!"

The lean young man looked sleepily at Millitranyi and his uniformed companions, and then at Venables. He rubbed his eyes and sat up. Millitranyi had apparently some theory as to the efficacy of early-morning arrests, for he had got up at dawn—and Venables perforce also—so that he could execute his warrant on Brightholme before the suspect was awake.

"Are you part of my nightmare?" mumbled Brightholme, looking at the General distastefully. At last he succeeded in grasping the situation. Then he went pale. "Good Lord!" he said. "Murder! That is absolutely absurd!"

"You will be permitted to make a statement in due course," stated Millitranyi in his parade-ground voice. "I warn you it is useless to deny the charge. The evidence is overwhelming."

"What ought I to do, Venables?" asked Brightholme uneasily.

"There is nothing you can do," answered Venables, "except go with Millitranyi's people."

"You will shortly appear before the Extraordinary Commission, who will examine you," went on the Chief of Police. He turned to his two assistants. "Bring him along about ten. Herreshyi will show you where he is to be imprisoned."

"Isn't he going to the State Prison?" asked Venables in some surprise.

"No. With extraordinary solicitude His Majesty has ordered that he be confined in the Palace prison." The Chief of Police looked disgusted. "Of course it is absurd."

"Oh, I didn't know there was a Palace prison," said Venables. "Where is it?"

"It is a small tower at the end of the Royal gardens. It was used for political prisoners of high rank. Goodness knows why Gustav has granted him a privilege which used to be reserved for the nobility, and then only for misdemeanours."

"I demand legal aid," said Brightholme suddenly.

"Refused!" answered Millitranyi shortly.

"Very well. I insist on sending for the British Consul."

The Chief of Police, who was just on the point of leaving the room, turned abruptly. "Indeed?" he said with a malicious smile. "You appeal to the British Consul? If you will kindly produce your birth certificate, to confirm that your father was British, the request will at once be granted!"

Brightholme flushed, and was silent.

Millitranyi smiled again. "Come on, Venables," he said at last. "I expect we both want some breakfast."

Brightholme managed to speak to Venables as he lingered in the room for a minute.

"I say, Venables, have they really got a strong case against me?"

The detective thoughtfully regarded Brightholme's face. It was a long face, with plenty of character. But now it was an extremely worried face.

"They have a remarkably good case against you!" answered Venables slowly.

The case was not, however, advanced by Brightholme's examination before the Extraordinary Commission. He refused to say anything, even a simple "yes" or "no." Millitranyi stormed, and the Public Prosecutor was alternately suave and envenomed.

"Why did you see the Queen on the afternoon of her death?"

No answer.

"*Did* you see her on the afternoon of her death?"

No answer.

"Did you say to her, 'This is the end of you'?"

No answer.

"Did you impersonate the Queen?"

The prisoner made as if he was going to speak, but refused to answer.

"*Dumb out of malice*," scrawled the Public Prosecutor angrily across the shorthand report. "Remanded in custody for a day. He may come to his senses by then!"

Brightholme was taken out, his face expressionless. "I am afraid you will find him an awkward prisoner!" said Venables prophetically.

The Tower Prison was a neat red-brick structure which had been built in comparatively recent times. It resembled in shape that prosaic object, a silo. Inside, Venables was told, it was "plain but comfortable." There was the warder's room, from which one ascended a spiral staircase that led to the sitting-room. Above that again, reached by a ladder, was the prisoner's bedroom. The flat roof was surrounded by a high spiked battlement some ten feet high, and in here the prisoner was supposed to take exercise. Surrounding the tower, but about thirty feet from it, was another high wall, also spiked.

The prison was now used for short detentions—drunken sentries, thieving servants, and so forth. Since Venables' arrival at the Palace and Gustav's accession to the Throne, it must be confessed that the Tower had become useful as a laundry. Behind its high walls it had been possible to hang up the washing out of sight even of the guests of the Royal garden-parties... The Chamberlain complained bitterly of the decision to shut up Brightholme in this place, but the King was resolute.

"Brightholme is entitled to it. His guilt is still in doubt. I would have given the same privilege to any other member of my

Household—even Robor, if he had not been definitely implicated by the signed statement of my mother."

In the evening Venables attempted to get an audience with the King. Luigi at first sent out the usual formal message, but when Venables became more pressing, Luigi came out and saw him.

"His Majesty is busy, he cannot possibly be seen. Can I give him a message?"

"I want to see him urgently, Pavellicini. Where is he?"

Luigi thought a moment. "I suppose I can tell you. He is interviewing Brightholme."

"What, in the Tower? Are you sure?"

"Of course. He left just now."

"But what on earth is his idea?" exclaimed Venables.

"You know how secretive he is, Venables. I rather gathered that he believes he can make Brightholme speak where the Commission could not."

"That may be!" Venables reflected for a moment. "I say, who went with him?"

"No one."

Venables stared at Luigi in horror. "He went alone? But what is he thinking of? I say, this is dangerous!"

Luigi looked startled. "I had not thought of that. After all, Gustav is tremendously strong. Brightholme is a comparative weakling. The King could squash him with one blow from his fist if he started to make trouble. Besides, would he dare to attack the King when he is a prisoner?"

Venables did not wait to answer Luigi's questions. He turned and raced down the corridor of the Palace out into the Gardens.

At the foot of the Tower the sentry stopped him. "Sorry, sir, no one is allowed to see the prisoner without a signed permission from the Chief of Police."

"But His Majesty has gone in there!"

"Well, naturally, sir, we could not stop *him*."

"Then I insist on going in too."

"Sorry, sir, it can't be done!"

"Don't you realize the King may be in danger?"

The sentry looked a little startled. "We could hear him if he called for help. Besides, the prisoner is unarmed."

"The Queen wasn't shot," declared Venables irritably. "Let me pass, and don't be a fool."

"Sorry, sir, we have strict orders. A signed permission from the Chief of Police!"

Venables lost his temper. "Get out of the way, you ruddy idiot," he declared. At that moment there was the unmistakable sound of a shot from the Tower above. The sentry's jaw dropped. Venables delayed no longer. Pushing past the sentry, he rushed through the warder's room. The warder had risen to his feet at the sound of the shot, but Venables dashed past and flew up the spiral staircase. As he expected, the door to the prisoner's rooms had been left unlocked by the King. He flung it open.

Venables paused on the threshold only long enough to take in what was happening. Brightholme and the King were rolling on the floor, closed in a death-struggle. The King was lying on his back, and Brightholme, his knee on his throat, was slowly throttling him with one hand and holding the King's wrist in the other. Gustav was gripping a revolver in this hand, and evidently it was from this that the shot had come. Brightholme was bleeding from a wound in his arm. This made him loosen his grip even as Venables ran forward, and the King, with a heave of his huge limbs, dislodged Brightholme and sent him flying against the wall. Venables helped the King to his feet.

"Are you all right, sir?"

The King wheeled round. "You, Venables, good heavens! You came just in time! In another moment I believe I should have been strangled, like my mother."

Brightholme said nothing. He glared at the King, nursing his wounded arm.

Gustav dropped into a chair, panting. "The man's strength is absolutely diabolical. He is only half my size, but I must confess he had me at his mercy. If you had not arrived…"

"You underestimated him, I am afraid, sir," said Venables. "He evidently knows ju-jitsu, judging by the grip he had on you then."

"I seem to have made a fool of myself," went on the King. "I came here to get some information from him about my mother's murder, and nearly got murdered myself. However," he added, brightening, "I suppose in a way I have done even better than I hoped. This attack on me will be conclusive evidence of the character of the man we have to deal with."

"It will," agreed Venables.

The sentry and the warder, who had rushed in on Venables' heels, had been astonished witnesses of the incident. Now the King turned to them.

"Get a doctor!" he said shortly, "and have the prisoner bandaged. Then—if the doctor permits—he is to be removed at once to the State prison. Go carefully, for he is a dangerous man!"

The two men moved forward towards Brightholme. He retreated a pace. At that moment there was a quiet voice from the door.

"Will you all have the kindness to put your hands up—except Mr. Brightholme!"

No doubt gangsters instinctively put up their hands when they are ordered to do so, perhaps even without looking for the firearm with which they are threatened. Normal persons, however, at first hesitate whether to take the request seriously. Then they look carefully at the person threatening them, to decide whether he means his threat.

Thus the King remained staring incredulously at the figure half-shadowed by the door. The warder and the soldier took two paces forward as if deciding whether to risk a shot. Venables put his hands up…

Princess Vera of Kossovia advanced another step. This time there was no mistaking her seriousness. The firm white hand holding the revolver did not tremble, and looked perfectly at home with the weapon. Her eyes were cold and fierce. She spoke again decisively.

"Get back or I shall fire without further warning. Stand up against the wall. Quick, now!"

The four men obeyed.

"But this is charming of you, Vera," said Brightholme enthusiastically. "You could not have come at a more opportune moment."

"Are you hurt?" asked the Princess, going up to him.

"Just a flesh wound. The bullet took off some of the skin as it passed. If you could tie up this handkerchief, it would stop me losing blood."

"Jan!" called the Princess. The Princess's equerry, already familiar to Venables, appeared in the doorway. He was grinning...

"Jan," said the Princess, "hold this revolver and remove any arms these gentlemen may have. Take care that they do not rush you."

Jan nodded and took the revolver. The Princess, with the utmost calm and almost professional neatness, began tying up the wounded man's arm.

The King looked at her, pained amazement in his eyes.

"Vera, what in heaven's name does this mean? Are you mad?"

"I am sorry to be so abrupt, Gustav," said the Princess quietly, "but Valentine is simply not going before your wretched Commission."

"Valentine now!" exclaimed the King. "As your future fiancé, I demand to know: what is this man to you?"

"Don't talk like a play, Gustav," said Princess Vera. "Valentine is my husband. We were married by my chaplain two days ago..."

"Vera," gasped Gustav, "you are absolutely crazy. Do you really understand what you have said?"

"Perfectly."

Gustav's face was scarlet with emotion. A vein thumped in the corner of his forehead. He moved his shoulders uneasily.

"Good heavens, am I mad myself?" he asked. "You, a Princess of Kossovia, have married a commoner?"

"Don't call my husband such insulting names," said Vera with a smile, as she tore a strip from the handkerchief. "He's a perfect dear."

"You're a fool," said the King abruptly. "The marriage is illegal."

"I know quite as much about the legal position of the Princess Royal of Kossovia as you do, Gustav—more, I think. I am twenty-five, and the marriage is valid..."

"Do you realize what you have done?" groaned the King. "This man is a common criminal. He will probably be outlawed by my courts if he leaves the country, and if he stays he will undoubtedly be hanged as a felon. This is the man you purport to have married!"

"My dear Gustav, don't be silly. Valentine never killed your mother or anyone else." She smiled tenderly at Brightholme. "He wouldn't harm a fly; would you, darling?"

"Not unless I prescribed for it, Vera!" answered Brightholme. He grinned, but looked a little tired and white.

"Vera, I make one last appeal to you. Consider my position. Discount for the moment any personal insult in your choosing a commoner..."

"You had better do that. After all, I was prepared to discount Rosa."

"Very well, let us say one wipes out the other. But putting aside personalities, do you realize what your action may mean politically? You run away with this man, who is wanted by our courts for murder. We apply for extradition. And he turns out to be your husband!"

"There is no extradition treaty between Iconia and Kossovia!" the Princess reminded him. "Really, Gustav, for a monarch you are extraordinarily ignorant of State affairs."

The King flushed angrily. "It may mean war."

The Princess laughed a trifle insultingly. "When Kossovia could crush you without troubling to mobilize! I think not, Gustav. I am very sorry, but much as I admire certain of your characteristics, I have taken an absolutely unconquerable dislike to you. I am sorry, but there it is. What is more to the point, I have taken a similar liking to Valentine, which, oddly enough, he returns. I am sorry to discuss all this in so unromantic a manner, but the love affairs of Royal persons tend to be somewhat business-like. And if you insist on discussing it in so melodramatic a manner you must expect me to take the opposite view."

"Oh, no doubt, like all the Forgerons, you can make a fool of me in an argument," said Gustav hotly. "Simply because I speak with feeling you call it melodramatic. Conceive my position. I have to announce to my Commission that my destined wife has run away with my mother's murderer."

"My dear Gustav, in a day or two your Commission will find out what fools they have made of themselves over Valentine. I advise you, as a wise ruler, to forget all about it and marry some other nice girl. Why not one of the old French semi-Royal titles? Some of them are charming girls. I could not hope to compete with their complexions for a moment. The Forgerons have always been freckled. Please excuse me for talking so much and keeping you waiting. Your arms must be getting tired. I must just tie this knot and then we shall go."

"Vera," said the King after a pause, "you will regret this. Do not be led on by your pride. The marriage can be annulled—quietly... no one need ever know. There is no need to marry me since you dislike me. I know I have been irritable and inattentive lately. All my worries... But I cannot see you wreck your life—you a Forgeron of Kossovia—by an alliance with an adventurer, a man of unmentionable birth—a man..."

"Do not make a fool of yourself, Gustav," cried the Princess imperiously. "One day you will realize what an ass you are, in spite of your superficial cleverness! I do not wish to discuss the matter further.

"There, darling," she added tenderly, as she finished the bandage, "I think that will be all right. I used to do nursing at the Royal Hospital, and I don't think I have forgotten. Do you feel well enough to travel?"

"I should never feel too ill to leave this confounded place," admitted Brightholme. "What shall we do with Gustav and Co.?"

"Jan," said the Princess, "you had better tie them up. You will probably find some rope in the warder's room. It won't be necessary to gag them, there is no one within earshot. Don't tie up Mr. Venables too tightly, poor lamb!

"It will not be much use following us, Gustav," she added. "We have Jan's aeroplane at the aerodrome waiting to take us straight to Kossovia, and we shall be over the border in half an hour. Make any statement you like about my sudden departure. I am quite ready to save your face by backing up any reasonable lie." She turned at the door and made a mocking curtsy. "I must beg Your Majesty's pardon for this abrupt departure. The King, my father, will write and thank you for your hospitality."

Lying tightly bound, in an uncomfortable heap on the floor, the four men found it difficult to converse, although they were ungagged. The King indeed made no attempt to do so. Charles searched his mind for suitable topics, but found none that seemed to fit in exactly with the place and the circumstances. He then made a prolonged struggle to free himself, but found that although he had been tied considerately, he had been tied efficiently. He resigned himself to wait...

It was Luigi who found them. He had become alarmed at the absence of the King, and after an hour had gone in search of them. His expression when he saw the bound figures of the four men was a mixture of surprise and stark terror.

"Are you all right, Your Majesty?... Thank God you are! What has happened?" he said as he freed Gustav.

The King jumped to his feet. His face was a study in misery and annoyance. He made as if to speak, and then closed his lips firmly. With a glare of concentrated irritation at Luigi, he strode from the room without a word.

"What has happened, Venables?" asked Luigi. "Where the devil is Brightholme?"

Venables looked carefully at Luigi's wide-open eyes and paused before speaking.

"What hasn't happened," he countered. "The whole works have started to go sky-high. And I've lost Queen Hanna's murderer!"

Chapter XXIV

THE NIGHT ATTACK

"Schloss Hoben,
"Kossovia.

"Dear Mr. Venables,

"We arrived here quite safely last night. My father does not yet know about Valentine. To be perfectly candid with you, I am a little alarmed at the prospect of having to tell him. However, it will be all right in a few days. Valentine sends his love. Take care of yourself.

"Yours sincerely,

"Vera, P."

"I don't know whether this note is confounded cheek or not," said Venables thoughtfully. "Well, I suppose it shows a pleasant nature."

"What has happened to Dr. Brightholme?" asked Miss Fotheringay, when Venables looked up from his letter. "I hear all kinds of rumours."

"He overpowered his guards and escaped," said Venables. "Why?"

"It is true, then! Really, it makes me shudder when I think he may be somewhere in the Palace, creeping around." Miss Fotheringay put her hands up nervously to her throat. "I am afraid he would have no cause to love me after what I told the Commission."

"You can take it he has left Iconia," said Venables shortly. There was a silence.

"How very odd," went on Miss Fotheringay after a few minutes, "that Princess Vera should have left so suddenly. I was expecting an announcement. It seems so strange to have a bachelor, or rather a widower King. The Princess left without a word of warning."

"I understand she was not feeling well," said Venables, supporting the story which had been concocted by Luigi and the Chamberlain. "She could not face an Iconian winter."

"Indeed! But I understood Kossovia was considerably more inclement than this country. It was the draughts in the Palace, I suppose. I always used to tell the Queen when I could do so respectfully: 'Your Majesty, they may say what they like, but I cannot believe all these draughts are good for one. Fresh air is all very well in its place, but surely not in the form of a draught.'"

The Chamberlain's dinner-table seemed strange and quiet without either Brightholme or Robor. The Professor peered benevolently round the table, but said little. The Chamberlain presided, when official duties permitted, courteous as ever, but reserved and quiet. The Wardrobe Mistress was alternately torpid and childish according to whether she was sober or not. Miss Fotheringay was disapproving, too obviously contrasting the events at the Milö Palace with the home life of English Royalty. Venables began to find the dinners a strain, and either had them at Isorb or served in his suite. And at the same time he began to find the Palace itself, which had started by being amusing, take on a queer, an almost ogreish atmosphere, whose tension one expected to be broken by some catastrophic surprise.

That night the tension was most noticeable. Venables looked round his room and asked the sprawling gods and goddesses, "What is going to be the next move?" They were unable to answer. Some move seemed called for, from what Venables had taken to calling the Opposition in his private thoughts. "The next move," he finally decided, "is obviously to get rid of the snooping detective. And as time is short it will probably be to-night."

Venables examined the huge oak door carefully. It was solid. There was a key, which he turned, but he knew the untrustworthiness of locks, and was pleased to find a large bolt.

A bolt is a fairly good safeguard, but not a perfect one. By jamming the handle of his safety-razor blade in the bolt, however, he made it as foolproof as possible.

As an added precaution he placed against the door one of the two marble statues of Hercules. It represented the demigod strangling Antæus, and was already a top-heavy production. The slightest movement of the door would upset it.

"That looks after the door," he said to himself with satisfaction.

He next examined the window. It was a casement window, looking out on the Courtyard, and it was provided with shutters. Venables closed these carefully, and then bolted the window. He secured this bolt from interference with a key which happened to fit the groove of the bolt snugly.

Venables surveyed his handiwork. "As far as may be we are safe against attack... One hates to be on the defensive, but I cannot remain awake all night with my hand on a revolver."

Venables slept. He awoke suddenly in the middle of a dream, in which he was Hercules struggling with some nameless beast which had pounced on him. And he found he was in fact being attacked. Some formless monster had him by the throat.

Had he not been taken completely by surprise, he could probably have defended himself. But the suddenness of the attack, waking him in confusion from his sleep, and the darkness of the shuttered room which hid his assailant, utterly disconcerted him.

His opponent had already pinioned his arms before he woke. He was dragged out of bed, and his head was hurled violently on the floor. Venables passed again into unconsciousness...

Venables woke to find his head alternately swelling and contracting with a feeling as if it were about to fly apart. He groaned and caressed his forehead. The apparent change in size ceased as he became more conscious, but the splitting remained.

He moved slightly, and as he did so a breeze ruffled his

brow. Was he lying on the floor of his room? If so, how did the window come to be open? He opened his eyes painfully and stared upwards.

Unless he was mad, he was staring at the night sky. And out of the sky above him loomed the tall shadow of some fantastic building. Venables groaned again and closed his eyes, endeavouring to pull himself together.

Then he attempted to scramble to his feet, and as he did so he slipped. He had been lying on a sloping stone floor. He scrabbled with his fingers at the stone, and he felt his legs kicking in air.

With a feeling of horror Venables realized that he was hanging on to the sloping stone by the mere friction of his elbows. The rest of his body was hanging sheer in space. And it was at that moment, with his brain cleared by the emergency, that Venables managed to grasp what had happened to him. He had been lying prone on a sloping stone ledge round some sort of tower. Above him was a blank wall. Below him was a drop of God knows how many feet. The night sky was around him, and below, like scattered stars, were the lights of Isorb. He was alone above the city, and below his kicking legs was a black gulf.

Venables felt physically sick as he clung grimly with his elbows to the ledge. He felt the sweat on his forehead chilled by the night breeze. With a strangled groan, he attempted to drag himself back on to the stone.

His left elbow slipped suddenly and he nearly panicked. He stopped struggling for a moment.

"You are merely doing some of your favourite rock climbing under unusual circumstances," he told himself firmly. "Pull yourself together!"

With one determined heave he got his knees on to the ledge and lay there for a little to recover. Then he sat up with his back to the wall.

An hour passed. "I'll not move till it gets lighter," he told himself.

The dawn slowly lightened in the sky, and as it did so his sur-
roundings took shape out of the bodiless gulf. He had been lying
half-way up the western tower—the belfry tower—of Isorb Palace.
The ledge was at the back of the campanile, and was the counterpart
of an elaborately carved cornice in the front. But as this ledge was
invisible from the ground, it had been left uncarved.

The Palace roofs stretched below him, forty feet or more. He
would have dropped on them, had he slipped, and his corpse would
have remained there for some days. He tried to remember whether
there were vultures in Iconia...

He flattened himself against the ledge and looked over it. The
overhang of the ledge was such that it was impossible to climb down
without a rope. Below him was the belfry, pierced with holes that
might, perhaps, give him enough hold to work his way down to the
roofs if he could only get past the first difficult bit. But it seemed to
him quite impossible.

Behind him was another blank wall. How the devil, then,
had he ever been placed on the ledge? He crawled along it and
found a door flush with the wall. It was locked from the inside, of
course. Venables had not even a penknife, and soon lost interest
in the door.

The ledge ended abruptly, so that it was impossible to climb round
the Tower. If only he could climb up the wall, and over the top of the
cupola on to the other side of the Tower, facing the street, he might
find, among the many ornaments of the front, sufficient foothold to
enable him to descend. In any case, once on the other side, he might
be able to attract someone's attention in the street below, whereas
here, overlooked by nothing but roof, it was hopeless.

At the far end of the ledge Venables found a ladder running
upwards. It was a thin ladder, and in order to clear the moulding
below the cupola which surmounted the tower, the ladder ran out-
ward from the wall at an angle, so that whoever climbed it would be
hanging a little downwards, and would need to get a firm foothold.

This did not worry Venables, who had a good head for heights. None the less, with one foot on the ladder, he hesitated.

Why, he thought, had his assailant left him in his present position? It would have been the easiest thing in the world, while Venables was still in his power, to have pushed him off the ledge, instead of leaving him there. After all, it was pure accident that Venables had nearly slipped off the ledge, and it would have been so much easier for the fellow to have given him the necessary shove while he was still unconscious.

There could be only one reason why he had not pushed Venables off into the void. He might be afraid that when Venables' body would be found, foul play would be suspected. Still, what was his motive in dragging Venables on to his perilous eyrie? If Venables escaped, his assailant's performance would have been without object. If he starved to death, if he slipped or fell, there would be just as much likelihood of suspicion arising as if he had hurled Venables into oblivion at once.

There could be only one possible explanation to the dilemma. The worst was still to happen to Venables; and it would happen in such a way that it would unquestionably appear an accident.

Venables looked at the ladder again. He shook it firmly, but nothing happened. He grasped the rungs as high up as possible and pulled. It seemed firm enough, although he thought he heard a faint click from the top. Then he braced his feet in a small pierced cavity in the wall, again seized the ladder high up and pulled at it until his muscles cracked. The ladder snapped suddenly at the base and fell with a clatter on to the ledge. Then it rocketed down the side and fell with a bang on to the roofs.

"That ought to wake someone," said Venables hopefully. But it did not seem to do so.

Well, at any rate that made his adversary's ingenious idea perfectly clear. The ladder had been sawn through almost entirely at the top, and probably weakened somehow at the base. Owing to the angle of the ladder, the leverage of any weight upon it increased rapidly as the weight rose. At the foot of the ladder its effect was negligible. But as the climber got higher and higher the leverage increased until the base snapped and the ladder folded outwards, plunging the unfortunate climber clear of the ledge on to the roof below. It was a delightful trap, self-adjusting for any weight. The lighter the person, the higher he had to go before the ladder broke, that was all.

No murder could have been neater. When Venables' body would at last have been found, there could have been no question of anything but accident. For some reason, it would have seemed, the detective had wished to explore the cupola in search of clues. Who knew why? Detectives were odd fish! Poor Venables had started to climb the ladder to get on the cupola. The ladder had been weak—it was so old. And so he had fallen. Very regrettable, but no one could suggest it was anything but accident. By that time the door leading to the ledge would have been unlocked.

How had his assailant got into his room? Venables wondered. Then, with a wry smile, Venables recollected the gentle fun he had poked at Millitranyi's search for a secret entrance to the Queen's bedchamber. He had discounted that, because such a means of committing the murder was too obvious not to be discovered at once. But in his case, where his death would have appeared an obvious accident, no one would look for a secret entry. That explained everything. His assailant had got into the Blue Room by a secret passage. The involved decoration of the room gave ample opportunity for concealing such a means of entrance. What a triple-dyed fool he had been to overlook it!

Perhaps the locked door and the shuttered windows of his room would give the show away? No, his would-be murderer would of course take care, before leaving, to open the shutters and lock and unbolt the door.

Venables shivered. It was partly apprehension, partly the unpleasant chill of the wind which was springing up, and which cut through his clothes like a knife. It was then it occurred to him to wonder why he was not wearing his pyjamas. He was fully dressed. Was this another freakish fondness of the murderer for dressing his corpses as shown in the case of Queen Hanna? Then Venables understood. The fact that he was dressed would make it still more certain that his fall from the ladder had been an accident. Whereas had he been in his pyjamas his nocturnal attempt to explore the cupola might seem eccentric, even for a detective.

At any rate he was grateful for the ingenious thoughtfulness of his murderer. An Iconian winter's day spent on the moulding round a tower was no joke. Venables wondered what it would be like if he were still there when night came again, and he had had no food all day. Already his hands were beginning to feel unpleasantly numb... But he resolutely put the thought away from him.

The morning wore on. Far beyond the Palace there were houses, people. He saw them as specks. And they saw him not at all, though he yelled at the top of his voice. Below, out of sight, he knew that sentries moved, but his voice was blanked and blotted out by the sheer bulk of the Palace which hid him from sight. He yelled until he was hoarse.

Another idea occurred to him. He took off his boots and hurled them at the roof, hoping that their clatter would arouse attention.

But no one saw. Noon came, and although the pale winter sun was welcome, he began to feel unpleasantly hungry...

Chapter XXV

THE VANISHED DETECTIVE

When the ladder which should have killed Venables fell clattering on to the roof at 4 a.m., it awoke Professor Carolos Andreyi. The Professor occupied a set of large rooms under the leads. These he was able to use as his bedroom, study, library, and for the storage of old dresses, stone fragments, mediæval weapons, fossils, and other of his prized antiquities of Iconia, which he jealously kept apart from the Royal Museum in the crypt. The rooms were old and uncomfortable, but their size and privacy endeared them to the Professor.

The ladder made an appalling clatter, and Andreyi woke up from the easy sleep of the aged with his heart beating violently. He did not realize the noise came from the roof. As it echoed through the high rooms, the Professor felt certain he heard a gang of burglars tramping about among his precious antiquities. He leaped out of bed, rushed into the storerooms, and found them empty.

The Professor felt quite sure he had not imagined the noise which had woken him. Obviously it was a matter that ought to be investigated. Could it have something to do with the other mysterious occurrences? He decided to consult Venables, who was in the same wing, although on a lower floor.

The Professor was devoid of fear, and he walked unhesitatingly down the dark stairs. He halted outside Venables' door for a moment and heard someone moving inside. The windows squeaked as someone opened them. He knocked on the door. Instantly the movements ceased. He knocked still more loudly. There was no response.

He tried to open the door. It was bolted. Placing his mouth near the crack of the opening, he shouted loudly. There was still no reply, but he felt certain he could hear the stealthy movement of feet.

Coming after the strange noises that had woken him, this odd reticence on the part of the English detective worried the Professor. He hurried downstairs, still in his dressing-gown, to the Corporal of the Palace guard on duty in that wing. The Corporal was fast asleep, a minor fault in the eyes of an Iconian sentry, and when he heard the Professor's story he was even inclined to be a little resentful of having been awakened. However, he came upstairs. He also could obtain no reply from Venàbles, even after hammering violently on the door with his rifle butt. The Corporal phoned the Bureau of Police, and the officer on duty decided to telephone to Millitranyi. Millitranyi made up in conscientiousness and zeal what he may have lacked in analytical power, and getting rapidly into a simple uniform, he hurried round to the Palace. It was he who gave the order for the door to be forced.

It took four men to force it. There was a crash as the door swung inwards and the statue fell. Antæus was rent from Hercules' arms and lay in fragments on the floor.

"Good heavens!" exclaimed Millitranyi. "Where is Venables?"

The room was empty. The windows were half open but the shutters were still closed from the inside. The bedclothes were scattered round the floor as if there had been a struggle. Venables' pyjamas, however, were neatly folded on a chair.

The Chief of Police stared suspiciously at Andreyi while his agents opened the cupboards and looked under the bed. "You are certain you heard someone in here?"

"I am positive," answered the Professor. "He was opening the windows and moving about, but when he heard me he stopped at once."

"Venables has obviously been attacked," said Millitranyi. "It must have been his assailant you heard moving about in here. But where have they both gone to? How could he have got through a locked door?"

"Perhaps he escaped through the window?"

"Impossible!" The General explained the obvious difficulties. "The shutters are still bolted from the inside. Besides, unless Venables was unconscious it would have been impossible to make him go down the wall of the Palace like a fly. And if he were unconscious it would have been more difficult still."

Suddenly the General beamed. "He must have used a secret entrance," he exclaimed. "Franceo! help me sound this wall."

The secret entrance was easily discovered. On one wall the fresco depicted a party of worshippers issuing from a temple door to offer a sacrifice to the deified Hercules. The temple door from which they came was cunningly painted so as to conceal the fact that it covered a real door.

Millitranyi hurried into the neighbouring room, which was empty. Here a tapestry concealed the corresponding secret door, which was provided with a handle. When opened, this door led to a small recess, as deep as the thickness of the wall, whose back was formed by the door leading to Venables' room. Obviously whoever the Professor had heard moving in Venables' room had left by this door. It was hardly a secret passage; it was merely a communicating door which had been concealed.

"It would be well," as the General said to the Professor with a wink, "not to inquire what distinguished persons have occupied these two suites in the past."

The General returned to the Blue Room. "This is all most unexpected," he complained. "Can that scoundrel Brightholme still be hiding somewhere in the Palace? Who else would wish to attack the detective?"

"I wonder why he removed Mr. Venables' body?" said Franceo with interest.

Millitranyi gave a start. "Good Lord, Franceo, don't start talking about the poor fellow's body at this stage. After all, there is no sign of blood. Let us assume he has been temporarily removed to some prison."

"He can hardly have been removed from the Palace without being seen, sir," said Franceo. "We know how carefully the outside of the Palace has been guarded since Her Majesty's death." The Corporal of the guard, who overheard this, blushed slightly.

"Then he is somewhere in the Palace, Franceo!" exclaimed Millitranyi. "We must find our esteemed colleague. We must find him before the day is out!"

"Yes, General, but how?"

"We must search the Palace from top to bottom. Every room! At once!"

"But, General!" protested Franceo, "that is a difficult task. And at this hour—with everyone still in bed..."

"We can be discreet," said the General severely. "Enough. Telephone at once for more men."

"But everyone is asleep, sir," reasoned his assistant. "They will be annoyed at being disturbed. His Majesty may be awakened by the noise."

"His Majesty *will* be awakened," answered the General firmly. "I am the Chairman of the Extraordinary Commission, and I know my duty. A colleague's life is in danger. A wanted murderer may be at large in this Palace. Enough. Telephone now. Remember—every room in the Palace, except His Majesty's bedchamber. No matter if it takes us until morning! Hurry now!"

The great search began. Heavy feet clattered. Indignant and sleepy Palace denizens turned unwillingly out of bed. The Professor assisted, unique in his knowledge of the topography of the Palace. But there was no sign of Charles Venables.

"Poor Venables!" Millitranyi began to say after two hours' fruitless search. "Perhaps after all..."

It was at this moment that Franceo approached him and saluted.

"Well, what is it?" asked the Chief of Police impatiently.

"If you please, sir, Miss Fotheringay refuses to let us enter her bedroom."

"Tell her I, Millitranyi, as Chairman of the Extraordinary Commission, demand this."

"Very good, Your Excellency!" Franceo left, but returned shortly afterwards. "Miss Fotheringay still refuses, sir. She requests you to remember that she is an English gentlewoman."

"She is an impertinent ——!" swore the General. He hurried into the wing in which Miss Fotheringay slept. Her door was locked and he knocked on it peremptorily.

"Open at once! It is I, Millitranyi, Chief of Police."

"Your Excellency!" answered Miss Fotheringay's indignant voice. "This is outrageous! Are you mad?"

"A dangerous murderer is somewhere in this building," said Millitranyi. "He has forced Mr. Venables to accompany him. We are searching for them both!"

"Don't be perfectly ridiculous," answered the lady irritably. "Do you suppose a murderer and his victim could be in my room without my knowledge?"

"That is our business, madam," said the policeman acidly.

"I refuse to open the door. I am not in a state to receive visitors. Go away." A silence followed.

Millitranyi was about to acknowledge defeat and turn away. Suddenly he stiffened. "I heard a man whispering in there," he hissed to Franceo.

"Kindly dress yourself sufficiently to receive us!" he said aloud in his most peremptory voice. "It is imperative that we search your room."

"I do not feel well!" squeaked Miss Fotheringay pathetically. "This sudden awakening has given me palpitations."

"I regret to hear it. Kindly open the door."

"I shall complain to the Chamberlain. Is this a palace or a tavern?"

"Kindly open the door."

"I refuse!"

Millitranyi laughed sardonically. "I propose to give you ten minutes in which to clothe yourself. At the end of that time the door will be broken down."

There was an ominous silence. Millitranyi, with a watch in his hand, counted aloud slowly. "One minute... two minutes... three minutes..."

At the end of five minutes the door was opened. Tight-lipped, enveloped in a huge flowered dressing-gown, Miss Fotheringay stood glaring in the doorway. "Enter!"

The General bowed. "I regret to have to inconvenience you, Miss Fotheringay. Excuse me." He walked inside.

His Excellency the Chamberlain stood in front of the fireplace. He was in his dressing-gown. His hands were clasped behind his back. His beard was a little tousled. He cleared his throat.

"No doubt you are surprised to find me here, Millitranyi?" he began heavily.

General Millitranyi gazed woodenly through the Chamberlain. "I see nobody here except Miss Fotheringay," he said. "My duty is to search this room for Mr. Venables. I do not see him here."

"Oh, that is very discreet of you, Millitranyi!" said the Chamberlain testily, "but it is too late to be discreet now. Not that I don't trust you, but your assistant is grinning like an idiot"—Franceo abruptly composed his face—"and I saw half a dozen members of the Household in the corridor."

"I regret extremely, Your Excellency—" began the Chief of Police, embarrassed. "If I had guessed the situation... Of course, Miss Fotheringay is very charming. The English style of beauty, eh?"

"Pray, what *are* you talking about, General?" interrupted Miss Fotheringay acidly. "In any event, I am not English but Scots." She turned to the Chamberlain. "Ferdinand, be good enough to explain our—er—position to the General. He is evidently under a misconception characteristic of this licentious country."

The Chamberlain frowned. "General, I have the honour to inform you that this lady is my wife!"

"Good heavens!" exclaimed Millitranyi. He recovered himself with an effort. "That is to say, congratulations, Your Excellency!"

"We have been secretly married for twenty years," went on the Chamberlain sadly. "It is the only thing in which I deceived Her Majesty. I asked her permission to marry, you know, and she absolutely refused it. She said that the Chamberlain of a Queen's Household must be a bachelor. A fixed idea of hers... And so we married without letting anyone know."

Miss Fotheringay sat down limply in a chair. "Oh dear, oh dear! I don't know what will happen now. It was very wicked of us to deceive the Queen. It was my fault. I became such a martyr to nerves. In this Palace, with these dreadful draughts! Not that that is any excuse, but still..."

The General observed with astonishment that the stern cheek of Miss Fotheringay, or rather of the Countess Mapponyi, was bathed in tears...

The Chamberlain patted her on the back. "There, there, Jean." He smiled at the General. "These English, you know. Outside, all is ice—reserve—phlegm. Beneath there is passion, tenderness."

"Indeed," said the General, interested. "I have known so few English girls."

"I am not English, I am Scots," repeated Miss Fotheringay mechanically. "How dreadful this all is," she snivelled. "Now everyone in the Palace will know. Not that Ferdinand has anything to be ashamed of. After all, the blood of the Stuarts runs in my veins... But it is so difficult to explain our having been married twenty years without telling anyone."

"My devotion to the Queen sufficiently explains it," said the Chamberlain proudly. "True, on His Majesty's accession I might have confessed the truth. But it seemed difficult after so many years... Poor little Jean, how you frightened her!"

An amazed voice from the door made them both turn. It was Luigi.

"What on earth is going on here, Millitranyi? What are you doing here, anyway? His Majesty sent me to inquire. You have woken him up. The whole Palace is in an uproar."

Millitranyi told him.

Luigi looked from Miss Fotheringay to her husband with an air of dazed astonishment.

"Good God!" he said, and walked out.

And the body of Charles Venables was still undiscovered. The morning wore on. They were exploring the cellarage now. And still there was not so much as a button or a handkerchief.

"It is incredible!" exclaimed the General, dusty and ruffled. "He must be somewhere in the Palace!"

"The devil has flown away with the interfering Englishman," muttered one of the scullery maids to the other, as they scoured a huge copper cooking-pot. "I heard the General Chief of Police say so. The devil was seen by seven different people as he flew out of the bedroom window carrying the Englishman under his arm. That is what comes of meddling with the Curse of the Herzvogins." The other scullery maid crossed her fingers.

"The solution is plain!" said one of the sentries, who considered himself a detective, and being anticlerical, was not influenced by the childish superstition of the scullery maids. "Her Majesty's murderer is a mad cannibal. Now he has eaten the Englishman."

At five o'clock in the afternoon the General abandoned his search in despair. He had had forty policemen at work continuously, turning out the Palace from top to bottom. Big as the Palace was, this had enabled him to explore every known room and cupboard, and nowhere was there a sign of the missing man.

"Let us not give up hope. To-morrow," he said, "we will start to tap the walls!"

*

But that night, soon after twelve o'clock, when the Palace was in bed, an eerie, a terrifying event took place. Loud and clear, in the silence of the night, the alarm bell of the Palace spoke. It spoke stutteringly, as if it was inarticulate with fear. It spoke incessantly.

The last time it had clanged out in the night watches was to announce the passing of the unquietly reft soul of Queen Hanna.

The inmates of the Palace rose, wide-eyed with conjecture.

"Run at once," said the Chamberlain, hurrying into his clothes. "Find who is doing it. It is a practical joke. In very bad taste!"

The messenger returned from the bell loft as pale as a ghost.

"May the angels protect us!" he stammered, crossing himself.

"What the devil is the matter?" asked the Chamberlain.

The messenger shuddered at the Chamberlain's choice of oaths. "The loft is empty. The bell is ringing itself."

"Don't be a fool," exclaimed the Chamberlain. He hurried into the Tower room. And in spite of himself he felt a cold thrill of horror when he stood in the bell loft. Above, invisible in the blackness, the great bell uttered its strangled and stammering cry. The rope hung vertically, trembling, moved by invisible hands.

The Chamberlain wiped the cold sweat from his brow and pulled himself together. "Get lights and ladders and climb up to the Tower. There must be someone up there doing this…"

There was. In the uncertain light of their lanterns they discerned a man hanging like some great bat, swinging perilously over the cornice of the campanile and kicking the bell into clamour with his feet. He was hanging on to a loop plaited out of his shirt, jacket, and waistcoat, which was perilously secured to the remains of the ladder-anchorage on the ledge. At each swing away from the bell he hung sheer into space, held only by his crazy fabric loop.

The key to the locked door leading on to the ledge was missing, but they got him down the ladder. He was hungry, cold, filthy, and white with fatigue.

"What on earth were you doing up there?" asked the Chamberlain, pardonably enough.

For the first time he saw the English detective look discomposed. Venables scowled ferociously and exclaimed in a voice of cold fury:

"I sometimes walk in my sleep! Get me some food and a drink!"

Chapter XXVI

THE SHOCKING EXHUMATION

The morning following Venables' airing on the campanile was the King's birthday. This was a festive occasion at the Milö Palace. The Sovereign held a morning reception at which the major nobles, State functionaries, and diplomatic representatives called to present their congratulations to the King.

These ceremonial occasions, Venables observed, always gave the members of the Household a temporary cohesion. They ceased to quarrel. The Palace became quiet. Even the guards about the Palace stood smartly to attention instead of lounging reflectively against the nearest wall when no one was in sight.

The Deputy Wardrobe Mistress, with whom Venables was somewhat friendly, passed him in the Winter Garden hot-foot. She gave him an expressive shrug, and Venables noticed a look of concern on her fat, genial face.

"What's the matter?" asked Venables.

The Deputy Wardrobe Mistress stopped, glad to unburden herself. "It's Naomi," she moaned. "She is in a dreadful state. At this hour, too! The worst of it is she refuses to keep to her room. She is insisting on coming down to take her place in the reception!"

"Can't you lock her in?"

"I daren't!" said the Deputy Wardrobe Mistress, rolling her eyes. "Her rages are terrible!"

"Have you told the Chamberlain?"

"He refuses to have anything to do with her. He says it is not his business."

"H'm! I suppose he hasn't recovered from the dressing-down he got when he complained about her before. Well, you'll have to let her come, that's all. Have you told the King?"

"It is impossible to get near him. He is busy working off the Cardinal and the Ambassadors. You know, perhaps, that it is Naomi's duty to present the wives and daughters of the smaller foreign people—*chargés d'affaires* and visitors, and so forth. Well, she is hurrying along now to do it."

"Oh, well, she'll probably pull herself together when she gets there. By the way, where is it? In the Throne Room?"

"No, the Banqueting Hall. Why don't you go there? As a member of the Household you are entitled to. The King is looking splendid."

The Deputy Wardrobe Mistress hurried off, apparently for no other reason than to be out of the way when Countess Naomi took up her post in the Throne Room.

Venables entered quietly. The Deputy Wardrobe Mistress was right. Gustav was looking magnificent in the all-white uniform of a colonel of the Royal Cuirassiers, with a silver helmet topped by an eagle, white gloves and boots, and a silver breastplate. The Banqueting Hall was draughty, and most of the guests looked cold and irritable. Fortunately they were not expected to stay long.

The Wardrobe Mistress was certainly an alarming sight as she waddled into the Banqueting Hall and took up her place near the Chamberlain. Her face was flushed and her breathing was stertorous. She looked pugnacious...

Venables saw her sway. She put out one hand and steadied herself against the King's empty chair. Gustav looked at her and instantly understood her condition. An odd look of blended irritation and pain came over his face.

As Venables prophesied, she had pulled herself together. She repeated the names of the ladies which were whispered into her ear with a hopeless incoherence that was, fortunately, only heard by the King and the negligible person who was being presented. But when her duties were over she let go the chair arm, stepped forward to mingle with the guests, swayed for a moment, fell, and lay there prone. There was an excited murmur.

The King glared at the Chamberlain. "The Countess Tacora is ill!" he said loudly. "Assist her to leave the room."

The Chamberlain hurried forward. Venables, always ready to help, assisted him. Between them they got the Countess to her feet, and half escorted her, half dragged her out of the hall.

In the corridor she mumbled something and attempted to struggle from their helping hands.

"Keep quiet, damn you!" hissed the Chamberlain, with murder in his eyes. He dropped the shoulder he was supporting and allowed the Countess to bump heavily on the floor.

"I say," Venables protested. "Steady."

"I could strangle her," exclaimed the Chamberlain, with suppressed fury. "It is dreadful that such an event should occur during my office. Bad as the Countess has been, she has never before been drunk on a State occasion."

"I don't think anyone noticed," said Venables soothingly. "It looked like a faint."

"Bah!" exclaimed Mapponyi disgustedly. "No one could mistake it."

Once back in the Countess's apartments, the Chamberlain unloaded his soul. The Countess Naomi lay back in a chair, regarding him vindictively and dizzily while he abused her.

"Enough," exclaimed the Chamberlain at last, out of breath. "Either you or I must leave the Palace. I shall see you to-morrow."

The interview next day was painful. The Chamberlain recounted it to Venables.

"I have dismissed the Countess Tacora!" he said abruptly. "I have told her to leave as soon as possible."

"Good Lord!" exclaimed Venables, startled. "What, without consulting His Majesty?"

"I am within my rights," answered the old man defensively. "As Chamberlain of the Household every office other than the military and secretarial posts is under my direct control. It is in my patent of appointment. The Countess's own patent is signed by me."

"And supposing she refuses to go?"

The Chamberlain shrugged his shoulders. "We shall see. I could do nothing else. How could I permit her to stay after what occurred yesterday?"

"My dear Chamberlain," said Venables. "Do you suppose for a moment Gustav will support you?"

"I expect justice from His Majesty," answered the Chamberlain. Venables shook his head pityingly.

The Chamberlain's valet entered. "What is it, Crispin?" he asked.

"His Majesty is outside," stuttered the valet. "He is making you a personal visit."

The Chamberlain looked a little pale and rose quickly to his feet. With a deep bow the valet opened the door and then fled.

Gustav was looking ferocious. He glared at the Chamberlain. "Good-morning, Mapponyi!" he said brusquely.

"Good-morning, sire."

Foreseeing an unpleasant interview, Venables made as if to go. But Gustav detained him with a gesture. "Be good enough to wait, Venables! I wish to have a word with you too."

Venables bowed.

"Mapponyi," went on the King, with dangerous quietness, "Luigi tells me that you have dismissed the Countess Naomi Tacora from her post as Mistress of the Wardrobe. He has, of course, been misinformed."

"No, sire!" said the Chamberlain. "I—"

"No?" interposed the King. "Do I understand that you have presumed to dismiss a senior member of my Household without consulting me?"

"After the disgraceful scene yesterday," stammered the Count, "I had no option."

"Precisely what disgraceful scene are you referring to? You can hardly mean the Countess's unfortunate illness. Or do you consider it disgraceful to faint? A rigorous standard, surely?"

The Chamberlain braced his shoulders. "Your Majesty, the Countess—with all respect—was hopelessly drunk yesterday. Her servants even—"

"Don't repeat servants' gossip to me," said Gustav furiously. "Do you think I have no eyes? The Countess was indisposed. Your attitude is in the highest degree impertinent and insulting."

"My patent authorizes me—" began the Chamberlain.

"Good Heavens!" exclaimed the King, "have you become a lawyer? Do you have to look at a patent to know what your duties are—you who have been Chamberlain here for thirty years? Mapponyi, you have acted unforgivably! This all arises from a despicable jealousy of the Countess, about which I have had to reprove you again and again. How dare you talk of disgraceful scenes, you who figured in a scene from a French farce—"

"Your Majesty," interrupted the Chamberlain against all etiquette, but goaded beyond endurance by this fresh attack, "I have already made my apologies for that concealment of my marriage. I repeat those apologies. When making them I put my resignation in your hands, and you were good enough to refuse it. I offer it to you again. But I beg of you, sire, to treat this woman—"

Gustav silenced him with a roar of rage. "Have you gone mad? Upon my soul, I believe you are on the point of giving me a lesson in manners. Pull yourself together. Remember who you are. In fact, silence!"

The Chamberlain drew himself up, his thin body unnaturally erect. He looked at the King. Two red spots burned on his cheeks. The old man faced the young man silently.

"You are dismissed from your post," said the King slowly. "I will consider whether, in view of your services, it will be announced as a resignation. You will hand over your Key to Luigi until we have decided on your successor. You will call the heads of the Household staff together and inform them of your demission of office. You will not tell them whether you have resigned or have been dismissed. You will then leave the Palace and return to your country seat, and there await the quietus of your accounts. At some later date I may permit you to return to Isorb. In that event I will let you know. Do you understand?"

The Chamberlain's breeding came to his support. His voice was calm as he answered, "Perfectly, sire! I regret that I am no longer able to serve Your Majesty as for so long I was able to serve Your Majesty's mother. I am an old man, and am not likely to live much longer. Nevertheless, such time as I have is always at the service of any member of your House. Have I your permission to retire, sire?"

"No," said Gustav irritably, refusing to allow Mapponyi even the luxury of a dignified exit. "There are a great many details I shall wish to discuss with you before you go. I wish to speak to Venables now."

He turned to the detective, who had been an embarrassed witness of the scene.

"Venables," he asked, his bright-blue eyes fixed firmly on the detective's, "where are my children, eh?"

Venables felt himself going hot under the collar. The look in Gustav's eyes was unmistakable. The King had found out. There was little purpose in denying knowledge of the children.

"I have reason to believe, sir, that they are now in Kossovia."

Gustav's eyes narrowed slightly. "Why did you not tell me this?" he asked quietly.

"I was told in confidence," replied Venables.

"Confidence, good heavens!" exclaimed the King. "Were you not brought here by me?"

"By your mother, sir," answered Venables.

"Do not attempt to quibble! Why have you at last broken this precious confidence of yours?"

"I have not, with respect. I gather that you had already found out."

"Your answer is impertinent," answered Gustav irritably. "I felt myself forced some days ago to employ, through Luigi, agents of my own. It was they who found out that Princess Vera has had the audacity to harbour my children. Venables, I can no longer trust you. You have not been honest. I will not say you have been bribed——" He paused. Venables continued to look impassively at him——"but that is an inference other people might draw. You have had unexampled freedom of investigation. Tell me truthfully, have you even the least idea who murdered my mother?"

"I have, Your Majesty; but until my investigations have gone further——"

"——You cannot tell me. What a childish excuse! You have done nothing. You have found nothing. You have abetted my enemies. You have involved yourself in ridicule. That Tower episode, for instance."

"I must apologize for that, sire," said Venables blandly. "My fondness for fresh air is always leading me into difficulties."

Gustav lost his temper. "Confound you, do you think you can be witty at my expense! I order that you cease your investigations forthwith. You will leave the Palace and Isorb to-night. Give up your card of authority to Luigi before you go. What are you waiting for?"

"A request, Your Majesty!" answered Venables.

"What is it?"

"The exhumation of Prince Maximilian takes place this afternoon. In view of its judicial importance, the Extraordinary Commission have ordered me to be present. What shall I do?"

"You will not go. Enough!"

Venables went.

"Well, I may as well have one last wander round the old place," he told himself. He decided to visit St. Boron's Chapel.

The Chapel interior was transformed. To-morrow was to be the postponed meeting of the Order of the Collar, at which King Augustus would be installed as Sovereign Prior. The crape hangings and drapery had been removed, and instead the walls were bright with banners and coats of arms. A red carpet stretched in front of the stalls of the Knights. The throne in which the Sovereign Prior would be installed had been erected in the chancel, ten paces from the tomb of St. Boron. At the foot of the tomb itself was the pulpit from which the Chaplain, His Beatitude the Patriarch of Iconia, would deliver his inaugural address. The flying and looping angels peered out from between faded and historic banners. The pews were ready, provided with gold-braided velvet hassocks for the Companions of the Order who would fill the body of the church.

An interesting Order. Venables had been dipping into the books of Mr. Lancelot of the Foreign Office, and had also spoken to Professor Andreyi about the Institution. It was more than an Order of Chivalry, it appeared. It had also acquired, as the years passed, a quasi-parliamentary function, almost equivalent to that of a Second Chamber. As the only Iconian Order, it had *ipso facto* enrolled every-one of distinction or birth in the little kingdom, and therefore it had been readily granted certain privileges that belonged more strictly to a Privy Council. A Privy Council did not, however, exist in Iconia.

The Order of the Collar was also a final Court of Appeal in any process of divorce, probate, religious establishment, or treason. It had the right of appointing the Regent during the minority of the Sovereign, and it was also its duty formally to summon the Sovereign to the Throne. When the mad King Maximilian the Second was deposed, this had been done by the Order of the Collar; although it must be admitted that jurists had always contested the legality of the action. Altogether, Charles Venables felt sorry that he would be unable to witness the ceremony of the installation to-morrow...

He wandered downstairs into the Museum. The Curse of the Herzvogins had been replaced, with another and grimmer addition to its legend. He strolled round the waxworks. Here, to-morrow, the Knights would move in procession round the images of the dead sovereigns of Iconia at the conclusion of the ceremony. He stopped in front of the empty frame intended for Queen Hanna.

And here, in the Museum, quite suddenly a light came to him.

"Good heavens! So that was it!" exclaimed Venables. "Why, or why didn't I guess it before? When it was staring me in the face!"

He returned thoughtfully to his room. His valet was already packing his trunks. "Chamberlain's orders, sir," the valet said, a trifle shamefacedly.

"Yes, quite right, Van!" said Venables absently. "Pack me enough things for two or three nights in a separate valise. I'll be back for it shortly."

Those members of the Royal Family who have not reigned are buried in the Herzvogin vault, in the Cemetery of St. Eleutheria. The vault is a massive and melancholy crypt of red sandstone, and looked none the less melancholy when, by the light of lanterns, Millitranyi, two police chiefs, and Drs. Brygidor and Achevin, with a retinue of carpenters, masons, and spade-bearers, descended into its chilly depths for the purpose of exhuming the remains of the ill-fated Prince Maximilian. The permit of exhumation had required the counter-signatures of several bureaucrats, and it was not therefore surprising that so long had elapsed before the actual disinterment could be carried out.

"It is ridiculous!" exclaimed Dr. Brygidor. "I am ashamed that a doctor of Robor's intelligence should have suggested such a measure. Nothing, absolutely nothing, of any consequence can be found after such a lapse of time! It might, of course, be possible to find traces of violence; but as for negative evidence, something proving that poison was *not* administered, for instance—why the idea is absurd!"

"I fancy it was only a device for gaining time," said Achevin. "Poor Robor, one can hardly blame him! What folly on his part ever to take a Court appointment. An intelligent man, too, in his way..."

A workman rubbed the accumulated mud and grime off a small tablet with a piece of sackcloth.

MAXIMILIAN FERDINAND-GEORGICUS AUGUSTUS,

PRINCE,

DUKE OF THERIA,

COUNT OF THE WESTERN PROVINCE,

HEIR APPARENT,

&C., &C.,

DIED

ÆTAT 2 YEARS 2 MONTHS.

The workman placed a wedge in the corner of the tablet. The work began...

The pathetically small coffin was at last hauled from its resting-place. The gilt crest upon the lead was faded, but the Royal seals, verified by Millitranyi, were still intact.

The coffin was placed upon the hastily erected table. The sounds of filing and tapping reverberated irreverently in the vault. At last the lid was free.

The surgeons drew on their gloves, Brygidor still grumbling to himself. The tart stimulating smell of disinfectants filled the air. They drew out the small bundle of faded linen cerecloths, only vaguely suggestive of humanity.

"Scissors," murmured Dr. Brygidor. "Good linen this."

The doctors started to unwind the bundle. "I say, that's odd," exclaimed Brygidor loudly. "There's something queer about this." A small pile of faded linen bandage grew beside them as they unwrapped the corpse. "What on earth is it!" muttered Achevin. "Quick, the light!"

"Good God!" exclaimed Brygidor, starting back from the table in surprise. "Millitranyi, what in heaven's name has happened here?"

For the corpse of the late Prince Maximilian, after an altogether surprising length of linen wrappings had been unrolled, had proved to be nothing but some lengths of lead piping...

Chapter XXVII

THE RESURRECTED PRINCE

That evening Venables took his bag and left for the station, after giving orders for his trunk to be sent on to England. He made his good-byes ostentatiously. At the station he got out of the Palace car, walked into the station and out through the other entrance. Here he got into a taxi. Venables had no intention of leaving Isorb.

"The Chancellor's residence in the Vio Victorio!" he said to the bushy-whiskered driver.

The Chancellor's secretary was at first doubtful whether His Excellency could see Venables. The message the English detective sent in altered his views. The Count Demetrior would see him at once.

The Chancellor was sitting by the fire in his study reading, wearing a dressing-gown and bedroom slippers. He apologized for his informality with a smile.

"When my work is over I like to lock myself up in my study with a bottle of port and a cigar, and a good detective novel!"

"I am glad to hear you like a detective novel!" said Venables dryly. "You should be the more prepared to understand the story I am going to tell you now."

"Really? This sounds interesting! Sit down, won't you? A cigar?"

"Thanks. First of all, then, I must inform Your Excellency I have been dismissed by the King. He ordered me to leave Isorb to-day."

Demetrior looked surprised. "I am sorry to hear that. Why? Don't answer my question unless you wish it."

"I was making too slow progress, he told me. He wanted to know why I hadn't yet discovered the murderer."

The Chancellor looked embarrassed.

"Ah, well, naturally we are all a little disappointed at that. I don't blame you for a moment, but the affair has been a blot on my term of office. It will take a little living down." He sighed. "I have lived down worse things."

Venables smiled. "It is nice of you not to blame me. But the truth is, the King dismissed me because I had found out far too much."

Demetrior ceased to smile. "Come, come, Mr. Venables! There is an insinuation in that remark which I regret. I am sure you cannot mean to suggest that His Majesty wishes to hamper the investigation?"

"I am going to suggest a great deal that you will find it difficult to believe," said Venables seriously. "May I ask you if you have heard the result of the exhumation of Prince Maximilian, which the Commission were undertaking this afternoon?"

"No, I have not. The exhumation took place after I left the Chancellery. In any case, I cannot imagine the result will be of much interest."

"You will find it of enormous interest," said Venables positively. "I was not present, but I can guess pretty well what they found. Your Excellency, will you oblige me by ringing up Millitranyi and finding out what has happened?"

Impressed by Venables' earnestness, Demetrior rang up the police Chief. The telephone conversation was a series of surprised "What's?" and "Good heavens!" He replaced the receiver and turned to Venables helplessly.

"You are right. An incredible thing has happened! Although the seals are intact, the body of the dead Prince has been removed."

"Removed is hardly the word I should use," said Venables with a smile. "Fortunately I know where the body is at the moment."

"We must replace it!" exclaimed Demetrior, with the practical mind of the politician. "As quietly as possible. We do not want a public scandal."

"I'm afraid the body won't fit in the coffin now," answered Venables, grinning.

"What?" asked Demetrior, frowning.

"It's grown, you see."

"What *are* you trying to tell me?" exclaimed the Chancellor irritably. "What do you mean? How could a corpse *grow*?"

"Prince Maximilian happens still to be very much alive," replied Venables slowly. "He is now a man of thirty-two. You will have difficulty in persuading him to be buried."

The Chancellor jumped and spilt the ash from his cigar down the front of his dressing-gown. "Alive!" he repeated incredulously. "Prince Maximilian *alive*? But how could he be? Why has nothing been heard of him? Where is he?"

"He has been living at the Palace for the last two or three years," answered Venables quietly. "He is at present in Kossovia."

Demetrior agitatedly dropped his cigar butt into his port. "For God's sake, man, tell me? *Who* is Prince Maximilian?"

"A man we used to know as Dr. Brightholme," replied the detective. "He is now the husband of Princess Vera of Kossovia. There is still a warrant out for his arrest for the murder of his aunt, Queen Hanna."

"But how can we confirm this? I find it difficult to grasp," exclaimed Demetrior confusedly. "It all happened so long ago. You say he was Brightholme, of all people! Surely you are wrong. I cannot imagine anyone less likely to be Prince Maximilian!"

"Are you so sure?" asked Venables. "Did you see the report of the examination of Miss Fotheringay by the Commission? It was testified that Brightholme was so like the Queen in appearance that he could give a plausible impersonation of her! The Herzvogin face, you see!"

Demetrior's face wrinkled with perplexity.

"Of course, I remember now! How blind we were. But this isn't enough, Venables! I do not doubt your assurance, but we must learn how it all came about. We must have witnesses, proofs. This is political dynamite. I hardly dare handle it."

"I suggest we send for Dr. Robor."

"Of course. I will ring for my secretary."

Ten minutes later his secretary hurried off with an order signed by the Chancellor to fetch Robor from the prison.

Robor returned with him in half an hour. He was still dressed in his own clothes as he was a prisoner under remand, but he was pale from the effects of confinement.

"Sit down, Robor," began the Chancellor sternly. "We want from you now the truth, and the *whole* truth. We have exhumed the body of Prince Maximilian."

The old man smiled maliciously. "Ah! and does it prove my innocence of the charge?"

"It does! But it suggests many other things. You must realize that the time for concealment is past! We know that Brightholme is Prince Maximilian."

Robor passed his hand nervously over his wrinkled face. "Ah, you know that, do you? I did not think you would guess it so quickly. Well, there is not much object in further silence. I confirm it. 'Brightholme' is the lawful Prince Maximilian."

The Chancellor shuddered slightly at the political prospect.

"Tell us how this came about," he said.

"It is not an easy story for me to tell," began Robor slowly. "It starts with a young princess and a young doctor. The young princess was a woman such as we shall never know again—like flame— imperious—the sort of woman who could make a man do what she wished. A queen by character as well as birth."

"The Princess Hanna," said Demetrior softly. "Yes, I remember the sort of woman she was. You, Robor, and the Chamberlain—even I—we are all old men who once fell under her spell."

"Yes, but you never knew how the woman could be at the one time fascinating and implacable. Her wickedness was on such a grand scale that it was almost a virtue. In those days it seemed to be part of her character, of her innate regality. Now I see it in a less rosy light. But in two things she was like a rock—her hatred of her brother, and her determination that she would reign. When her brother was king she attacked the first obstacle. It was his only child, Prince Maximilian. He fell ill of some childish complaint. I was called to attend him. Hanna sent for me. She commanded me, she implored me—" The Doctor bowed his head wearily. "I don't know how to describe her peculiar method of entreaty. All I know is that I loved her, and before I left her I had heard myself agreeing to that crime."

"You agreed," exclaimed Demetrior, with a kind of horrified fascination, "to the murder of the Heir Apparent!"

Robor nodded. "It was easy enough to agree. But as soon as I had left her I knew I could never carry it out. As a man I might have done it. As a doctor it was impossible. It is not one's mere oath that stops one, it is second nature. One cannot deliberately mix a poison in a healing draught. But I knew my Princess, and away from her one's head cleared a little. If she did not employ poison it would be some other means—perhaps a hired assassin." Dr. Robor looked up earnestly. "Do not ask me to explain what motives lead me to try to save Maximilian. A cynic would say it was ambition, foresight. A sentimentalist, pity for a helpless infant. A lover, a desire to save the Princess from herself. I myself do not know. But I decided to save it. I took the nurse—long dead—into my confidence. She worshipped the child and helped me. We announced that it had died, and allowed the Chamberlain, as was his duty, to inspect it while it was unconscious under a sleeping draught. That and my death certificate were sufficient. It was we who claimed the duty of winding it in the shroud... The child was smuggled away to England to be educated and brought up at my expense."

"Did the Prince know his history?"

"Yes, from the day he was twelve years old. During the years that followed we waited. As long as Hanna was on the throne we knew that, in spite of his legal claim to the throne, her position was so secure that, even after his majority, she could crush him like a fly. Hanna meant more to Iconia than a mere legal form. But all the time the Queen never guessed. I admit it was I who persuaded Maximilian not to attempt to regain the throne while Hanna lived. It was not only from motives of political expediency. My love for the flame-like Princess lived on as respect for the ageing Queen. But, as her health failed, as I too grew old, I introduced Brightholme into the Palace as unsuspiciously as possible. Already the Queen showed evident signs of repentance for her usurpation, of an intention to make amends.

"Everything seemed set for our *coup d'état*. On the night of her murder Maximilian visited her and told her the truth. She begged him to proclaim it. 'It will be the end of you,' he warned her. 'I can't expect you to have much mercy on me,' she replied half-jokingly. These words were heard by Miss Fotheringay. And then, before she could abdicate, she was murdered! Our whole plan collapsed. If Maximilian revealed himself then, he would inevitably be suspected as the murderer. Gustav would have no difficulty in getting his succession attainted. So Maximilian decided to keep incognito until the murderer was discovered. The rest you know, and how by a strange chance Princess Vera fell in love with him, and he with her. At last he told her the truth about his identity. They married and fled to Kossovia."

There was a silence.

"Tell me," said the Chancellor at last, "how did Maximilian's father, Franceo, come to die? Was that by a hired assassin of the Queen?"

Robor shook his head. "No, I swear it was not. Certainly, after she thought I had killed Maximilian, she kept on pressing me to poison Franceo. I was always able to make excuses. He was assassinated by some madman, and the Queen told me seriously that it was a Providential approval of her plan. There could be no mistaking the genuineness of her surprise, so I knew she had no part in it. I admit she would have been glad enough to have done so, she hated him so bitterly."

The Chancellor leaned his elbows on the table and looked thoughtfully into space. "The Herzvogins seem to have been true to type throughout the ages. I can't imagine anything more awkward happening... Do you realize that Prince Maximilian, as the son of King Franceo, is really entitled to the throne? Augustus is a usurper."

"I realize it," answered Venables, with a smile. "So does Gustav, I imagine."

The Chancellor started. "Do you really believe the King knows that Prince Maximilian is alive?"

"He has known it for the last few days," admitted the detective. "And he knows I know. Hence my dismissal."

"Oh, I see. And he has kept his knowledge dark. That means he will fight." The politician plucked savagely at his grey moustache. "I don't like this, Venables. I don't like it at all! It's not at all the statesmanlike thing to do, to upset the Succession like this. The King may not be generally popular, but the army like him. I think they would follow him. After all, he has been crowned in good faith. And he is Queen Hanna's son! If he likes to fight Maximilian—"

"You may take it that he will fight—to the end," Venables assured him.

"Then I don't like it the least bit," said Demetrior firmly. "Maximilian will have to sue to establish his legitimacy. Even supposing the King allows it—the hearing will take months and months. There is ample time for Gustav to get ready to fight. Why, it will mean a revolution before we know where we are!"

"But after all, Prince Maximilian is entitled to the throne," pointed out Venables.

"No matter. Plenty of kings have kept their throne with worse title to it than Gustav. Your Tudors and Hanoverians, for instance." The Chancellor's wise face was clouded with perplexity. "After all, the throne is a mere symbol. Legitimacy is a symbol. Gustav is all that a symbol should be. The King exists for the State, not the State for the King. Can I, as Chancellor, justify the possibility of tearing the State in two because of a legal quibble about relationship? You know, Venables," he added slowly, "I think I shall come down on Gustav's side."

"I wonder if you will?" said Venables quietly, "when you have heard *all* that Robor has to confess?"

Demetrior frowned. "Oh, there's more, is there? Well, Robor, we want the *whole* truth, as I said before."

"Your Excellency," said the Doctor solemnly, "I have told you all I dare tell you. The other thing I have sworn by all that I hold holy not to reveal. I cannot, I will not reveal it."

"Supposing the Queen herself were to give you permission," said Venables gently.

"She alone could release me from my oath," agreed the Doctor. "And she is dead."

"Dead, but not dumb," answered the detective, opening his bag. "I have here a document which I feel justified in producing, now that my investigation has reached its close. It is the last message of Queen Hanna, the message of which Rosa gained possession in order to blackmail Gustav."

"But we have seen that," exclaimed the Chancellor. "It was the confession which originally implicated Dr. Robor."

"No. That confession you saw was the document which the thief substituted for the original—or rather thought he had substituted. Actually, I had already taken a copy of the document, although the envelope containing the copy was apparently still sealed. The thief secured and destroyed the copy only. I kept the original. It is similar to the substituted message in its opening, but goes on to tell much more. The end, I fear, will shock you. You need hardly be surprised that I kept it back until I was sure of everything, until you would no longer think it the ravings of a lunatic..."

Venables unfolded the document and read it out.

It ran as follows:

"The State Office,
"Milö Palace, Isorb.

"We, Hanna, by the Grace of God, etc., being now come to a state wherein we regret and would expiate the wickedness of our younger days, do hereby make declaration that in the year of our Lord 1902 we did procure our Physician, Benedict Robor, to slay by poison the Prince Maximilian, our nephew, then Heir Apparent, which crime we now wholly detest and do denounce.

"But by the mercy of God it has this day been made known to us that He inclined the heart of Benedict Robor to mercy, so that he preserved the young Prince from our designs, and bred him up, and the Prince is now living, which we take as a sign that our sins may find mercy and forgiveness, thanks to the intercession of our holy ancestor, St. Boron.

"Wherefore upon this day, the Feast of our holy ancestor, St. Boron, we do as token of our contrition solemnly and for ever abdicate our titles as Queen and Monarch, and renounce our inviolability as Sovereign Prior, and give over all privileges or prerogative of blood or office whatsoever, having by this, our last Act, appointed our nephew Prince Maximilian to succeed us as King, nor by this abdication do we deny his right to depose us and annul our Acts as unlawful and *ultra vires*, but we do commend our person to the King's justices, that they may have mercy upon us, and our Acts to the prudence of the King's Councillors."

"Well, we know all this," said the Chancellor.

"Wait," said Venables, "listen to this."

"And further, we do now confess the heinous cheat we have put upon the State, in commending to them the so-called Prince Augustus as our heir and the son of our body, the said person being in fact the lawful son and heir of the late Count Tacora and his wife, our Mistress of the Wardrobe; Wherefore by this, our last Act, we do withdraw and annul all those privileges he has enjoyed as our son and Heir Apparent, to which he has no manner of right or claim.

"Given under our Great Seal at our Court of Milö.

"Hanna, Queen."

There was silence for a moment after the reading of this document. The Chancellor took it from Venables' hands and perused it again as if he found himself unable to believe the words he had heard spoken. At last he turned to Robor. "You knew all this?" he said gravely.

"I knew it!" answered Robor solemnly. "But I should never have revealed it unless the Queen herself had confessed it. But now I feel myself released from my oath. You may remember the circumstances in which Prince Augustus was born. When the event was announced as expected the Princess Royal retired to her country seat. Almost at the time of the birth the Countess Tacora's child was reported to be ill. I attended it. Its death was announced. In reality the child was smuggled back to the Princess Royal and given out as her child. This was while Prince Maximilian was still officially alive. But the ease with which the substitution could be effected suggested to me, a few months later, the means by which Prince Maximilian could be saved."

"But why this extraordinary substitution? It sounds insane."

"You must remember Queen Hanna's hate of her brother. It was not enough that his line should be eventually wiped from the succession. Her line must succeed. As her physician I was forced to tell her, some years before, that she would never bear a child. Therefore she determined to adopt one. But an adoption is not recognized in the Succession, and therefore it was necessary to make the adopted child appear her own."

"I understand. But did the Countess Tacora know of this?"

"Most certainly."

Demetrior looked incredulous. "She allowed her own child to be taken away from her?"

"Yes, to become King of Iconia. You must remember that the devotion of the Tacoras to the Herzvogins has reached a climax in her case. She almost worshipped the Queen. She would have given life, land, anything for her, and, as a final sacrifice, even her child. It was a terrible error. Only the Queen's overmastering personality made it possible. The conflict between her devotion to the Queen and her frustrated mother-love almost unhinged her mind. She became neurotic. Eventually she took to drink. The Queen, naturally, overlooked her faults in view of her great sacrifice. The King overlooked them——"

"Because she was his mother? But did *he* know that?"

"Towards the end, yes," admitted Robor. "I am certain of it."

The Chancellor dug his fingers into his hair. "Good heavens, this is a worse problem. I'm damned if I know what to do."

"It seems to me fairly obvious," said Venables. "Gustav must go."

"But is it so obvious? All this involved story has got to be proved. Most of the actors are dead. I can see attempts to stop the trial, and even a revolution. Gustav knows everything, and he will use all his prerogatives. Can one blame him? My whole instinct is to hush it up. What if he is a Tacora? They're quite as old blood as the Herzvogins. I don't mind who rules."

"Naturally, as a politician, you must play for safety. But does it occur to you to wonder," asked Venables gently, "who murdered Queen Hanna?"

The Chancellor turned white. "My God, I'd forgotten that! Venables, you're right. Gustav must go. We must depose him. We must do it quickly, no matter if it isn't altogether legal. We must telephone for Maximilian to fly here to-night. Above all, the army must be presented with a *fait accompli*."

Venables nodded. "If I read my history correctly, the last deposition of a King was undertaken by the Order of the Collar. There is a meeting of the Order to-morrow. It seems to me you'll have to get busy between now and the morning."

"That's true," agreed the Chancellor. "Do you know everything, Venables?"

"No," said Venables slowly. "I always believe in keeping something back."

Chapter XXVIII

THE LAST EXPLOSION

I t was morning, and the Chapel of St. Boron was a tapestry of living colours. In the chancel of the church the Knights, looking more than life-size in their billowing cloaks and robes of scarlet and white, sat like effigies on their carven thrones. All of them were old in years, most of them were of ancient blood. These petty chieftains of the tiny estates which dotted Iconia came up to the capital for the most famous of Iconian ceremonies, fully conscious that they were part of a unique past. They were as proud as princes and as poor as peasants. Their faces, unremarkable separately, gave in mass an odd sensation of power. Those accented cheekbones, sparse beards, heavy brows, and the yellowish skin of age, made them seem an assembly of dead knights, resurrected for some wizard ceremony.

Above the thrones hung the banners. Some of them, Venables knew, had been borne in that last Hungarian battle, when Iconia's cavalry, having gained by lot the station of honour in the right wing, had met the shock of the Turkish Janissaries and rolled them back. One banner at least had floated over the bulwarks of the Iconian galley in Lepanto...

The nave itself was bright with scarlet, where the seventy Companions sat in their short red cloaks. The front pew alone was sober black and white. Here sat the Clerks and Keepers of the Order in their black gowns and white wigs. In the gallery sat certain privileged ladies, officially not "in the Chapel," and inconspicuously dressed in black.

Venables had a unique view of this bizarre but historic spectacle, for, thanks to the Chancellor, he had been smuggled into a tiny room, above the sacristy entrance, built in the thickness of the wall. It was provided with a small window, through which the whole Chapel could be seen, while the observer remained invisible. Tradition declared that it was from here the mediæval lepers were allowed to view the services, without danger to the faithful. History, in the person of Professor Andreyi and Mr. Lancelot, declared less romantically that it was used by such members of the Royal Family in the past as had become nuns in an enclosed Order.

Sounds were not so clear. The voices of the choir came dimly and inarticulately, in the clumsy vocables of Icon, that ancient dialect, long forgotten by the peasant, but still used for a part of the Church liturgy.

From where he watched Venables could see the recumbent figure of St. Boron staring stonily at the roof, the banners among which the angels dived and glided, the stiff Byzantine saints regarding the colourful Companions with rigid disapproval; the lights from thousands of candles glittering fugitively on the thin iron collars which encircled the gaunt throats of the Knights.

The choir's voices died away. The organ paused, then swelled into a march. The hundred bearded and yellow Iconian faces turned towards the door. The King entered.

The office of Sovereign Prior, in which Gustav was now to be installed, was considered by Iconian jurists as the culminating office and function of the monarchy. Feudal forms still dominated Iconian politics, in spite of the Constitution and the Distribution Act. The nobility and Civil Service still formed the final arch of the building of the State, and the keystone was the Monarch. The members of the Order of the Collar were composed exclusively of these ruling classes. Thus the ceremony of the creation of Sovereign Prior, in the course of which the members of the Order swore fealty to their head, was also an oath of obedience of nation to King. Indeed jurists sometimes argued that not until the King was installed as Sovereign Prior were the nominally independent landowners of Iconia his lieges and subjects...

The King was wearing the simple white tunic of a novice, for no member of the Iconian blood royal might become a member of the Order of the Collar except as Sovereign Prior. He was followed down the aisle by his two sponsors, the Warden of the Royal Forests and the Marshal of the Nobility, both Knights Grand Cross of the Order.

Gustav walked up to the Prior's throne, bowed to the Deputy Prior and the Chaplain of the Order—the Patriarch of Iconia—and stood at attention. Not until invested with his Prior's robes was he entitled to sit on the throne.

Erect at his lectern at the foot of St. Boron's tomb, His Beatitude the Patriarch of Iconia looked at Gustav. The Patriarch was not lacking in courage. As a comparatively young man, a new-comer to his office, he had publicly rebuked Queen Hanna for her neglect of the ceremonial rights due to her predecessor and brother, King Franceo. Age had given him added assurance and a new dignity. Yet even his hand trembled a little as he turned the pages of the Order of Service, in which had been incorporated, for this day, new and unprecedented matters.

His yellow shaven face, with its small brown eyes, showed none of his concern, however. He looked calmly at the King, and leaned a little forward. His voice was clear and ringing.

"Do you, Augustus Crispin Maximilian Herzvogin, King, swear to uphold the Royal and Peaceable Order of the Collar, without change of rite or alteration of precedence, according to the Rule established by your most holy ancestor and predecessor, St. Boron, King and Confessor?"

"I do," answered Gustav loudly.

"And will you freely accept of the fealties of the noble Knights and worshipful Companions, as head and leader of the Order?"

"I will."

"And do you accept as Sovereign Prior not to lead them against any manner of enemy inside or outside the realm, save only the Saracens?"

"I do," answered Gustav. Here, however, modern conceptions of sovereignty had intruded an interruption into the ancient ritual.

"His Majesty the King of Iconia," interposed the First Sponsor, Count Herreshyi, "asserts his right as Sovereign of Iconia to lead his subjects against all manner of enemies inside or outside his realm."

The Chaplain, as by custom, acknowledged the gloss with a bow. Then His Beatitude closed the Order of Service. His hands shook a little with excitement, but his voice was firm as he spoke to the Herald. The Herald bowed to the Deputy Prior and the candidate, and then his clear voice filled the church.

"Let any Knight who has aught to protest against the installation of Augustus Crispin Maximilian Herzvogin, King, as Sovereign Prior of the Royal and Peaceable Order of the Collar, now come forward, or for ever hold his peace. And on his part his Sponsor and Champion, Count Herreshyi of Gortin in the Eastern Province, doth throw down his gage, and will maintain the same with his life against the body of any Knight."

Bored and a little sleepy, the Marshal of the Nobility Count Herreshyi, that vapid descendant of an illustrious line, dropped an embroidered silken glove on to the velvet cushion proffered him by a page, who bore it to the Deputy Prior in the top left stall, who placed it in front of him.

A queer silence followed. And then there was a strange, an unprecedented phenomenon. Venables heard the rustling and scuffling in the chancel as the noble Knights rose to their feet and assembled in a disorderly manner round the King. The worshipful Companions pressed forward to the very communion rails, which were now locked and closed. But no one spoke.

The King was unfamiliar with the details of the ceremony. But it was clear that something was wrong. He looked round for the quiet efficiency of his Chamberlain, but his seat was empty. The Chamberlain, in disgrace, had remained in the country.

Gustav whispered to his champion. Marshal of the Nobility Count Herreshyi looked round angrily. "Get back," he muttered. "Don't crowd. The ceremony is not yet over."

The scuffling continued. Gustav was now completely hemmed in by the Knights of the Collar. He turned slowly round. Everywhere were dour, almost menacing, yellow faces.

Like most unrehearsed movements, the scene was not dignified. It resembled a disorderly mob of schoolboys. Yet in its silence and its unexpectedness it was profoundly frightening. The possibility of real danger at that moment seemed to strike the King. His lips tightened. He glared at those grave old faces nearest him. "What the devil does this mean?"

"Make way for the Chancellor," shouted someone on the fringe of the crowd. A lane opened suddenly.

Count Demetrior, hardly recognizable in his robes, walked briskly up to the King. In contrast to other officials, the Chancellor was never ordinarily seen in anything but civilian garb, at its most dressy a frock-coat. This fact, with his urbane deprecating manner, gave one an impression of someone mild and ineffective. Now, however, in the imposing insignia of Knight Grand Cross, he suddenly became remarkable. Venetian Doges, Renaissance Ministers, gorgeous in ducal or cardinatial robes, had just the same shrewd and worldly expressions.

"What does this mean?" Gustav asked him furiously.

The Chancellor made no answer, but calmly pulled out from under his robes a sheet of paper, on which he had evidently made some notes. The King made a hasty step towards him. The surrounding Knights, without actually laying hands on Gustav, crowded in on him and kept him back from the Chancellor.

The Chancellor did not look up. He took out a pair of spectacles from his robes and adjusted them. Then he started to read from the paper in a low business-like voice, as if he were skimming through the report of a public company.

"On behalf of the members of the Royal and Peaceable Order of the Collar, I challenge the birth, breeding, and station of the present candidate, and maintain that he is not eligible for the honourable office of Sovereign Prior, in that he could not be the rightful wearer of the Crown, inasmuch as the rightful Monarch, the most high and mighty the Prince Maximilian, eldest son of His late Majesty King Franceo II of Iconia, is still alive: *Item*, he is not a Herzvogin, but the lawful son of the body of the present Countess Tacora: *Item*, his past crimes do render him unsuitable to be a member of this honourable Order, of which crimes he will, on leaving this sanctuary, be duly arrested and impeached. Now, in lieu of maintaining the same against his Champion with my body, I do, as provided for in the Rule of this Order, call upon the members of this Order to decide between us by vote. And I now ask the Noble Knights and Worshipful Companions, each by lifting up his right hand and answering quietly and without disorder *Nolo* or *Volo*, whether or not they wish this candidate to be rejected."

The Chancellor paused for breath and pocketed his spectacles. The Herald put the question to the Order, and as had been arranged at their midnight meeting the red cloaks fell fluttering back as the right hands were lifted in the air.

"*Volo!*"

"The candidate is rejected," stated the Chancellor formally, and was lost to sight again among the Knights. The Marshal of the Nobility, unaware of the impending catastrophe, started to protest violently. He was swept and hustled from the King's side, and found himself almost in a moment thrust into the sacristy. With that helplessness which even the bravest man feels when suddenly surrounded by hostile fellow creatures, Gustav looked round for help. But none of his intimates, neither Luigi nor the Chamberlain nor any of his suite, was there. Even his other Sponsor had silently melted away. The faces round him were strange to him. He had considered these rustic landlords unimportant and ineffectual…

He made as if to force his way out of the hostile crowd, then he dropped his hands.

"What do you want, gentlemen?" he asked firmly.

The silence gave way to a disorder hardly suitable to the sacred character of the Chapel. "Depose him!" shouted a Knight. "No, no, abdicate!" cried a Companion. The Herald called for silence, and got it at last.

"This is rebellion," exclaimed Gustav. "Are you mad? Every one of you is indictable for treason." His words were drowned in angry cries.

The Deputy Prior, in the nave, walked heavily to the lectern through the crowd. He was a short, fat man with a large black beard. Gustav remembered him as a successful racehorse owner who had caused excitement by introducing innovations in the rotation of crops on his estate. A negligible man, and now he, Gustav, was being hushed into silence to hear him speak.

"Augustus Franceo Maximilian Tacora, known as Herzvogin," the Deputy Prior began, "as it has been sufficiently proven to us that you have no right or just succession to the Crown of Iconia, we, the Order of the Collar, Custodian Interregnum of the said Crown, do demand of you to surrender it and all its privileges, the same being usurped and pretended by you without substance or fact."

"Answer, 'I surrender the Crown,'" whispered Gustav's neighbour threateningly. The King paused, his huge body towering over the men around him. He seemed about to try to fight his way out of the crowd. Then a voice was heard to shout furiously: "Murderer!"

Gustav winced. Then, "I surrender the Crown," he said firmly, "under protest."

The Deputy Prior acknowledged this response with a perfunctory nod. He turned over a page. "And on behalf of the Order I do call His Majesty, King Franceo III, formerly the high and mighty Prince Maximilian, only child of His late Majesty, King Franceo II, to be installed as Sovereign Prior of the Order, to whom the noble

Knights and worshipful Companions will freely pay homage as liege lord. God save the King!"

"God save King Franceo III!" shouted the Herald.

Gustav was hustled into the sacristy. He did not hear the shouting in the gallery as the Countess Tacora, protesting violently, was also ejected. The Knights and Companions hurried back to their places. The Deputy Prior wiped the sweat off his brow. Everything, on the surface, was as it was at the beginning of the ceremony. The organ struck up the slow strain of a march.

The doors opened again. Prince Maximilian, *alias* King Franceo III, *alias* Dr. Brightholme, a slight figure clad in the white robe of a novice, supported by two sponsors, advanced to the chancel to be enthroned and receive the homage of the Order...

"Good Lord, how like his aunt!" exclaimed the Deputy Prior to his neighbour.

Charles Venables, however, at a much earlier date, had been more struck by the likeness between Maximilian's lean elfish features and those attributed by the contemporary sculptor to that pious and ascetic man, St. Boron, King and Confessor.

Chapter XXIX

THE REAL REGICIDE

The deposed King was taken from the sacristy to a little vestry which adjoined the Chapel, and was used for the storage of robes and vessels.

His deposition still required certain further acts to acquire the force of law throughout Iconia. But the midnight sitting of the hundred members of the Order of the Collar, convened with such secrecy and dispatch by the Chancellor, had in effect settled the issue. It had made Maximilian lawful King, under the style of Franceo III, and had settled the date of his Coronation. It had formally declared that the deposed King was not a Herzvogin but a Tacora, and it had stripped his person of Royal privileges and prerogatives.

When Mr. Lancelot, at a later date, came to comment on these events in his *Revised History of the Kingdom of Iconia*, he remarked on the speed with which the Council of the Order accepted the facts presented before them, and acted on them, in marked contrast to ordinary judicial process. "But," as he pointed out, "although a judicial body, the Councillors of the Order are not lawyers. On the contrary, they are blunt men, farmer-nobles one might call them. They are used to making quick decisions on matters of business. They know nothing of the laws of evidence, but they know that farm and State affairs brook no delay. Many of them, moreover, remembered the rumours which had been current at the time of Maximilian's supposed death and the posthumous birth of an heir to Queen Hanna. They now believed these rumours, and acted immediately. In doing so they undoubtedly saved their country from the evils of

236 Christopher St John Sprigg

civil war, and a civil war with that most barren of all battle cries, Legitimacy. Augustus was faced with an accomplished fact before the Palace had the faintest suspicion of what had been planned. That strange—in our eyes perhaps grotesque—ceremony appertaining to the investiture of the Prior of the Order of the Collar was chosen with good reason for this *coup d'état*. On the one side Augustus was placed in the always humiliating position of a man seeking election. On the other hand the forces which planned his deposition had all the legal, traditional, and personal prestige of their Order. Augustus was eliminated in a few minutes, without a single blow being struck in his defence."

Mr. Lancelot's comment is just, as his comments always are... Gustav certainly looked a beaten man as he sat in the vestry, staring gloomily in front of him. He had taken off his novice's tunic. Underneath he wore an ordinary lounge suit. Two policemen stood near him watchfully and a little apprehensively. He looked up when Charles Venables came in.

"I suppose all this was your idea?" he asked slowly.

"More or less," admitted Venables. "I am afraid it was rather a shock. But it was the only way. You know they like you in the army, and we dared not risk that."

"Yes, they like me. Odd, isn't it?" said Gustav, with a bitter smile. He relapsed into silence. "Where's Luigi?" he asked, after a pause.

"He has been sent for," Venables told him. Luigi had indeed been called by a message which told him that the King wished to see him, but somewhat cruelly gave him no inkling of what had just taken place.

The messenger returned to the hall with Luigi. Luigi looked surprised when he saw the King.

"You called me, Your Majesty?"

Gustav opened his mouth and then closed it without saying anything. He waved to Venables and turned his back sulkily on them both.

"Your employer is no longer to be addressed as 'Your Majesty,' Pavellicini," Venables told him. "He has just been deposed by the Order of the Collar. They have ruled that he is to be known by his correct title of Count Tacora."

Luigi turned dead white. He looked unbelievably at Augustus, whose dejected back was self-explanatory. Then he seemed to pull himself together with an effort.

"Is this a joke?" he asked.

"Joke, who's talking about a joke?" boomed a voice from the door. It was Millitranyi's. He entered fussily, and was helped off with his Knight's robes by a policeman. He turned to Gustav and spoke more gently. "I am sorry about all this, Tacora, but I must do my duty. I have to arrest you for the murder of Her late Majesty Queen Hanna. Here is the warrant."

Gustav pushed it brusquely aside. He rose to his feet. "I have been deposed," he said indignantly. "I have agreed to my deposition. Why trump up this charge against me? I am powerless. Why kick me?"

Millitranyi reddened. "Trump up this charge! I do not like that expression!"

"It is the truth," said Gustav hotly. "You know it."

"I do not wish to discuss the matter," answered Millitranyi stiffly.

"Listen, Millitranyi. I swear I am innocent!" exclaimed Gustav. Then he dropped his hands helplessly. "I see you have made up your mind. Very well. Where are you taking me?"

It was at that moment that the occupants of the vestry became aware of a scuffle outside. The policeman on duty was having difficulty in fulfilling his instructions to keep everyone away from the King. His respectful remonstrances showed that it was someone of importance. The next minute the Wardrobe Mistress had pushed past him into the room.

Her black dress and veil were torn. Her hair was tousled. Her eyes were red, and her cheeks unpleasantly puffy.

She went up to Gustav, who was looking gloomily at the wall. She seemed to be a little afraid of him. "Will you ever forgive me?" she said gently, touching him on the shoulder. "I did it for the best." Her voice faltered as she made this always unconvincing excuse.

Her son nodded abruptly and uncomfortably. "Of course," he mumbled.

Something in Millitranyi's impatient attitude made her look at him more attentively. "What do you want with Gustav, General?" she asked. "Why are you here?"

The Chief of Police shrugged his shoulders. "I am sorry to tell you, Countess, that your son is under arrest."

"On what charge?" she asked.

"The murder of Queen Hanna!"

What followed was a lesson to Venables, for it taught him that it is impossible to foretell what human beings may not do, and that their wild actions have a habit of suddenly and irretrievably upsetting the best-laid schemes.

The Wardrobe Mistress's face went white and queer. There was no particular expression in it—it just seemed to collapse. She turned to Luigi with a sudden animal cry. "You beastly little Italian rat!" she sobbed. "You caused all this! It would never, never have come out if you hadn't been here. My son was a decent boy, and you led him astray. He never murdered the Queen. Never, never, never! You did it. No Tacora could lift a hand to a Herzvogin. His very blood would refuse. You did it... You murderer!"

The shot rang out almost simultaneously, and exploded in that high vaulted stone room with an almost appalling reverberation. The Wardrobe Mistress, her hand shaking with excitement, had pressed the muzzle of her revolver against Luigi's breast. He had tried to thrust it aside with one hand even as she fired. The bullet shattered his ribs. He seized the revolver instinctively and pitched forward on her. Whether he pulled the trigger himself, or whether the fright made her press her finger, it was impossible to tell. Her

arm was against her own side, and as they both fell to the floor—
the Wardrobe Mistress's face pale with fright at her own act—the
revolver went off again. She was killed instantly...

With the second shot half a dozen people came from the Chapel
where the noise of the first had been heard. Dr. Robor was among
them. Venables was already kneeling by Luigi's side, and had stripped
off the Italian's coat. Robor helped him, and shook his head as they
exposed the wound.

"A few minutes," he said in a low voice. Already it was plain
that the mists of death were gathering over Luigi's eyes. He looked
glassily into space.

"I tried to help the King..." he murmured vaguely, out of the
darkness. He groaned. "Gustav never... knew..."

"Listen!" Venables urged the waiting crowd. They bent lower.
The detective whispered urgently into Luigi's ear.

"Do you want to make a confession?"

The dying man lifted a hand.

"You murdered Queen Hanna?" went on Venables.

The Italian seemed to lie there immobile. In reality he was gathering all his efforts for his last words. They came at last.

"Yes... I killed her... the wax..." A thin bubble of blood spumed
his lips. Luigi was dead...

"It seems to me I have had a rotten deal," complained Gustav to
Venables. "You knew I didn't murder Hanna, and yet you let them
go through that farce, even down to arresting me."

"It was essential," Venables explained. "The fact that the
Order of the Collar and the Chancellor thought you were a murderer gave that extra impetus needed to make them act promptly.
Otherwise they would either have tried to hush the whole affair
up or proposed that it should have been thrashed out in a formal
legitimacy suit. Either would have resulted in Prince Maximilian
losing his rights."

"Well, you might have considered *my* feelings," went on Gustav. "Just conceive what it feels like, after being a royal highness or a king all one's life, to be a plain person."

"It must be rather a relief, I should have thought. I notice Your Excellency is leaving for Paris to-night alone—a thing you could hardly have done if you had still been King of Iconia."

"Oh, I won't deny that it has its compensations. Still, I insist that I was treated abominably. After all, 'Murderer' is not the kind of name one ought to hurl about at random."

Venables looked at the blond giant enigmatically.

"I think I had some justification. After all, although you *weren't* a murderer, it wasn't for want of trying. Remember the Imperial Tokay? And the scene with Brightholme in the Palace prison? And my adventure on the Palace roof?"

Gustav frowned, attempted to look surprised, and, as the other's keen glance continued, blushed in spite of himself.

He grinned at Venables and threw up his hand.

"You win! Yes, I can't deny the poisoned wine. But after all I think blackmailers deserve what they get, and you cannot conceive how diabolically infuriating Rosa was."

"I can," answered the detective. "But she could be quite delightful at her best, I feel sure."

"Hmph," grunted Gustav noncommittally.

"And how are the children?" went on Venables.

Gustav's face brightened. "Splendid, thank you. Really, when I heard that they had proved so obstreperous with Vera at Schloss Hoben that they had driven her and Maximilian out of their minds, I nearly died of laughter. And then to think that they ran away from the Schloss and came back here—incidentally taking with them all the more portable animals from Vera's private zoo. I haven't had the heart to punish them. Vera has always been so sure she was the only person who could control the children, you know. She didn't realize what every parent learns, that children will be quite obedient when you are a visitor in the home and they are anxious to impress you. But if you are so rash as to take them into your own home it is a very different matter!"

"Well, I hope they will be all right now."

"Oh, I understand them, you know. You were right about one thing. I don't think I will separate them yet. If I hadn't been so worried at the time I should never have thought of doing it. I shall be able to give more time to them now. By the way, what was the idea behind encouraging them to run away?"

"Vera and Max thought you were the—er—culprit," explained Venables. "And I am afraid that for a time I toyed with the idea myself..."

"Well, well," said Gustav philosophically, "I can hardly blame any of you. In fact, I must admit I quite like Maximilian—or Franceo as he calls himself now. I suppose I should really hate him for having got my job, but you can take it from me, Venables, that although there is a great deal of enjoyment in being a king, in the long run the advantages outweigh the disadvantages in a country like Iconia. For one thing, one's subjects—in bulk—smell so abominably... And then the Chancellor treats one as if one were a complete idiot, which may be true, but I should have thought common politeness would have prevented him showing it... Then there is the eternal difficulty of keeping within one's income.

"I'm not sure that the worst thing isn't the incredible boringness of even the best people once you are King. They seem incapable of making a single intelligent remark. It is as if one paralysed their brains. Of course one has the pleasure of being able to be rude to them, but then you know they cannot answer back, and believe me that takes half the satisfaction away." Gustav reflected. "No, on the whole, I still think the worst thing is that difficulty of keeping within one's income—the continual worry to keep down expenses, with everyone in the Palace trying to grab a little. It gets on one's nerves. I don't see how this Palace can be run at all without the Chamberlain."

"I understand he is back again?"

"Yes. We had a little farewell party last night—Max and Vera, and the Chamberlain and I. Max insisted on finishing up the Tokay. The Chamberlain nearly had a fit, but he recovered after drinking a bottle of it." Gustav winked. "You may be sure I sniffed mine carefully, but there was no poison... I think we all got a little drunk... Oh, by the way, while I remember it, Max gave me a little memento to present to you as a souvenir of this affair."

Gustav pressed something into his hand and stepped into the train, which had been due to depart half an hour earlier. According to Iconian practice, therefore, it could shortly be expected to leave. Indeed, even as Venables opened the package, the train started to move off, and the detective looked up to see Gustav's blond head and beefy arm thrust in farewell from a receding carriage. He responded, and then finished opening the package.

Inside was coiled a silken cord, faded and frayed. It was worthless in substance, invaluable in associations. It was the Curse of the Herzvogins.

A card was pinned to it. Scrawled in King Franceo's firm handwriting, Venables read the words:

"Keep it; and prevent it doing any more harm!"

Venables picked the cord up by one end and regarded it thoughtfully. Tradition proclaimed it to be the very cord which the early Herzvogin had twisted round the neck of Augustus the Clerk. The cold voice of history, in Professor Andreyi's person, asserted it to be a fragment of a fairly recent bell-pull. Whichever it was, in its pretensions, its glamour, and its tawdriness, it seemed a fit symbol of the Iconia he was leaving by the next train...

(Which may be skipped by the incurious reader)

Letter from Mr. Charles Venables to Superintendent Manciple

(Reproduced by permission of Mr. Venables
and the publishers of the *Art of Criminal Investigation.*)

The Constable Express,
January 12, 19——.

My Dear Manciple,

I understand from your letter that there were several details
which puzzled you in the brief description I sent you of the events
following on the murder of Queen Hanna. I expected you to say
that. The narrative I sent you was only an outline. I intended
to fill in the details as soon as I had time. I do so now. The train
has stopped in a plain absolutely destitute of scenery, and shows
every intention of stopping here indefinitely.

First of all, you want to know exactly how the murder was
executed. It was a simple puzzle in bi-location, and I could kick
myself for not having discovered the essential clue earlier. You
will remember that Gustav and the Chancellor saw the Queen
in the State Office *after* guards had been set at the door of her
bedchamber, where she was later discovered dead. Actually the
Queen was not in the Office then at all. *At that very moment she
was lying dead in her room, strangled by Luigi.*

When the Prince and the Chancellor opened the door, they
expected to see the Queen. Luigi had told the Prince she was in
there, and the Prince had told the Chancellor. What they really

saw was her wax effigy, apparently leaning forward over the desk in sleep. The face had been touched up, and in particular the eyes had been repainted to make them appear closed. The figure had, of course, been clothed in the dress which the Queen had been wearing that day, and which had been removed from her corpse by Luigi.

The one risk was that the Prince might have investigated the effigy further—tried to wake it, in fact. But I learn that when the Prince and the Chancellor opened *their* door, Luigi—who you may remember was on guard outside the State Office's other door—came into the room, pointed to the Queen, and made clear in pantomime that she was asleep. They withdrew at once, of course.

I always suspected that the Queen could not really have been asleep in the State Office. Until I remembered the waxworks, on the last day of my stay at the Palace, I could not see how the Prince and the Chancellor had been so deceived. It was obvious on the face of it that there had been some impersonation, but I could not imagine who had done it. The idea that Brightholme, for example, could have misled anyone, in a strong light, and with his face motionless, was an idea I never entertained for a moment. It was an idea only Miss Fotheringay could suggest and Millitranyi believe.

A wax effigy is the one thing that is—apart from movement—absolutely lifelike. We all know the dummy policeman at the waxworks who is always being spoken to by visitors. Give the Queen's effigy an excuse for being motionless—sleep—and at once it is impossible for anyone to detect the fraud, without actually touching it. That is, of course, providing the effigy is a good one, and these Royal wax figures were all excellent.

After his *alibi* had been established, Luigi removed the waxwork into another room and hid it. He took off the outer clothes, tied them into a parcel, and in the confusion following on the discovery of the Queen's death was able to bring them back into the bedchamber and throw them under the bed. This made it less obvious to us why the Queen's corpse should have been dressed in the clothes of the Order. Actually the reason was that these were the only clothes available in the room which Luigi could substitute for the dress he wanted for his wax effigy.

The wax effigy also explains the incident of the shot ghost. The sentry met Luigi carrying it downstairs to put it back in the storeroom of the crypt. The sentry shot at the effigy, and, as he says, the chest "caved in"—for it was only wax. Naturally there was no blood. The sentry's torchlight only fell on the effigy's face and shoulders, otherwise he might have been made suspicious of the sitting posture of the figure... or have recognized its bearer...

I don't know how Luigi accounted for the destruction of the waxwork to the sculptor. Perhaps he passed on some imaginary explanation of the King's. But anyway, the niche which ought to have been filled by the Queen's effigy was empty when I went down there on my last day, and that gave me the explanation of everything.

I am afraid Luigi was not disinterested in his murder. He was merely thinking of keeping his own position. As personal private secretary to Count Tacora he would be nothing. As the King's secretary he might hope eventually to be the *eminence grise* of Iconia.

At first no one except Dr. Robor and the Wardrobe Mistress knew the revelations Queen Hanna was going to make on the Feast of St. Boron. But everyone at Court knew she was going to tell *something alarming*. It was the Wardrobe Mistress who eventually gave the secret away to Luigi inadvertently. She was drunk, of course... Luigi was horrified. He started planning at once—first threatening the Queen with mysterious notes, finally killing her when he found he could not frighten her into silence.

The Wardrobe Mistress, with the queer fitful memory of the dipsomaniac, remembered later that she had told Luigi everything, although at the time she was completely drunk.

From that moment she divined that he was the murderer. Hence the dreadful scene in which they died...

The worst mistake Luigi made was in confiding his discovery to Rosa. Or perhaps Rosa found out accidentally? I think that is more likely. Anyway, Luigi had made the additional mistake of keeping that document in which the Queen confessed so much. This clearly shows that he was not disinterested in his murder. For if he had been he would have destroyed such a damaging document at once. Instead he kept it. It might come in useful at some future date, should his influence with the King weaken...

Rosa stole it. And being a fool, she began to use it actively. Luigi was content to remain in the background, having secured his position by the murder. Rosa wanted to use the document to improve her position. She began to blackmail Gustav. It was then, for the first time, that Gustav learned everything—that Maximilian was still alive; that he himself was not the rightful King. He took the shock amazingly well. I don't know whether he guessed that Luigi had killed the Queen. Perhaps he suspected it, but preferred to shut his eyes... Anyway, from that moment until the end he was simply Luigi's tool.

The first step was to crush Rosa. They decided the simplest method was to poison her. You ask how the King could have poisoned Rosa when the wine was poured by Robor into apparently empty glasses. I am bringing back for you the fragments of Rosa's broken glass to show you how it was done. There is a tiny hole in the bottom of the bowl and the walls are double, as in an "unspillable" inkwell. The poison drops through the hole, and when you invert the glass the poison runs into the walls. The glass is opaque enough to make it invisible. When you turn the glass the right way up and pour the wine in, the poison runs to the bottom again and is taken up by the wine.

Of course I never smelt the poison. That was my excuse. Actually I recognized those glasses. There is a picture of a similar glass in Revalli's *Methods of the Borgias*, and they were extremely popular in Renaissance Italy. Eventually they became so well known that they were given up by all the fashionable poisoners as being insufficiently subtle. Directly I saw them I suspected poison. Rosa was the obvious victim, and the ostentatious way in which Gustav took care that the glasses should be inverted, and that someone else should pour out the wine, betrayed the amateur poisoner.

The neatest touch was that Gustav had poisoned his own glass. Of course, when Rosa dropped on the floor in convulsions, he would have put down his glass in horror, and it, too, would have been found to be poisoned... Quite a clever alibi...

I was beginning to see my way a little more clearly then. I must confess I never suspected Gustav's legitimacy at first, until Professor Andreyi told me of the Countess Tacora's "indifference" to her child's "death." But I *had* guessed that Maximilian was alive. And I guessed he was Brightholme. Brightholme had certain Herzvogin features quite distinctly. You can see them even in that photograph. A likeness to St. Boron...

The trouble was, how long would it be before Luigi, who already knew from the Queen's confession that Prince Maximilian was alive, guessed Brightholme was he? I was concerned for Brightholme's safety, and his love affair with Princess Vera did not make it any easier. Meanwhile, Brightholme, primed with the true facts by Robor, had thought, naturally enough, that Gustav had murdered the Queen. Eventually he had told all this to Vera. Needless to say Vera lost interest in Gustav as a husband after that. Also she began to feel sorry for the children—the children of a murderer—and encouraged them to rebel against their father. After they had run away, she sent Brightholme to the circus to smuggle them to her castle in Kossovia.

Luigi and Gustav guessed that Brightholme was Prince Maximilian after Miss Fotheringay had told of his interview with the Queen. After that his life was definitely not safe. I was glad to see him arrested, and gave the Commission all the encouragement I could in doing so. I thought he would be safer in prison. It was then that Gustav, inspired by Luigi, made his final attempt to get rid of Maximilian. He was placed in the Palace prison. The idea was that Gustav should interview Brightholme secretly, and shoot him, afterwards asserting that he had done it in self-defence. Directly I heard that Gustav was interviewing the prisoner alone I guessed what he had in mind.

Unfortunately Gustav was a half-hearted murderer. Perhaps he hesitated to shoot in cold blood. Anyway, Brightholme had time to jump on him and avoid a mortal wound. I came in time to prevent anything worse happening. Gustav was the stronger, and in another moment would have been able to finish Brightholme off. Then Princess Vera arrived and got Brightholme away from the Palace safely, if rather spectacularly.

Yes, I had given her the tip...

It was about this time that I veered round to the view that Luigi and not Gustav was the Queen's murderer. For I felt sure that whoever murdered the Queen would not have bungled the shooting of Brightholme...

You were puzzled by the intrigues centring round the stolen confession. When I got the document back from Rosa I was very much embarrassed by it. If I revealed the document at that stage, Gustav, with his position as King *de facto* if not *de jure*, could hush the whole affair up. For I did not as yet see how the murder was committed, and unless I could prove to the Chancellor that Gustav had gained his Crown through a murder, I guessed— and I was proved right—that the Chancellor's instinct as a politician would be to hush the whole affair up. And I wanted to see Maximilian have fair play... After all, I had been retained by Queen Hanna, and I felt my duty was to try to carry out her last wishes...

If, on the other hand, I handed over the document to the King without revealing it, it would be destroyed, and with it my hope of clearing up the case.

I compromised. I kept the original and put an excellent forged copy in the envelope. Then I told the King and Luigi that I had not yet read the document, and I told them where it was. Of course Luigi stole it.

Here Luigi showed cleverness. If he had been content to destroy the document, there would always have been the unexplained mystery of what the Queen's revelation was going to be. It would always have been a centre for whispering and rebellion. So he substituted another document, which made a partial revelation—not enough to shake Gustav's position, but enough to account for Queen Hanna's remorse. It did not give much away, for pretty nearly everyone at the Palace suspected that Maximilian had been poisoned by Robor at the Queen's orders.

The one danger was that Robor might give the show away when he was accused. But they relied on his loyalty to the Queen and the ease with which Gustav could shut him up if he started to make what at first would appear to be fantastic assertions. Later on, I learned from him, they kept him quiet by promising him a pardon after a few weeks had elapsed, and things had blown over. Unfortunately his demand for an exhumation—made before the pardon was promised him—had been granted by the Commission, and it was impossible for Gustav and Luigi to stop it without exciting suspicion. No doubt they would have been able to hush matters up. After all, there were many possible explanations for the lead piping. They might have suggested that Robor had destroyed the body himself to prevent a post-mortem revealing the presence of poison. But before an explanation was even asked for I had acted...

This second document was forged very badly as compared to *my* forgery. Even the Public Prosecutor saw the difference between its handwriting and that on the pardon granted to Robor by the Queen so long ago. He jumped to the conclusion that the pardon was forged. For different reasons, both Gustav and I insisted that the pardon was genuine. Any further comparison between the two writings would have revealed the forgery of the confession, and might have been fatal to both our plans...

I don't know the exact stage when Luigi guessed I knew everything. He acted promptly when he did. I fancy he planned everything, but I imagine it was Gustav, with his strength, who carried me on to my uncomfortable perch... Overlooking the secret door was my first big mistake in the investigation. Headstrong pride, Manciple! The second mistake was when I let the Wardrobe Mistress shoot Luigi. Two big mistakes in one investigation! I can see you shake your head and frown. These amateurs!

Well, it's all blown over now. Max, as King Franceo III, makes a good king, I understand. Responsibility has toned down even *his* levity. He does not make such a good figure in a uniform as Gustav did, of course, but then Gustav was unique. By the way, Mapponyi has been appointed Chamberlain again. Miss Fotheringay that was—his wife—is Mistress of the Wardrobe. The only complaint Queen Vera has to make about her is her mania for putting draught-protectors under the doors...

I am afraid the outcome has been morally unsatisfactory. It is true the murderer is dead, and it might seem at first sight that morality is satisfied. But is it? The Wardrobe Mistress, whose life was a poem in self-sacrifice, is also dead, after being mentally moribund, for that matter, for ten years or more. Queen Hanna, one of the wickedest women I have met, if you analyse her actions impartially, is now spoken of in Iconia as Hanna the Great. Rosa, who caused so much trouble, is the reigning toast of Bucharest. She sent me a signed photo of herself the other day! Finally Gustav, who tried to murder Rosa, who attempted to assassinate Brightholme, and nearly killed me, is having the time of his life spending the Tacora fortunes in the gayest cities of Europe.

Yet, somehow, I cannot feel upset about it. Hanna was an impressive figure. Rosa was quite amusing. And I liked Gustav. The world would be dull without them, and the more I see of bores the more I like murderers.

Yours sincerely,

Charles Venables.

P.S.—Would you tell Lancelot of the Foreign Office when you see him again, that I have some corrections to suggest for the next edition of his handbook, *The Antiquities of Iconia?*   C. V.

Available from Moonstone Press
by Christopher St John Sprigg

DEATH OF A QUEEN

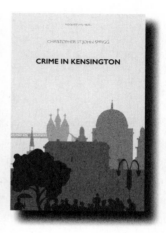

CRIME IN KENSINGTON

THE PERFECT ALIBI

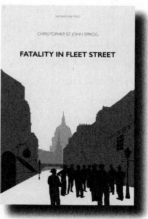

FATALITY IN FLEET STREET